THE IMMIGRANT

Also by Charles Clark

Trails to Dos Encinos

Return to Dos Encinos

Suit Up in Scrubs

Dark Side Hospital

Code Pink

The Immigrant

A Novel

Charles Clark

iUniverse, Inc.
New York Lincoln Shanghai

The Immigrant
A Novel

Copyright © 2008 by Charles Clark

All rights reserved. No part of this book may be used or reproduced by any means, graphic, electronic, or mechanical, including photocopying, recording, taping or by any information storage retrieval system without the written permission of the publisher except in the case of brief quotations embodied in critical articles and reviews.

iUniverse books may be ordered through booksellers or by contacting:

iUniverse
2021 Pine Lake Road, Suite 100
Lincoln, NE 68512
www.iuniverse.com
1-800-Authors (1-800-288-4677)

Because of the dynamic nature of the Internet, any Web addresses or links contained in this book may have changed since publication and may no longer be valid.

This is a work of fiction. All of the characters, names, incidents, organizations, and dialogue in this novel are either the products of the author's imagination or are used fictitiously.

ISBN: 978-0-595-47471-4 (pbk)
ISBN: 978-0-595-71223-6 (cloth)
ISBN: 978-0-595-91743-3 (ebk)

Printed in the United States of America

To my wife, Joyce

Acknowledgments

Special thanks to:

Camille Whitworth—Attorney, formerly with Immigration and Customs Enforcement (ICE)

Elizabeth Susser—Language Translation

Dr. Sergio Avalos—Physician, former resident of Monterrey, Mexico

Dr. Juan Bahamon—Physician, former resident of Colombia, South America

Dr. Salvador Zamora—Physician

Jack Peterson—Health Industry Consultant, Peterson and Associates

Kay Clark—Artist, cover graphics

Danny Clark—Photography

Chapter 1

▼

Houston, Texas—Wednesday, November 15, 2007

Megan Andrade glanced at her watch—ten minutes early, just as she had been most mornings. Neatly arranged on her desk were the same deportation documents that she had not had time to finish reviewing the day before. She had no sooner faced her computer to start her work than her friend, Jaime Cordova, from Detention and Removal, tapped on her office door.

"Hi, Megan," he said. "Looks like you're getting an early start."

"Don't tell me you're bringing more for me to do," she said without looking up.

"No … uh, no," he replied. "It's not that. I need a favor."

"Sure, what's going on?"

"I have an illegal from Mexico in my office … an eleven-year-old boy. He was brought in by a Border Patrol agent—picked up by a constable at a wreck scene and turned over to the agent. I'm having trouble communicating with him."

"Why is that?" she asked. "You don't need me; you speak Spanish as well or better than I do."

"I think he understands most of what I'm saying," he said. "I don't think it's language. The boy has no physical injuries … just scared, almost in a shocklike state. The chief thought you might be able to get him to talk."

"How about family—any other family members in the wreck?"

"He's the only survivor … a horrible accident. I have sketchy reports: his mother and father were killed, the *coyote* was killed instantly also."

"How sad … the little boy is all alone."

"Yeah, and we can't get any information from him," he said. "Do you have a few minutes to try?"

"You knew how I would answer that before you asked."

Jaime laughed. "Guess I have been around you long enough to know. The chief said you would."

"Let me finish this one report, and I'm with you ... won't take long."

"I'll wait."

* * * *

"How's Jeff?" asked Jaime, as they headed toward his office.

"Working too hard," she answered. "His law firm is considering making him a full partner. Right now he's trying to be as productive as possible. Today he's trying a case out of town—won't be home until almost midnight."

"I'm sure he'll make partner," said Jaime. "You two make a good pair. I see you starting early every morning and staying late at night. Ever regret working for ICE?"

"It's tiring work and it's depressing at times, but I like it. How do you hold up to it ... seeing these destitute people flooding in here, only to have to be deported?"

"It *is* depressing. These people need so much help. Seeing this boy, thinking what he faces now without parents ... this is about the worst I've seen in a long time."

"What's his name?" asked Megan, as they approached Jaime's office.

"Ignacio Narvaez," replied Jaime. "It has taken all morning just to get his name. Take your time with him. We might have rushed him too much earlier—you'll see what I mean. I'll wait outside."

In the far corner of the large conference room, Ignacio sat on the floor with his legs pulled against his chest. His head rested on his knees as he stared vacantly toward the outside window. He didn't move when Megan and Jaime entered.

"Ignacio," said Jaime. "This is Megan. She's here to help you. She's going to ask you some questions."

Ignacio looked at Megan briefly, his face devoid of any expression of recognition, and then turned back toward the window.

Megan froze in her tracks; her raised eyebrows and dropped chin reflected her expression of astonishment. She stared at Ignacio for a few moments, shook her head, and edged back toward the door without speaking. Jaime came to her side.

"Megan ... are you all right? What's wrong?"

"I ... I don't know ... he, he resembles...."

"I'm sorry ... we can wait."

"No, no … I can do it." She turned back toward Ignacio, appearing more composed. "I apologize, Jaime. I'm all right."

"Are you sure you're all right?"

"I'm fine. Give me some time with Ignacio."

"I'll be next door if you need me."

✴   ✴   ✴   ✴

Thursday, November 16, 2007

Megan rounded the last turn of the five-mile running trail and headed for home. She could feel the perspiration drip from her scalp, across her wet face, down her neck, and into the fabric of her already sweat-saturated tank top. She checked her watch. The heat must have slowed her pace—the early-morning temperature was unusually high for mid-November. By now she should have been in the elevator and on her way to her tenth-floor apartment.

Maybe it wasn't the heat that had slowed her, but rather the lingering memory that kept flashing through her mind. It was as clear as if she were watching an instant replay of events of the day before: the visual image of the frightened, wide-eyed, eleven-year-old boy—the lone survivor of the ill-fated trip from Mexico. The horrible, fiery freeway accident had taken the lives of his mother and father as well as that of the *coyote*—the man who made his living by escorting Mexicans, illegally, into the United States.

Except for an occasional unpleasant experience like that of yesterday—trying to interview the young boy and trying to comfort him at the same time—a day never passed that she wasn't thankful she had chosen immigration law as her specialty. Graduation from law school, with her exemplary scholastic scores, had brought attractive offers from law firms, but something drove her toward working for ICE, the Immigration and Customs Enforcement Service. Sometimes she asked herself why she had chosen this career path. There had to be a reason. *It certainly isn't as rewarding financially as some of the other offers, but self-satisfaction doesn't carry a price tag,* she reminded herself.

Situations like the one she had just faced, however, infuriated her because they emphasized the blatant disregard the *coyotes* held for human life. They lived to profit from the hopes of the poor, helpless masses in Mexico who were only striving to improve their way of life. How could anyone be so cruel? How could they take money from families who had scrimped and saved for years to accumulate enough to cover the cost of crossing the border, and then treat them like animals?

She remembered the incident her office had investigated a couple of years earlier—immigrants had been left locked in an airtight trailer truck for hours without ventilation, food, or water. Megan shook her head trying to clear her mind. *What did those people feel when the heat and thirst became unbearable, when the air became so oxygen depleted that they fought for a breath of fresh air?*

Now on the tenth floor, Megan walked back and forth the length of the corridor outside her apartment. She stopped briefly at each end to gaze through the large floor-to-ceiling windows at the view below while she followed the muscle stretching cooldown routine that her trainer had advocated.

She reached for her key in the pouch around her waist. She didn't need it. Jeff had left the door ajar again. She wished he would be more careful about locking it when he rushed off each morning. But there was no changing his habits; she had long since given up—cabinet doors left open, newspapers strewn on the floor, dirty dishes left out. But she could live with that.

Since the door was unlocked, she knew Jeff had already left for work. She wished he were still there, as he was on Saturdays and Sundays, so she could hop in bed and awaken him with kisses. With her despondency over the orphaned illegal immigrant, she would love the secure feeling of cuddling close to Jeff. She really hadn't had time to talk to him about the child since he had been so late getting home last night. However, she was sure that the reason was mostly because she had avoided it.

She was trying to forget the memory of that little boy's sad eyes. But why ... why was she having so much trouble erasing the image of that kid from her mind? Was it the shock of seeing his close resemblance to her brother? After all, the boy was just another of the many pitiful wretches that she encountered almost every day in her work. But there was something different about this orphaned boy. He had been so frightened that he hadn't even shed a tear over the death of his parents.

Megan stood still for a minute trying to recall the boy's name. She had heard it—an unusual name—but she couldn't recall it. A wave of guilt swept over her. Had she forgotten his name, or was she just suppressing the fact that tragedies like that could happen? Often the immigrants were referred to only by number at the office. She had never liked that policy. It was so impersonal—especially in this case.

She took a few seconds before bathing to study her image in the bathroom mirror, looking for any telltale signs of gray streaks or wrinkles. *I think I look older,* she thought. *Maybe it's just my short hairstyle—makes me look like a mature career woman.*

She finished her shower and her makeup routine, downed a quick Instant Breakfast, and dressed for work. All the while, during every quiet moment, the picture of the boy's face crept back into the memory neurons of her brain.

Driving to work, fighting the early-morning traffic, she became obsessed with thoughts of her first chore of the day: check with Jaime Cordova. He could give her more detailed information on the boy. She could find out where he was being held, if any family member had been located, and if anyone had taken time to console the frightened waif over his loss. She finally remembered his name: Ignacio! That was it … Ignacio Narváez. His friends and family at home probably used a shortened version.

What family did he have left in Mexico? There was so much to learn about this child. Even though this case was one of thousands processed by ICE every month, there was something about this undocumented immigrant that captured her interest—something different. Hopefully the chief investigator would allow her to pursue this case.

She maneuvered her Mazda 550 Sport Coupe in and out of traffic, competing with the dozens of other motorists, all trying not to be late for work. Her thoughts turned to Jeff. He always made the trip into the city early enough that he avoided this "racetrack" ordeal every morning.

She wondered what would become of their relationship. Would she and Jeff ever marry? Funny that such a thought would come to mind at this time. Could it be related in some way to her recent experience with Ignacio?

What was happening to her? She had dedicated her life to a career that did not include domesticity or parenthood. Now she could hardly think of anything other than the plight of that poor eleven-year-old who no longer had parents or a home. And, added to that line of thought, she was questioning what the future held for her relationship with Jeff. How could that be of any relevance to her concern for an orphaned immigrant?

Of course, she always became nostalgic this time of year. Maybe that explained her quandary. Thanksgiving and Christmas celebrations were family days. The same dilemma would arise again this year: Where would they go during the holidays?

She shuddered at the thought of spending any part of the holidays with Jeff's parents, Harmon and Jeanette Harrison. They were well-known in Houston for their philanthropy and social status, and never missed a chance to boast about it. It had always struck Megan as strange that Jeff rarely recited any experiences that he had had as a child with his father. *I guess I'm comparing Jeff's relationship with his father to the relationship I've always had with mine,* she thought.

Megan reminisced about the time last year when she and Jeff went to his sister's wedding. She had been miserable during the entire visit. Jeff's mother and her snobbish River Oaks friends had treated her like some tramp from the trashiest part of town. The vivid memory of meeting Jeff's mother flashed through Megan's mind:

> "Let's see ... you're home is in ...?" the stocky-built, graying icon of Houston society asked. Her glasses hung from the tip of her nose as she scanned Megan from head to foot.
>
> "Laredo," Megan replied, her head held high, as her eyes searched the room for Jeff to come to her rescue.
>
> "That's on the Mexican border, I believe, isn't it?" She asked as if she meant to say: *it's an undesirable neighborhood.*
>
> "That's correct," Megan answered. "I spent my childhood in Laredo ... that's in Texas, you know. I was born in the United States," she added with a whiff of sarcasm. "I am a citizen of the United States."
>
> "And your parents?" she asked, with a smirk on her face, totally ignoring Megan's comment. "Where do they live now?"
>
> "My father and mother own a jewelry store in Nuevo Laredo, Mexico, but they live in our family home in Laredo ... where I grew up."
>
> "You have a lot of immigration problems along the border, don't you?" she said with a nonchalant demeanor that was on a par with asking about the weather. "And I read about all the killings and shootings."
>
> "My father and mother deal with it," Meghan snapped, trying to control her irritation from the woman's innuendos. "The immigration issues are not limited to the border cities, in case you didn't know."
>
> "I am somewhat familiar with Laredo," she said, again ignoring Megan's remark. She pushed her glasses back in place. A frown wrinkled her forehead. "We send one of our debutantes to their George Washington Celebration every year. Personally, I have felt it was a waste of time and effort. I presume that you were a debutante in Laredo, were you not?"
>
> "As a matter of fact, I was. And the George Washington Celebration *is* a very significant event for both Nuevo Laredo and Laredo," she said, determined not to let the woman intimidate her.

Megan shook her head to break the trance. She remembered how ruffled she had become at the remark about the celebration. Megan's thoughts shifted back to Jeff. She recalled how he had tried to reassure her after she had been the target of his mother's abrasive behavior. "Forget it," he had said. "That's just her typical conduct any time I have ever brought a guest home. I should have warned you."

Now she wondered: *Where do I stand with Jeff? I care for him and I know he cares for me, even if his mother doesn't think I measure up to her social standards.* She and Jeff had enjoyed a comfortable cohabitation for over three years. Why should she be concerned now?

What had happened to her that had triggered these thoughts that were whirling through her mind? Maybe it was just because she had been shocked into the realization that, at nearly thirty years of age, she was unmarried and childless.

She parked in her usual spot, walked to the elevator entrance, and went straight to her desk. First, she needed to get the chief to authorize her to investigate Ignacio's case, and then she had to have Jaime find out where Ignacio was domiciled. She cleared her desk of the usual early-morning mundane tasks, left voice mail messages for Jaime and the chief, and put in a call for Jeff.

"Hey," he answered after only two rings.

"Remember me?" she said. "We've hardly spoken in two days."

"Yeah," he said, "I've missed you."

"We need to talk," she replied, with a determined tone to her voice.

"What's up?" he said. "This doesn't sound like you."

"I just need to talk to you. I'll tell you later."

"You've piqued my curiosity. Must be serious."

"I think it is. I just want to talk to you."

"Can we have lunch?" he said.

"I hoped you'd ask. Let's go to that deli where we went when we first met in law school."

"Is this National Nostalgia Week?"

"Stop it, Jeffrey! I'm *serious* about talking to you *seriously*."

"I'll be there."

Chapter 2

▼

Megan arrived first and ordered for both of them: a corned beef on rye sandwich—Jeff's favorite—and her usual, a smoked turkey on wheat with mustard. She picked a booth in a remote corner while she waited, hoping the cacophony of voices echoing off the walls and ceiling wouldn't be too distracting.

"You're worried about something?" said Jeff as he scooted into the seat across from Megan. He began adding sugar and lemon to the glass of tea that Megan had ready for him.

"Yeah, I was called to Detention and Removal yesterday to help interview an eleven-year-old boy from Mexico whose parents died during the crossing process."

"Was that the kid who was the only survivor of an accident? I read something about it."

"Same one. He is a beautiful child. He is so scared; it just made me want to cry … the way he looked at me with those big, 'maple syrup' eyes. I can't get him out of my mind."

"You joined me for lunch just to tell me about another illegal Mexican who got caught crossing the border?"

Megan didn't answer. Her unblinking eyes fixed on Jeff as if she were startled by the look of indifference on his face. After a few painfully silent seconds, Jeff looked at Megan.

"What's wrong?"

"Jeff, I asked to see you because I need your help. I don't *know* what's wrong with me. I just can't get it out of my mind. That child needs me. I have to do something to help him."

"This *is* important to you, isn't it ... this thing about the orphaned boy?" he said. "I apologize for my trite remark. Sure, I'll help you. If it's serious for you, it's serious for me."

"Thank you," she said. "You sound more like yourself now."

"Tell me more about the boy," he said, as he pushed his sandwich plate aside.

"Look, I know there are thousands of pitiable cases similar to this, but there is something different about this one. I almost fainted when I walked in to interview this child yesterday. He looked so much like my younger bother that died years ago ... when I was just a child. It was an eerie feeling; I thought I must have been having hallucinations. I have such an intense feeling that this little boy needs me."

"I'll do anything I can to help you; I'm just a little curious why you feel so strongly about it," he said. "Do you think it has anything to do with the loss of your brother? I know you have always seemed reluctant to talk about it ... always makes me think it must have been some tragic occurrence."

"I don't know ... maybe so ... it *was* tragic," she replied. She silently stared into emptiness for a few seconds before facing Jeff again. "I just don't know what's wrong ... I just know that I needed to talk to you," she said. "Do you think it could be because I'm almost thirty ... wondering if my life has meaning. Where am I going? What's my purpose?"

"Maybe you're thinking of 'feathering a nest.'"

"Maybe so." She looked longingly into his eyes. "Whatever is going to happen to us, Jeff?"

With a now-softened look of concern and a tenor of sincerity, he said: "We may be able to make some long-range plans for ourselves before too long. I think the law firm is going to make me partner soon."

"Great news, Jeff! You've worked so hard to get there."

"We've both worked hard these last few years to get where we are; we really haven't taken time to explore our relationship as closely as we should have," said Jeff. "It might be a blessing that you have these thoughts racing through your head right now. Maybe it's time we took a closer look at ourselves. I think both of our lives have meaning ... for each other."

"Jeff, do you ever think about what it would be like to have a baby?"

"Funny that you should ask," he said. "I've wondered lately what it would be like. One of the younger members of the firm is married and his wife is pregnant with their first. He's so excited about it ... brings copies of the sonograms to the office. He already knows it's a boy."

"I don't think I'd want to know," said Megan.

"I agree. I'd rather wait until the baby was born to know ... besides, what difference would it make?"

"You sound like me. Maybe it's because we've been together so long that we think alike."

"I think it would be cool to have kids," said Jeff. Before continuing, he gazed out the window for a few moments, as if in contemplative thought. "I've thought a lot about the kind of father I'd like to be ... as different from my own father as possible. I'd spend time with my kids ... do things with them, teach them values, get to know them better as they grew older."

"You'd make a good father," said Megan. "You remind me so much of my own father."

"I've heard you talk about your mom and dad," he said. "You had something growing up that I never had. My sister and I were closer to our nanny and our chauffer than we were to our parents."

"I've never heard you talk much about your family, except your sister," she said. Megan chuckled. "What do you suppose your parents think about your living with a Mexican girl from Laredo?"

Jeff was quiet for a short interval, again gazing across the room before answering. Finally, he turned to Megan with a facial expression of solemnity. "You know what? I don't care what they think. I don't remember a time in my life that I ever did anything for which the sole purpose was to please my parents."

"It doesn't surprise me to hear you say that," she said. "I guess that's one instance where we're different. I lived to please my parents, especially my father."

"You had good reason to," said Jeff. "Your parents were concerned for your welfare ... still are, from what I hear you say about them."

"Always will be, I guess," said Megan. "On another subject, before I forget to ask, what are we going to do about holidays this year?"

Jeff grinned. "Not with *my* parents, if that's why you asked. I've been meaning to tell you—my sister called me at the office a couple of days ago," he said. "She and her husband would like us to go to Cancun with them during the holidays. I think she wants to get to know you better."

"I'd like that. It would be a much-needed retreat for both of us."

"I had thought about going to Vail, skiing, like we did two years ago," said Jeff.

"We did have a great time ... we need to go back sometime. But this year, I like your sister's idea."

"So do I," he said, "but, back to the present, what are you going to do about the kid ... what's his name?"

"Ignacio. Ignacio Narváez," she said as she stood and gathered the empty plates to take to the trash receptacle. "I've got to interview him again today and get started on my investigation of his case. And I know you probably need to get back to your office. Can I get more tea for you?"

"No, thanks. I do need to get back," he replied. "But what can I do to help you with Ignacio? That's the most pressing issue."

"Just stay close to me," she said. "I just have an ominous feeling about this case … and about myself. I need you, Jeff."

"Look, I'll be there for you … whatever you need," he said. "I can see how important this is to you, *and* how worried you are about it."

"I was hoping you'd understand."

"My knowledge of immigration law is limited, but I'm available otherwise. What do you do when you investigate a case like this?"

"Try to seek out the details—where did the immigrant come from, what family he has in Mexico, how he crossed, and something about the *coyote* if possible. This case is going to be difficult … trying to get full information from an eleven-year-old. It'll take a while before he's ready to talk, considering the emotional trauma he's been through. I'll need some time to get close to him."

"Yeah, I see what you mean. I think your encounter with this boy has had an impact on you," he said.

"That's putting it mildly. I don't understand it, Jeff. I know it sounds weird, but I feel that Ignacio has been brought into my life for a reason … I feel that I've known Ignacio forever."

"Sure, everything happens for a reason, Megan. Look … I don't remember much Spanish from school, so I won't be able to talk to Ignacio, but I might come in handy in some other way."

"Thanks, Jeff. I'll welcome your assistance. I know so little about eleven-year-old boys."

"Megan, please sit down again for a minute before you go," said Jeff. "I hear your obsession for helping this boy, and that makes me wonder if your goals in life are changing. You've always been career oriented. What's happened?"

"I can't explain it," she replied. "Ever since I saw that poor, orphaned child, it's as if my world of today has crashed around me. Maybe I *do* want to build a nest and have children … I don't know. I guess I don't understand it myself. I don't know how else to tell you."

Jeff's unblinking stare at Megan, his forehead wrinkled in a shallow frown, lasted an uncomfortable few moments without his saying a word. Megan held eye contact and never moved.

"You *are* serious, aren't you?" he said. "It's not just a hormonal thing, is it?"

"I don't know, Jeff," she said, "If you were not serious a while ago about our building a life together, please say so now. Do I detect some second thoughts on your part?"

"No … no, I meant every word I said." He took her hand. "I know that we need to start planning our future. I guess I'm just not sure that I'm ready—or capable even—of assuming all of the responsibilities that go along with marriage. But I'm sure of one thing: I want us to spend the rest of our lives together."

"I feel the same way, Jeff, but some day we have to tell the world. I want to have a baby some day, Jeff. I want you to be the father, but not if we're not married. I guess too much of my old-fashioned culture is showing."

Megan continued to look him in the eye without speaking. She stroked his smooth cheek with her free hand and slowly slipped her other hand from his grasp. "I wish you would think about it, Jeff." She stood and turned to go.

* * * *

Megan had taken only a couple of steps toward the exit door when her cell phone vibrated. It was Jaime Cordova.

"Megan, the Ignacio Narváez case is getting more complicated. I sent you an e-mail earlier."

"I was out for lunch … has anything happened to Ignacio?"

"No, he's all right," said Jaime. "It's just this: the boy has a canvas tote bag that he's been carrying ever since he arrived. One of the attendants at the center has tried to get him to surrender the bag. The ICE agents suspect he has something that he picked up at the accident site that might be critical to an investigation of his case. Every time anyone gets close to him he grabs the bag and recoils like there's something in that bag that he is protecting. When you interview him again, the chief wants you to try to find out what it is."

"The greedy attendants at the center probably think he is carrying money. I doubt they're concerned with the thoroughness of the investigation … just looking for something of value to pilfer," said Megan. "Get him away from the center, Jaime. I'll be back shortly. Jeff and I just finished lunch … been getting his advice on this case."

"Jeff's going to help you?"

"Yeah, he's offered to. I need his support in dealing with this little boy. Anything wrong with that?"

"No, as long as you remember that you are responsible."

"Jaime, just from my one visit with Ignacio, and now, from what you just told me, it's going to take time to get through to him … build trust and friendship so he'll open up to us. I have a feeling that there's more to this case than meets the eye. There's no telling what we might uncover. Do you have any more information on Ignacio and his family?"

"Only that one of the guys in detention thinks he may have a sister. Ignacio yells something about a sister any time anyone gets close to the canvas bag he carries."

"That's strange. Why would he mention a sister? There was no one other than Ignacio in the truck with the parents. We've got to find out more about the circumstances of the crossing.

"Looks like it *is* gonna be complex, Megan … but I know you're on a roll. I've seen you like this before," he said. "I'll have Ignacio brought to the conference room."

"Thanks, Jaime. With Jeff's help I should be able to give you a report soon. If I can only get Ignacio to talk. I have a feeling he probably has an incredible story to tell. Do you suppose Ignacio has a sister who is still in Mexico? The parents would not have left her behind if she were a child."

"I've wondered about that. If he has a sister, there may be other family members we can find."

"Thanks for the info, Jaime. I'll see you at the office."

✳   ✳   ✳   ✳

Jeff had stood close by while Megan talked to Jaime. "I could hear only one side of your conversation with Jaime," he said, "but it sounds like there's plenty of work ahead on this case."

"Sure you want to get involved?"

"Absolutely! I'm not going to let you have all the fun. I'm going to check in at the office … I'll be right behind you."

Chapter 3

Driving back to her office, Megan replayed in her mind her talk with Jeff. He seemed to be hesitant about making any long-range plans. Was he trying to justify living together without marriage—over an expended period of time? *I hope I didn't sound too dogmatic when I expressed my beliefs,* she thought. *What if I lose him? I couldn't live without Jeff.*

They probably should have had this talk a long time ago. Maybe this was the best way for it to happen—her dilemma over Ignacio bringing the issue to the surface. If Jeff had some reservations about their future, she was better off knowing now.

As she neared her office, she felt tightness in her throat, and her eyes became misty. She was struck by the realization that she *could* lose Jeff. She then would be just like Ignacio—she would be alone. What would life be like without Jeff? They had been together almost four years, ever since their second year in law school. She wondered if he was having the same thoughts. But right now she had work to do.

She tried to avoid eye contact with anyone in the office as she made her way to her desk to check her messages. There were three e-mails from Jaime Cordova. Ignacio was being held in the old Oakmont School building that had been converted to a detention center for illegal aliens being held for deportation.

My God! she thought. *Surely they have not dumped that poor child into the same holding area with the dozens of others. This soon after such an emotional happening in his young life he should be with someone who can comfort him. He desperately needs counseling. Besides that, there are always a few criminals among groups of immigrants who have been apprehended.* She called Jaime.

"Jaime, what the hell is going on?" she yelled. "You can't house an innocent kid without parents in the same place with all those others."

"Cool it, Megan," he said. "It's just for one day. We don't have any other place for him right now."

"Well find a place, dammit!"

"What's with you and this kid?" he retorted. "He's just another illegal immigrant … just like the hundreds of others we deal with every month."

"He is not!" she said, and then caught herself from further admonishing Jaime. There was nothing Jaime could do. She never remembered a time when they had had an orphaned child to process. "I'm sorry, Jaime. I've just been struck with the plight of this poor child."

Jaime laughed and then said, "Hey, I understand. It's the motherly instinct showing." He was quiet for a few moments. "Maybe there's an answer to this problem, Megan," he added finally. "We're trying to find relatives, but it will take a month at least. Let's talk to the chief … see if he can arrange something safer for the boy in the meantime. What do you think of that approach?"

"Sure, let's give it a try," she said. "I just want to get Ignacio out of that detention center. You know better than anyone how illegal immigrants are abused in those centers. The incident with his tote bag is a typical example. He's just a child, Jaime."

"Megan, it's obvious that you're serious about the welfare of this boy … whatever the reason," said Jaime. "Maybe you could convince the chief to let you take temporary custody of Ignacio."

"You've got to be kidding, Jaime. He'd never do that. What would I do with Ignacio? I can't take off a month from work to take care of a child in my home, and besides …" She stopped. The realization hit her: she would have to talk to Jeff and get his approval first.

As though Jaime knew what she was thinking, he said, "I'll bet Jeff would enjoy having a kid like this around. The chief would give you a month off."

Megan was silent. Maybe she and Jeff *could* keep Ignacio until some relatives were found. They could hire a sitter to stay with Ignacio during the day—maybe someone who could teach him English. She wouldn't *have* to take off work.

"Megan … are you still there?"

"Yeah, Jaime, I'm here," she answered. "Could you arrange to have Ignacio brought here for me to interview?"

"Hey … you're thinking, aren't you?"

"Let me talk to him—away from the others."

"I'll let you know when he's here."

"Just get him out of that old school building."

* * * *

Ignacio was escorted into the conference room—still with the same vacant look on his face. He clutched the soiled, tattered canvas bag as though he were afraid that someone would snatch it away from him. When he saw Megan stand to meet him, a faint smile of recognition appeared but quickly faded into an expressionless portrait.

"Hi, Ignacio. I'm glad to see you again," said Megan, speaking in the Tex-Mex conversational Spanish that she had learned in her childhood. She realized that her Spanish likely would not be in the dialect that Ignacio was accustomed to, but she felt sure it was close enough that he would understand her. "Do you remember me?"

The boy looked at Megan and nodded his head slightly but didn't speak. Instead, he turned his saddened eyes toward the window and sat with a stone-faced stare.

Megan closed the door so they could be alone. Rather than sit across the table from Ignacio, she sat in a chair next to him. She thought that probably he had been interrogated so many times by immigration officers seated in front of him that he was frightened to a point of being speechless.

"My name is Megan, Ignacio," she said.

The boy, showing no response, kept staring out the window. Megan placed one hand on his shoulder and reached out with the other to hold Ignacio's hand in hers. He made no effort to pull away.

"I know you must be very sad and frightened, but you are going to be all right," she said. "I will be your friend and I will take care of you. You will stay close to me until we can get you back home to your people ... to your sister. Do you understand me, Ignacio?"

He nodded but made no attempt to speak. When Megan mentioned his sister, he pulled his tote bag closer to his side.

"You don't need to talk to me right now," she said. "I know how scared you must be. You can tell me about yourself later. Also, Ignacio, you won't have to go back to that place where you stayed last night. You will stay at my house, so I can protect you."

Ignacio turned to face Megan, and looked at her carefully as though he were seeing her for the first time. His eyes appeared slightly glazed with tears forming.

He smiled—not a broad smile—but a smile. In a soft, barely audible voice he said, *"Gracias, señora."*

My God, I've done it, she thought. *Now I have to plead with Jeff to agree to our taking Ignacio home with us. We will either have to find someone to stay with him or I'll have to take off work. What will the chief say?*

✳   ✳   ✳   ✳

Robert Schneider, the chief investigator in the Houston division of the Immigration and Customs Enforcement office, was known for his strict adherence to protocol. He had been with the agency for twenty-four years and had helped shape most of the policies of the old Immigration and Naturalization Service. Always strict in enforcement of the rules, he had been consistently fair in any decision related to the treatment of illegal aliens. Any customs or immigration officer who ever showed anything but humane treatment of an immigrant was severely reprimanded.

Now he had an eleven-year-old boy who had been orphaned as a result of an intoxicated *coyote*'s disregard for the welfare of the illegal immigrants he was transporting. What could he do with the child? This problem, along with his graying hair and the growing prominence of the wrinkles in his face and neck, reminded him that he was getting older and needed to take more time off the job. He found himself becoming less tolerant and more irritable with the influx of immigrants from Mexico.

Whatever would the answer be to the escalating issue: industry in the United States exploiting the availability of cheap labor? They should be prosecuted if they hired an illegal worker. But that was only one solution.

His thoughts shifted back to Ignacio. It would take weeks to find Ignacio's relatives in Mexico. He couldn't release the boy to just anyone, unless he was certain of a kindred relationship to that person. One thing he was sure of: he wouldn't allow the boy to be housed in the same detention center with the other detainees.

Robert had never faced a problem like this. Perhaps the state's Child Protective Services agency could help—find a foster home for Ignacio. But what about the problem of security? What if the boy escaped? What if he became ill or was kidnapped and exploited? There was no way around it. Ignacio had to be kept under special custody—safe and secure custody—until he could be deported.

Robert's deliberations were interrupted by a call from his secretary, Amanda Taylor, who reminded him of Megan Andrade's request for an appointment.

"What does she want?"

"I'm not sure. Jaime says it's important and that you need to see her as soon as possible."

"I hope she's not sick or pregnant. We can't afford one more person absent right now with the volume of deportees we're dealing with."

"When can you see her? You have a cancellation. You're free from one to three o'clock this afternoon."

"Who canceled?"

"The Homeland Security guy for this region. He wanted some assistance at the airports. Jaime handled it."

"Good for him. Yeah, let me talk to Megan this afternoon."

"I suggest you talk to Jaime first, so you'll be prepared for Megan's visit."

"You said you didn't know what Megan wanted."

"Just rumors that are going around."

* * * *

"A surprise visit, Megan!" said Robert. "To what do I owe this delight?"

"Cut the crap, Rob," said Megan, with a smile. "With the enigmatic information network you have in this department, you know everything that's going on in ICE."

"All right … all right, out with it. What do you want? Are the rumors true? I've heard how intent you are to help this boy."

"Look, I know and you know that you have a problem," said Megan, her unblinking eyes focused on Robert's. "I'll get right to the point. Get me temporary custody of Ignacio Narváez … for at least six weeks. I'll take the burden of this kid off your shoulders. I'll need the department to pay for a sitter during the day."

"I can't do that, Megan," he replied. "That's never been done before. You are an employee of the department. A step like that would leave me open to criticism. It's just out of the question."

"Then what are you going to do?"

"What about asking Child Protective Services to place him in a foster home?" he asked. "Can that be done?"

"He's not eligible for CPS," said Megan. "He's not a resident of Texas."

"Then he will have to go back to the detention center. We don't have funds to cover individualized care for immigrants."

"You'll have criticism and legal action that you wouldn't believe. What happens if he's molested? You'll have every human rights organization and every news media in the country to deal with. He has to be placed. I'm giving you a way out, Rob."

"Can you find a judge who would grant custody to an employee of the department?"

"I'll have one before the day is over."

Robert, with a deeply creased brow, stood and stared out the window without speaking. After a minute or so, he returned to his desk, stared at Megan while he stroked his clean-shaven face, and shook his head.

"If you get me in a jam with the department …"

"Look, Robert, I'm your attorney. I'll make sure whatever we do is legal and that the department is protected."

"How am I going to explain the cost of someone staying with him during the day?"

"We'll let Jaime worry about that," she said, as she bounced out of her chair and prepared to leave. "Thank you, Rob. You'll be glad some day that you did this. Then we are in agreement … right? Oh … Jeff's on his way over. He's going to help me with Ignacio."

"You young guys are going to send me to my grave."

"Don't leave. I'll have some papers for you to sign in a few minutes," she said as she closed the door to Rob's office and hurried off.

She needed to get the custody papers completed and filed before Rob found some reason for not signing them.

Chapter 4

Megan glanced at her watch. She would have to hurry and get the custody papers ready for Rob's signature and ready to send to a judge. Next on the agenda would be to take Ignacio to the nearest kids' clothing store—probably some place like Gap Kids. Jeff should be here soon to help with shopping. She knew so little about a boy's clothes preferences at this age. *God, how I hope Jeff agrees to my plan to take custody of Ignacio,* she thought. *He said he would help me. Surely he hasn't changed his mind.* She passed by Amanda's desk on the way to her office.

"Thanks for arranging my time with Robert, Amanda. I'll be back in just a few minutes. Don't let him leave before he signs some papers for me."

"Oh … Megan," she replied, a sly look on her face. "There's a man here to see you. I put him in your office."

"Who is it?"

"I didn't get his name. All I could do was gawk at his good looks."

"What does he look like?" asked Megan.

"Sort of a cross between Tom Cruise and Brad Pitt," said Amanda.

"And he has black hair, deep blue eyes, and is dressed like he had just left a men's clothing store," said Megan.

"So you know it's Jeff?"

"Just guessed."

Megan could feel her heart thumping in her chest, wondering how Jeff would respond to her plan for Ignacio. Her hand trembled as she opened the door to the corridor and headed for her office.

Through the window she could see him sitting in a chair with his back to the door. There was no question—it was Jeff. Even without seeing his face, she'd recognize him anywhere—his erect posture, his squared shoulders, his head held high. She paused a few seconds before opening the door, still wondering how she was going to handle this. *What will he say when I announce that Ignacio will be staying with us until some member of his family is found?*

She hurried through the door and went straight to her computer to prepare the custody papers. Jeff jumped to his feet.

"Hey, Jeff ... glad you're here."

"Am I interrupting something?"

"It's all right," she answered, "I have to get these custody papers signed as soon as possible. The chief agreed to give us custody of Ignacio until he could be returned to his family."

"What?" he exclaimed. "You're assuming custody of this boy ... he's going to be living with us?"

"It will only be for a month or six weeks. We've got to get him out of that detention center."

"You should have waited and discussed it with me first," he said.

"I'm sorry, Jeff, I didn't have time ... just got the chief's approval a few minutes ago. I never thought of this option until Jaime suggested it."

"I'll be sure and thank Jaime," said Jeff, his voice oozing sarcasm.

"Look, Jeff, we don't have to do this. It's not final until I sign it," she said. "Let's spend some time together with Ignacio this afternoon and then discuss it later—before you jump to conclusions. I want you to be convinced that it's the right thing to do."

"I like that idea," he said. "I know you're determined in your plans for Ignacio. You must've looked at other options ... haven't you?"

"We've looked into every possibility," she said as she walked to the printer to retrieve her documents. "There are just no safe places for him to stay."

"I have some news that you might want to hear," said Jeff. "I just found out. At the meeting at the office this morning, the firm voted to take me in as a full partner ... starting immediately."

Megan whirled to face him. In her haste, her custody papers sailed across the floor. "Jeff!" she cried. "Congratulations! I'm so happy for you! I know how hard you've worked to make partner."

Jeff started helping her pick up the scattered pages. "I was hoping you'd think it was good news for both of us," he said. A broad grin creased his face.

"Of course it is," she said as she pulled him up from the floor for a hug and a sloppy kiss that left lipstick smeared across his lips.

Megan bundled the papers and headed for the door, Jeff started to follow, but Megan stopped him. "Wait here," she pleaded, "I have to get signatures on these. I'll be back in a few minutes, and then I'll introduce you to Ignacio."

*   *   *   *

"Megan, have you thought of all the possible consequences of what you're doing?" asked Jeff when she returned and then darted out again. He followed, working hard to keep up with her. "You know very little about this boy. Think of all the diseases he might be carrying. Can we trust him to stay in our home while we are away? Even if we have a caretaker with him, he could escape. We would be responsible."

"You're talking like a lawyer now. Wait till you see him … you'll be impressed," said Megan as they raced to catch the elevator to go up to Detention and Removal. "You know Jaime Cordova."

"Sure, I know Jaime … I've seen him in here several times," said Jeff, still trying to match Megan's fast pace. "I heard your side of the conversation earlier when he called. Tell me again, what is his position with ICE?"

"He's in charge of Detention and Removal. He has Ignacio there now. He's still trying to get Ignacio to talk."

As they approached Jaime's office, Jeff asked, "Does Ignacio understand any English at all?"

"Not yet," she replied. "That's one of my goals—to arrange lessons."

"So right now he won't understand what I say and I won't be able to understand him."

"I can translate, and he can read body language. Try to show compassion. He is so scared. I think he'll feel more secure when he sees the two of us together … maybe feel like he belongs."

"Megan, I'm not into these psychosocial issues like you are. I feel sorry for these people, but I'm not interested in their cultural survival."

Megan stopped in her tracks, scowled at Jeff and said: "Why don't you just leave? No one is stopping you. You've contributed nothing but criticism of any plan to care for Ignacio. I can handle this by myself. Just go."

"Don't be so sensitive. I'm just concerned that you might be doing something that you'll regret later," he said.

"If you are sincere, you'll help me rather than delivering your innuendos," she said as she struck off down the corridor again. Jeff followed, shaking his head in bewilderment.

Jaime met them at the door. "Hey, Megan, heard you got the chief to agree."

"Yeah … thanks for your help, Jaime. You remember Jeff."

"Hi, Jeff. What a treat … huh? You get to participate in the national illegal immigration crisis." Jaime grinned and slapped Jeff on the back.

"He's not overwhelmed with joy, Jaime," said Megan.

"I'm still in shock," said Jeff. "Is all of this legal? I can just see someone serving citations on us if we do anything for this boy that could be construed as compensation to an illegal immigrant for work. Or what's worse—cited for child labor violations."

"Hey, man," said Jaime, as he nodded toward Megan. "You don't need to ask *me* a legal question. Anyway, Ignacio is legal now with the papers Megan has … he's not a *documented* immigrant, but he's in the country legally as long as he's in your custody. Wait till you see this kid, Jeff. He's a lovable child. I wish I could take him home. My wife would love it."

Jeff chuckled. "Maybe we could cut a deal."

"I don't think you'd risk it," said Jaime, pointing to Megan. He turned to Megan with a serious look on his face. "Megan, there's just something strange about Ignacio. I've been trying to get through to him—you know, get him to talk about his home and family. I can't get anywhere."

"So I've heard. It'll take time," she said. "Jeff and I will work with him. We'll be there to listen when he's ready to tell his story. Did you get any information at all?"

"I'm pretty sure he does have a sister … he won't talk about her. When his sister is mentioned he turns his head and acts like he is going to cry. He holds onto that canvas bag he's carrying. He carries it with him wherever he goes. I tried to get him to let me watch it for him while he went to the bathroom—no deal. He won't turn it loose."

"Probably his only remaining link to his home and family," said Megan. "I agree it's strange. He's just a scared boy, Jaime. Nothing more about his sister, then—how old she is or where she lives?"

"Not a clue. When I tried to get information about her, he became tense, seemed more fearful."

"Those are the keys, then, Jaime—his sister and the canvas bag that he protects."

"Good luck, guys." Jaime laughed. "Maybe what you're doing will catch on in the community. Maybe you're starting a trend."

"Don't count on it," she answered and nodded toward Jeff. "You see how *he* thinks ... like most people about immigrants. Do you have time to take us to Ignacio?"

"Sure, he's still in the same conference room. I'll tag along and show you which room he's in—make sure you don't get lost—then I'll leave. You don't want too many people around if you expect him to open up."

Megan and Jaime, a continuous dialogue going about Ignacio—in both Spanish and English—took off down the corridors side by side with Jeff trailing behind trying to keep up.

"Was he injured at all in the accident, Jaime?"

"It's a miracle," said Jaime. "Just a few scratches. That pickup they were in was demolished. The driver and the boy's parents were killed instantly. The boy was thrown out and rolled down a grassy incline. They found him wandering around in a sort of shocklike state."

"Has he had the usual medical clearance?" asked Megan.

"Yeah, he's clean. He'll need some immunizations. You'll need to get that done in the next few days. Keep your receipts; we'll pay for them. I think he's desperately in need of grief counseling right now."

"I agree. There's so much to do in taking care of a boy this age—food likes and dislikes, clothes, English lessons." Then she added in Spanish, "I hope Jeff will go along with it."

"He doesn't seem too eager, but I predict he'll change after he's been around the kid for a while."

"I hope so," she said.

"Here's the conference room. I'll leave you here. With the papers you won't have any trouble getting out of the building."

"I want to stay here and talk to him for a while," said Megan.

"Sure. Good luck."

Ignacio, his head drooped, the same dejected look on his face, was seated in the same chair that he'd been in when Megan last saw him. His canvas bag rested in his lap, the shoulder strap around his neck. Megan studied the bag for a moment. It obviously was handmade out of a piece of scrap material. The flap that closed it was held in place by three evenly placed buttons. The button holes were made with precision sewing, and the double-layered shoulder strap was anchored in place with triple layers of stitching. *Whoever made this is a good seamstress, and it wasn't done overnight,* thought Megan. *Why is he so protective of it?*

Ignacio looked up when they entered and smiled briefly in recognition of Megan. He glanced at Jeff with a look of bewilderment and immediately clutched the bag lying in his lap.

"Hi, Ignacio," said Megan, speaking Spanish. "I want you to meet my friend. This is Jeff. He and I live in the same apartment … the home where you are going to live for a while."

Jeff, expressionless, arms crossed, leaned against the wall across the room and nodded at the boy. Ignacio didn't acknowledge Jeff's gesture. He turned back to Megan.

"Your husband?" he asked. A faint blush bathed Megan's face.

"Not yet … but someday soon. How are you feeling, Ignacio?" she asked.

"Good, señora," he said and cast his eyes toward the floor again.

"I'll bet you are hungry, aren't you?"

Ignacio jerked his head toward Megan, started to answer, and then looked away.

"Have you eaten anything today?"

He hesitated and finally shook his head.

"Then you and Jeff and I are going to find some food. We'll do that first and then we'll go shopping for new clothes and whatever else you need."

* * * *

Megan took Ignacio's hand in hers. With the canvas bag securely strapped around his shoulders and cradled in his other arm, Ignacio walked as closely to Megan as he possibly could. They exited the building and strolled along the sidewalk. Jeff dutifully followed a few steps behind.

Speaking in Spanish, Megan asked, "Anything special you would like to eat, Ignacio?" Ignacio didn't answer but shook his head.

"I'll bet you would like a hamburger or cheeseburger, wouldn't you? Have you ever eaten a hamburger, Ignacio?"

Again, he shook his head.

Using a few key words that she thought might trigger some response from Ignacio, Megan kept a semblance of dialog in Spanish going with the boy as they walked down the street.

Jeff had remained silent during the entire scenario. Finally, he said. "I'm beginning to feel left out here. I guess I'll leave you two to your fun and get back to the office."

"Sure, if that's what you want," said Megan. "I had hoped you'd help me introduce this child to his new world, but I can handle it alone."

"Look, I think it's commendable that you're dedicated to this 'help for humanity' thing, but you know I can't understand a word you are saying. You could at least clue me in every once in a while … like, where are we going right now?'"

"Oh … I'm sorry, Jeff," said Megan. "I was inconsiderate. I'll try to remember to give you a few translated words. We need to feed Ignacio. He probably hasn't eaten since last night in the detention center, and most likely not even then. I suggested a hamburger, but I'm not sure he has any idea what I'm saying. I'm not even sure if there is a Spanish word for hamburger. I really need you to come with us, Jeff."

Jeff increased his pace until he was alongside Megan and Ignacio. He avoided eye contact with Megan and was silent for a couple of prolonged minutes.

Finally, he pulled Megan and Ignacio to a halt. "Megan, you know, as we walk along here, I look at Ignacio, and I think of the life he's had and the grief he's dealing with. And then I think of my own childhood. I was a spoiled brat at this age—never wanted for anything, and threw a fit if I didn't get my way. Now, I'm acting like my own eleven-year-old self. I'll try to do better. Yeah, I'll help you with the boy. I apologize to you … and to Ignacio."

Jeff picked up his pace, walked alongside Ignacio, placed his hand on the boy's shoulder, and pulled him closer. Ignacio didn't pull away. He looked at Jeff and smiled faintly.

Megan, grinning and misty eyed, stopped abruptly and pulled Jeff's head down for a kiss. "Where can we find a good cheeseburger?" she asked.

Chapter 5

▼

"I like your hamburger suggestion," said Jeff. "It's probably a little soon for Ignacio to be taken to a 'fancy' restaurant."

Once inside the Burger-Deli, Ignacio, a tight grip on Megan's hand, moved closer to Jeff. His eyes roved constantly, suspiciously scanning every corner of the room and every person.

"He's frightened, Megan," said Jeff as he gently rubbed the boy's neck and shoulders.

"Probably the first time he's ever been in a place like this."

"I think it's more than that," said Jeff. "He acts as if there's someone or something that he's fearful of."

"Maybe you're right. Maybe we'll know more if we can ever get him to talk more," said Megan. "Go sit with him and I'll order for all of us. I know what you want … I'll get the same for him."

Jeff placed the boy in a booth first and then slid in beside him. Ignacio watched every person who entered. If anyone walked toward their booth, he became tense, grasped his canvas bag, and moved closer to Jeff. Jeff responded by placing his arm around the child's shoulders and trying to divert his attention by motioning to the menu tent-card in the center of the table. Megan soon returned with the hamburgers, french fries, and drinks.

"Do you want me to sit next to Ignacio?" she asked. "In case he needs some help with his cheeseburger?"

"I can handle it," said Jeff. "He acts like he's terrified of every person in here, especially if they come close for any reason. You're right—he needs a lot of reassurance."

"We'll have to stay close to him any time we're around a lot of people," she said. "Do you think we should cut the burger into smaller pieces?"

"No, I don't think so," said Jeff. "He's too old for that. He'll catch on as soon as he sees us eating."

Jeff put the sandwich in front of Ignacio. As soon as the aroma hit his nose, his eyes brightened and he stared at the food. Jeff tousled Ignacio's hair with his hand and grinned. The boy looked at Jeff and returned the grin—one broad enough to produce the heretofore unseen deep dimples, one in each cheek.

Jeff took his own sandwich, unwrapped the waxed paper covering, and took a deep bite. He grabbed a napkin and wiped the drippings from his chin. Ignacio watched Jeff's every move. Jeff nodded toward Ignacio's burger.

Ignacio repeated the unwrapping process, trying to copy Jeff as best he could. One small bite led to another, and another, each followed by a indisputable look of enjoyment. For the first time since he had been in their custody, his eyes truly sparkled.

Jeff grinned and his eyes softened as he looked at Megan who was trying to constrain her chuckling.

"What do you think of that? Whatever you name it: he likes his cheeseburger."

"Don't tell me you don't do well with children," said Megan. "Your performance is an award winner. I laughed trying to keep from shedding a tear. He likes you, Jeff. I think he feels safe when he's around you."

"I wish we knew why he's so frightened."

"We'll find out later if there is anything other than just being in a foreign country," said Megan.

"I have a feeling that there's something else we don't know about."

"There's an ice cream parlor a few doors down," said Megan. "Do you have time to go there before you go back to your office?"

Jeff looked at Megan sheepishly. "I called in while you were ordering. I'm not going back."

"Great," said Megan, smiling. "We're off to get ice cream, and then we'll go shopping for clothes."

Ignacio, his canvas bag held closely to his side, held Jeff's hand as they exited the Burger-Deli. A short walk brought them to the Marble Slab Creamery. Outside the entrance, a bicycle parking rack contained no fewer than five or six bikes, all colorful racing types. Ignacio pulled away from Jeff momentarily to examine the bicycles. Smiling all the while, he stroked the leather seat on one, grasped the handle bar, and whirled the pedals.

"I see what's in store for us—find a cycle shop and get a bike for Ignacio," said Jeff. "I can teach him to ride."

"Did your dad teach you to ride when you were little?"

Jeff frowned and looked away for a few seconds before answering. "Our chauffeur taught me how to tie my shoes, how to skate, and how to ride a bicycle. How about you?"

"My dad," she said. "When I was five or six years old. Then I helped my little brother when he got his bike. I can teach Ignacio."

"Why don't you ever talk about your brother?"

Megan stiffened. Her eyes showered Jeff with fire. "Why are you asking me about my brother?"

"I just wondered why you hardly ever mention him—you know, what he was like, what happened to him."

"It has nothing to do with Ignacio," she said, her face contorted into an umbrageous stare.

"Megan, why are you so upset? What did I say to trigger this sort of reaction?"

"There are some things we just don't talk about," she answered and turned to walk away. Ignacio dropped Jeff's hand and followed Megan, an anxious look on his face.

"Now you have Ignacio disturbed, Megan," said Jeff. "Come back here. We'll talk about it later."

Megan stopped and glanced at Ignacio. She smiled at him, took his hand, and returned to Jeff's side. She pulled Jeff's head down and kissed him. Ignacio grinned.

"I'm sorry, Jeff," she said. "I behaved badly. Yeah, you're right … we need to talk about it."

* * * *

Now with new clothes and a full stomach, Ignacio still clung to his tote bag with one hand and held on to Jeff with the other. He appeared a little more relaxed and occasionally asked Megan a question. Megan's cell phone rang and she flipped the lid open. It was Jaime Cordova.

"Megan, we just had a visitor … looking for Ignacio. I have a weird feeling about the guy."

"What do you mean?"

"I don't know. His questions didn't seem appropriate," he replied. "He was just a little too curious about Ignacio. He wanted to know where Ignacio is. Said he needed to interview him, but he couldn't produce any credentials to show that he was entitled to investigate the accident."

"What did you tell him?"

"I had to tell him that you had temporary custody of Ignacio. That seemed to disturb him. Wanted to know why Ignacio wasn't in the detention center. I just didn't get a good feeling about the guy. He had already been to the pound where the wrecked truck was taken."

"What did he look like?"

"He looked scary ... a big guy, forty to fifty, clean shaven, lean, and muscular. Had a sort of cynical attitude when he asked questions," Jaime paused. "He was not Hispanic; had an accent that sounded like East Coast or European. He wouldn't leave a card or a phone number. Said he'd be back."

"Thanks, Jaime. Jeff and I are headed for home," she said. "Call me if you hear any news. I don't know what to think about the mystery man. He probably *is* an insurance adjuster of some sort."

"Maybe so. Megan, he said one thing that disturbed me: He said that he suspected that some valuables had been taken from the pickup truck at the accident site. He asked if we knew anything about it.

"I'm sure you told him that we had nothing to do with the accident scene report."

"Yeah ... he said he'd probably need to get a lawyer to get the information he needed."

"I'll see you tomorrow. We're on our way home."

"How are you doing with the boy?"

"Ignacio ate like it was his last. You should see him in his new clothes," said Megan. "I think we're close to getting him to warm up to us."

"How's Jeff holding up?" asked Jaime.

"Fine." Megan laughed. "Right now he's worried how he's going to get Ignacio into his new pajamas tonight at bedtime. And I'm worried about how I'm going to convince him that he needs to brush his teeth before going to bed."

*   *   *   *

Megan left her car at her office building and all three climbed into Jeff's car. By the time they reached their apartment, Ignacio—securely belted in the front seat beside Jeff—had dropped off to sleep. Jeff guided his car into his parking slot but was a little slow in braking. The car bumped forcefully into the concrete wall. The abrupt stop jarred Ignacio awake. He sat upright, screaming with widened eyes and an expression of panic on his face. His screaming brought both Jeff and Megan to his side.

"Mamá! Papá! Ayúdame ... Ayúdame ...!" He struggled to climb out of the seat belt. He looked at Megan and then at Jeff. His eyes became misty, and he hung his head as though embarrassed by his outburst.

"It's all right, Ignacio. You're with us now. You're all right," said Megan softly, trying to comfort him. In English, she added to Jeff, "He was calling for his mama and papa to help him, Jeff."

Jeff loosened Ignacio's seat belt, and Ignacio fell into Megan's arms. She couldn't restrain her own outright sobbing as she held him close to her chest. Jeff hovered over both of them and tried to hide the tears that were forming in his own eyes.

"He had a flashback to the wreck tragedy," said Jeff. "How sad. He's really all alone, Megan."

"Imagine the turmoil going on in his mind right now," she replied. "He needs us, Jeff."

"I agree," said Jeff, as he leaned across the console, wrapped his arm around Megan and Ignacio, and pulled them closer. "There's so much more to learn about Ignacio—so many unanswered questions."

※ ※ ※ ※

They made no effort to exit the car; instead, they stayed clustered in the front seat. Ignacio snuggled close to Megan. No one spoke a word for a full two minutes. Megan embraced Ignacio and swept her face across his head of fine-textured black hair. She remained motionless except that she had begun to cry. Without looking up she finally spoke, her voice muffled.

"Jeffrey," she said, a long pause followed.

"Yeah," he answered. When she called him Jeffrey, he knew something serious was coming. He braced himself.

"I was ten years old ... Andy and I were in the swimming pool in our backyard. Mom and Dad were at the store; the housekeeper was inside the house. We were both good swimmers. Andy was six. I was convinced from the time I was a small child that my role in life was to take care of Andy. I loved that little kid, Jeff. He was always happy. You could never be sad around him. He found happiness every minute in every thing he saw or did, always laughing and giggling."

Megan stroked Ignacio's cheek and neck, pulled him closer to her chest, and began crying uncontrollably, finally stopping long enough to continue.

"Are you sure you can do this, Megan?" asked Jeff.

"He was in the far end of the pool … the deep end," she said as she struggled to speak, her chin trembling. "He called out: 'Meggie, Meggie, help me! I can't move. Meggie …' I can still see the frantic look on his face when I close my eyes. He was thrashing around trying to stay afloat. Something was wrong.

"I swam to him just as he went under. I dived after him and tried to pull him up. He grabbed me and pulled me down. No matter how hard I tried I couldn't bring him to the surface, Jeff. I tried and tried. I had to come to the surface to get a breath of air and then I dived down again and again and again …"

"I'm so sorry, Megan," said Jeff.

Although Ignacio couldn't understand a word Megan was saying, he must have sensed the gravity of the message she was conveying to Jeff. He reached out and took Megan's hand in his. He stayed still and quiet while Megan, fighting tears, tried to continue.

"That's the story of my brother, Jeff. He drowned while I was taking care of him. Just in a flash he was taken away from me. I've never been able to talk about the void it left in my life. Everyone said that I did everything I could … that I shouldn't feel guilty. But I failed him, Jeff … I failed him … I failed …"

Chapter 6

▼

Six Days Earlier

Ciudad Mante, Mexico—Saturday, November 10, 2007

When the whistle blew, signaling the end of another work week at the sugarcane refinery, Rafael Narváez tossed his gloves in his storage box and picked up his jacket that he had left there at 6:00 AM when his day had started. He stopped next at the cashier's window to report his hours and pick up his pay for the week. He needed to hurriedly count the pesos, as he did each payday, to confirm that the count was accurate.

He looked at the big clock in the cashier's cage. He had only a few minutes if he wanted to hop on the flatbed truck for his ride back to Ciudad Mante; if the count had been wrong he wouldn't have time to challenge the cashier anyway, so he crammed the pesos into his pocket and ran. If he missed his ride, he would have a ten-mile walk at night, fraught with the danger of being robbed. Somehow, highway thieves always knew when workers got paid.

Once on the truck, he put on his jacket; the wind on the open bed was chilling, just as it was every morning when he rode the truck *to* work. Riding along the highway, Rafael tried to calculate mentally how much money he had stashed away over the last six or seven years. With this week's pay he felt sure that he had reached his goal.

Time was passing so fast. Ignacio was eleven now and would be twelve within a few months. Esmeralda was thirteen already and fast becoming a woman. He had to make some decisions soon. In the deep spheres of his brain, the driving force to make a move kept creeping to the surface. He wanted to take his family across the border into the United States and start a new life. If his calculations were correct, he could finally start planning his move now.

He felt in his pocket and patted the pesos from the last week's sixty plus hours. Most of it would go into his savings box. In the other pocket was the letter from Julio, his friend in Houston, who told glorious pictures of life in Texas and of the amount of money he earned. He sent money back to his family in Guanajuato every month.

Rafael thought of following the same path—go to America alone and send money back home. But he couldn't bear the thought of leaving his wife and two children. If he could accumulate enough cash, they all could go and make a new life for themselves.

He was determined that was the best way. Even if it took longer to raise enough money, Rosa and the children would benefit if they could stay together in the new country. He had talked to his co-workers and friends in the village about his plan. They all said the same thing: if he was determined to go and take his family, now was the time, while he and Rosa were young and strong and while the children were young.

Once in Ciudad Mante, Rafael hopped off the flatbed truck, waved to his *compadres*, and started the three-mile trek to his home near Cuauhtémoc. The walk along this familiar path didn't pose any threat of danger to Rafael; he had made this trip so many times before. He knew every crook and turn along the way as well as the identity of every villager's home. But as a safety measure, before he started the walk to Cuauhtémoc, he removed his shoes and placed the peso bills inside.

As he trudged along, the folded pesos in his shoes made him feel as if he were stepping on stones; but every step triggered greater anticipation of leaving soon with his family for the trek to *El Norte*. The first thing he would do when he reached his home would be to put a generous portion of the money into his savings box—after he had counted the total amount again—as he did every week. For so many years he had saved and saved; he knew he was close to having enough money now for all four members of his family.

* * * *

Cuauhtémoc, Mexico—Saturday, November 10, 2007

Once home, Rafael removed the pesos from his shoes and set aside a small portion of his pay for their basic needs. He placed the balance in his savings box—after again counting the total amount in the box. Rosa seemed exceptionally taciturn as she scurried about the kitchen preparing an evening meal for her husband. *She must have had a difficult day with the children,* Rafael thought. *She's upset about something.*

"Where are Nacio and Esme?" he said.

"I sent them to bed early," she said. She continued fixing Rafael's dinner without further word.

"Anything happen today?" asked Rafael.

Rosa hesitated before answering. She took the warmed tortillas off her stove, wrapped them in a hot, wet piece of cloth, and placed them on the table alongside his food.

"A runner came with a message," she said, finally, without looking up.

Rafael arched his eyebrows—an expectant look on his face—paused at eating and waited for her to explain.

"What was the message?"

"From your friend, Julio. Some man will be in Ciudad Mante this Sunday to talk, if you are ready," she said, a downcast look on her face.

"Good ... good," said Rafael, "Where will I find him?"

"On a bench in the plaza ... the runner said the man would be wearing a pink shirt."

"Must be the same man who helped Julio go across ... good news, Rosa," said Rafael. He pushed his food aside, jumped to his feet, and reopened his savings box. Once again he counted the pesos. "We have enough!"

"Are you sure this is what you want?" said Rosa. She avoided looking at Rafael. "When the messenger came to the door, I was afraid that was what it was about. That's why I sent the children to their beds early, so they wouldn't know that we might be close to leaving."

"You know it's the best thing to do," said Rafael. "Nothing is ever going to change around here. If we want to better our lives—yours, mine, and the children's—we've got to make the *El Norte* trip."

"Do you think it's safe for Ignacio and Esmeralda? I worry about them, Rafael."

"I worry about all of you, but we've decided that I should not go alone."

"No ... no, I don't want you to go by yourself," she answered.

"Julio says his friend will take care of everything," he said. "We'll ride the bus to Monterrey. The man will pick us up there, take us to Nuevo Laredo, and get us across. Then he will pick us up on the other side for the rest of the trip."

"What about getting around the check stations?" she asked. "That seems to be where there's so much danger—walking at night through pastures with snakes. I hear scary stories."

"Julio says the man will tell us what to do." said Rafael. "He'll take care of us. This is a good time to go; there will be a bright moon and the weather will be cool so we won't have to worry too much about snakes. Also, we won't have to walk very far before the man picks us up again."

"I don't want to go," she said, as she blotted tears from her face. "We have everything we need right here, Rafael."

Rafael ignored her comment and gazed out the doorway with a faraway look in his eyes—the same fixed look that had signaled his yearning to leave these last few years. He finally turned back to his wife.

"If we're ever going to escape this place, now is the time," he said. "With the money we've saved, plus the money I borrowed from Julio, we have enough for all four of us to go."

* * * *

Rosa cringed when they talked about making the escape to *El Norte*. She had never been convinced that the benefit of going was worth the risk. Almost daily, when she joined the other wives at the river on washday, she heard stories about villagers dying of heat stroke, snake bite, starvation, or some fatal accident on their way to America. And so many had been caught by the *Federales* and sent back to Mexico—their money gone. But if Rafael said go, that's what they would do. The men made the decisions; it was not her place to question Rafael's decisions.

She, herself, was not afraid to make the trip; she was strong enough to withstand the dangers and hardships they would have to endure, but what about the children? Ignacio was only eleven and Esmeralda almost thirteen. Could she and Rafael protect them if they were threatened in some way?

But she did not want Rafael to go alone, even though that seemed to be the usual plan followed by the others who had elected to go to *El Norte*. What could she do? Since neither of them had family left that Rafael could turn to for advice, maybe she could get him to just go talk to Father Armando. But she was reluctant to suggest it.

Rosa looked about the interior of their dirt-floored *jacal*, the two-room, thatched-roof hut that her now-deceased uncle had given them when they married. Until the present, their life in Cuauhtémoc had not been all that bad, as far as she was concerned.

They lived comfortably. They had plenty of food, the village had schools now, and they had so many friends—all living within their means, just as they were.

However, the children *were* getting old enough that they each needed a separate room to sleep in. Esmeralda had already started her *regla* and was getting more curious by the day.

The man who had been the husband of Rafael's sister who died last year said he would help him add on a room, but Rafael said he didn't want the man around his children. Rosa wasn't sure why, but he must have had his reasons. She had wished Rafael would use the money he had saved to pay someone to fix up their *jacal*.

And they had been promised that they would have electricity in the village before too long—even electric stoves. She laughed at the thought. She couldn't imagine how it would be not to cook over an open fire. The village had made a few improvements every year. They now even had a well close by so they wouldn't have to carry water from the river.

They had been told that the river water was contaminated—whatever that meant—and for them not to drink it. But that didn't make sense; she had drunk water from the river ever since she was a child and nothing bad had happened.

If they left their home, what could she take with her? How could she get along without her *metate* to grind corn for tortillas? She had heard that, instead, they would have to buy tortillas already made from the store. What would they taste like? They couldn't compare with the tortillas that *she* made—the ones that her mother had taught her how to make years ago. She just wasn't sure if she was ready for all of these changes in her life.

But there was something that kept making Rafael think that he had to move on—to go to new places. She couldn't explain why he was so determined. Why couldn't he be satisfied with living in one place? Maybe he's like his grandfather. Ever since she and Rafael had been married, she had heard the story of how Señor Narváez had walked all the way from Ecuador to Mexico when he was a young man.

She wished Rafael had never gotten so involved with his friend, Julio. It seemed as if Rafael wanted to do everything Julio had done. If Julio had made it, in spite of the hazards, and had thrived in America, so could Rafael. And now he would show Julio what *he* could do: he would bring his family with him.

* * * *

"Why are we going this way, Esme?" asked Ignacio. He hastened his pace to keep up with his sister as they made their way through the thick foliage to the river, careful to avoid scratches from the thorny bushes and to avoid stepping on scorpions.

"Hermelinda may want to go to the river with us," she answered. "Try to be nice to her today, Nacio. And don't stare at her lip."

"Why is her lip like that?" he asked.

"She was born that way. It can be fixed, but she would have to go to the city and her parents don't have enough money to have it done."

"Papá talks about all of us going to *El Norte*. I hear him talking to Mamá. He says they have good doctors there."

"I don't want to leave here … leave our friends," she said.

"You don't want to leave Guillermo, do you?" he teased. "I saw you looking at yourself in Mamá's mirror this morning; and I saw you brushing your hair."

"Stop it, Nacio!" she said. "I'll dunk your head in the river again."

"Maybe Guillermo will go to the river with us," said Ignacio. "Then he can push you on the swing his papá made from the grapevine hanging from that big tree. He likes to watch your dress blow over your legs."

Ignacio raced ahead to avoid a slap from Esme.

"Just don't expect me to push you on the swing," she replied. "And I'm going to tell Mamá how you ripped your pants on that mudslide into the river."

"I don't want to leave either, Esme," said Nacio. "Why does Papá insist on going?"

"Mamá says it's because he wants better things for all of us. I don't see that it's all that bad right here."

"I don't either. What can we do?"

"Nothing," she said. "We just do what Papá says."

"They say that we have to walk through snakes and thorns, and that we have to go without water and food," said Nacio. "I'm going to tell Papá that I'll just stay here. I'm not going."

"He won't let you stay," said Esme. "Who will take care of you?"

"I'll run away. He can't catch me."

"Oh, yeah … you're so brave," she said, her face twisted into a smirk. "You'll do what Papá says, just like I will."

"You're afraid to run away with me, aren't you? You're afraid … just like all girls. You'd be scared."

"I'm going to tell Papá what you said, Nacio."

"And I'm going to tell him you don't want to leave Guillermo."

Esme took a small branch from a bush and chased Nacio, swinging the whip as she ran after him.

* * * *

Cuauhtémoc, Mexico—Sunday, November 11, 2007

Without waking Rafael, Rosa stood and quietly searched for her *manta* before going into the kitchen to start a fire. In the early morning, the air was cool enough for her to wear a shawl until the sun rose. She would let Rafael sleep since he didn't have to go to work on Sunday.

The children were already up and out. They likely had already joined the other children at the river's edge where they played games and sometimes tried to catch a fish or a frog. Esmeralda and Ignacio wanted a dog like some of their friends had, but Rafael had forbidden it … said he didn't want another mouth to feed.

Rosa enjoyed this time of the morning. She could sit in front of their hut and watch the sun peak over the mountains. The valley below came alive with sparkle as the sunrays bounced off the lingering layer of mist that blanketed the area in the early morning. This was a time she could be alone with her thoughts—while the firewood she ignited turned into coals, just right for cooking.

She would miss everything she experienced this time of day when they moved to *El Norte*: the beauty of the countryside, the early-morning sounds from the valley, their friends and neighbors. Would the children be truly happy with the change? What about the dangers? Could they chase off every morning on their own to play and visit with new-found friends? How she wished that Rafael would change his mind; but he was determined to leave.

She reminisced about the days when they had chickens running around in their small yard. Rafael had sold all of them and put the money in his savings box. She missed not being able to walk into their makeshift chicken pen to gather eggs every morning. The children had fun chasing after a hen when she wanted one to fix for a special meal. Now the only eggs or chickens they had were the few that their neighbors occasionally gave them. She felt like crying, thinking about making such a drastic change.

* * * *

Rafael stirred about, ate the now-cold tortillas and beans that Rosa had prepared for him. He looked for her and the children and surmised that they had gone to the river as they did almost every day. He dressed, retrieved his savings box from its secret hiding place, and hurried toward the village and the plaza.

Just as he had been told, the runner in the pink shirt sat on a park bench. He was munching on fresh roasted corn that he had bought from a vendor. Rafael sat beside him and—as he had been instructed—remained silent and waited for the man to speak. The *hombre* kept gnawing on the corn cob the best he could, considering his shortage of teeth. He glanced at Rafael, finally.

"You're Julio's friend?"

"Yes, sir," he replied.

"You have all the money?"

"Enough for the crossing. I will need to borrow a few pesos from a friend that I work with for the bus trip to Monterrey."

"Julio told you how much you would need?"

"Yes. He said to pay one-half for the four of us to cross and then the other half when we get to Houston."

"Right. Señor Jimbob will meet you in the *Gran Plaza* in Monterrey in three days—on Wednesday. Are you ready?"

"We will be. How will we know Señor Jimbob?"

"Just wrap this pink bandana around your neck," he answered and tossed Rafael a swatch of pink cloth. "He'll find you."

"Then I don't need to pay you anything now."

"No, Jimbob will pay me. I have written your instructions on this paper. Give this to Jimbob when you get to Monterrey. That will show him that I sent you. He will explain the crossing to you and your family."

"Are you sure he'll pick us up?"

"Yes," he answered. "We mustn't talk too long. The *Federales* are looking for runners. I don't want to go to jail."

"*Gracias, señor.*"

He stood, covered his pink shirt with his coat, tossed the corn cob into the gutter, and ambled away.

* * * *

Three days—seventy-two hours! And they would be on their way. Rafael floated on air all the way back to his home. He was anxious to tell Rosa. They had to hurry and pack the few belongings they would take with them. First they had to decide which few things they felt were most important.

Rosa would have to split the seams in his coat and hers in order to hide the money they had saved, and then sew the coats back again. Julio had told stories of thieves spotting villagers on their way to *El Norte,* and stealing their savings.

He had saved a large piece of canvas from an old tarp that he had salvaged on the highway one day. Rosa could make tote bags for each of them to carry their belongings.

He had waited so long for this day. He would send word that he would not return to the sugarcane refinery. When they got to America and he found a good job, he would make far more in one day than he made in a month at the refinery. He knew Rosa was saddened about leaving, but once in America she would make new friends and enjoy her new life. And the children would have school and entertainment that they had never dreamed possible. A whole new world awaited them.

CHAPTER 7

▼

Nuevo Laredo, Mexico—Tuesday, November 13, 2007

James Robert Clifton, known as Jimbob by most of the barkeeps in Nuevo Laredo, staggered into the Blue Eagle Men's Club and managed to find an empty seat at the bar. Through the smoky haze he could barely make out the silhouettes of the patrons that filled every chair. Some were content to drink and visit; others concentrated on the *Daily Racing Form* before placing their bets at the off-track betting window.

Jimbob glanced around the room. Other than Beto Jimenez, the bartender, he saw no familiar face. He tried to shake the cobwebs from his brain and remember why he had been forced to leave the last cantina he had visited. Then he remembered—he again had picked a fight with a stranger over a disagreement about the impact illegal Mexican immigrants had on America's workforce.

Jimbob made a good living smuggling workers into the country to take the jobs that lazy Americans refused to do. So ... he believed he had every right to defend his position. Of course he should have been more selective in choosing his adversary. The president of some ironworkers union had probably not been a good choice.

He liked the Blue Eagle better anyway. If anyone looked for him to do a job, they could leave a message at the Blue Eagle, and Beto would always promptly pass it on to him. And Beto would never have thrown him out like that bastard did at the other cantina. Jimbob felt at home at the Blue Eagle.

With the help of his feet, firmly planted on the brass rail, he shifted his heavy torso to the edge of the barstool as he reached for the drink Beto placed in front of him.

"Heard you got into another fight," said Beto as he marked up a new tab for Jimbob.

"How the hell did you know?"

"You oughta look at yourself in the mirror. And news travels fast in this town, Jimbob. Scared some of my regulars back this way."

"If you'd hire some of them pole-climbing dancin' girls you wouldn't lose your customers in the first place."

"Believe not, I'd have to hire a bouncer to settle all the fuckin' fights," said Beto as he wiped the countertop and pushed a bowl of peanuts toward Jimbob. "Oh, dammit, I forgot to tell you. There was a fellow in here looking for you."

"Yeah?" Jimbob came alive. "What'd he want?"

"Said you'd know. He was a big guy—tall but not fat. Looked like someone you'd see in an old war movie. Dressed like a World War II German SS officer. You know … mean looking, short haircut."

Jimbob paled and looked around the room.

"Oh, shit!" he said. "He's not still here, is he?"

"Nah. Said he'd come back later. He didn't leave a message."

"I think I'd better leave."

"Too late," said Beto, looking over Jimbob's shoulder. "I see him coming through the door."

Bernie Hefferman took a seat at the bar next to Jimbob. He tossed a twenty on the counter and ordered his drink. He avoided eye contact with Jimbob.

"Give the son of a bitch sitting next to me another one of whatever he's drinking," said Bernie. "Make it a double. He'll need it by the time I'm through with him."

"I'm gonna pay you, Bernie," said Jimbob. "Just lay off. I've got a big job starting tomorrow. Gonna pick up four. They've got the money, enough to pay you what I owe. Trust me, Bernie."

"Trust you? You sleazy bastard," said Bernie. "Chacón sent me here to take you out after the way you fucked up that last job. I'm gonna give you one more chance. And the only reason I don't burn you right now is that Chacón has a package that needs to be delivered to Houston in a hurry."

"Why don't you or Horse take it?"

"Chacón's afraid for any of us to do the job—afraid we'll be picked up by customs or the FBI if we try to cross the border. We're all on their watch-list."

"What's in the package?"

"None of your fuckin' business."

"What's in it for me, Bernie? How much?"

"Your goddamn life … if you don't fuck up again. If you pull it off, Chacón will make it worth your effort."

"That other deal wasn't my fault, Bernie. I told you what happened."

"Yeah, but you left out what happened to the five grand."

"What do you mean?"

"There was five grand missing when you delivered the cash after the exchange. It didn't just disappear, Jimbob. Besides, we know you paid off a bet shortage right here in this hellhole—almost the same amount."

"Just give me a little time, Bernie. I'll make it good."

"Cut the shit, Jimbob. You've got two options. Either take this job—I talked Chacón into giving you another chance—or I won't be at all friendly when I see you again."

"When do I have to go?" asked Jimbob.

"Tomorrow night. The package has to be delivered by eight o'clock the next morning. Forget about your goddamn pickups and get this package to Houston."

"Come on, Bernie. I can't let my runner down."

"When's your next trip coming up?"

"I'm waiting on a call from my contact in Monterrey. Last time I talked to him he said I needed to be there tomorrow for the pickup. I don't want to lose my guy in Monterrey, Bernie. He gives me too much business."

"Then you should be back here from Monterrey tomorrow night?"

"Yeah … easy. When can I load the package?"

"Tomorrow night. I'll have everything ready—the package and your instructions. Don't mess with me this time, Jimbob."

"Where do I meet you?"

"Come straight here when you get back. I'll leave a message where I'll be."

"Why can't you tell me what's in the package, Bernie?"

"Because you don't need to know, *shlepper*," said Bernie, a scowl on his face. "Why don't you cut your hair, Jimbob? You look like shit with that long hair covering your fat head."

"What's a *shlepper*?"

"Yiddish for jerk. Make sure you bring me the money tomorrow."

"I've gotta have expense money … *mordida*," said Jimbob.

"Look, you can pay off your wife's brother in the Border Patrol when you get back from Houston."

"How did you know about him?"

"Look, dumbfuck, Chacón knows everything about everyone he deals with. That's why he's a winner and you're a loser."

"Fuck you, Bernie," said Jimbob, his eyes ablaze. "I don't have to put up with all of your insults."

"Then prove me wrong. Now, get the hell out of here and pick up your four passengers. You leave for Houston tomorrow night … have to get there by eight the next morning."

Chapter 8

▼

Monterrey, Mexico—Wednesday, November 14, 2007

They stepped off the bus within a short distance of the *Gran Plaza* in Monterrey. With saddened eyes, Rosa, Esmeralda, and Ignacio silently sat on one of the benches, under a large shade tree while Rafael, his pink bandana clearly visible, paraded expectantly back and forth.

Each family member carried a canvas bag that Rosa had meticulously made, staying awake most of the last two nights in doing so in spite of the almost continuous flow of tears dropping on her work. Even with the lively activity in the plaza, she found herself dozing any time she became still for a short time.

Esmeralda, still tearful from the sporadic spells of sobbing after telling her friends good-bye, sat motionless on the bench and stared vacantly into space.

Ignacio, restless from waiting and having nothing to do, left his sister and mother on the park bench and walked alongside Rafael.

"Where do we go from here, Papá?" asked Ignacio.

"The man named Jimbob will pick us up here and see that we get across the border safely."

"Are you afraid, Papá?"

"No, *mi hijo*," he answered. "Everything has been taken care of."

"Why do Mamá and Esme cry all the time?"

"They are just nervous about going to a place they've never been to before. Women are like that. They worry a lot."

"Mamá has cried for two days. She visited every one of our neighbors. She doesn't think it is a good idea to go to *El Norte*."

"Once we are in America, she will feel better. What do you think about going?"

"If you think it's best, it must be all right," said Ignacio.

"You have to be brave, Nacio. If it's worth having, it's worth taking a risk for. It will be a while before Mamá and Esme see that."

"When will the man pick us up?"

"Should be soon. The other hombre said to watch for a blue truck."

✷   ✷   ✷   ✷

Jimbob circled the *zócalo* looking for his passengers. On the third round he saw the pink scarf around Rafael's neck. At the same time he saw the other three members of the family. Then he realized: the runner had said four passengers, but he hadn't said that three were the man's wife and his two children. *What the hell? A wife is bad enough, but two young children?* He had never faced this before.

He debated about turning around and leaving. He couldn't be responsible for a group like this. The risk of getting caught by the Border Patrol was too great. But this man was Julio's friend, and he didn't want to disappoint Julio. He couldn't afford to lose that contact; Julio referred too many "passengers."

And I need the money now more than ever, he reminded himself. *Bernie Hefferman is waiting for me in Nuevo Laredo—waiting for me to return with a partial payment on the debt. If I try to escape the debt payment, Bernie will track me down until he finds me. Then that will be the end of Jimbob Clifton.*

He decided to go for it. He wasn't worried about the crossing, but what about the treks around the check stations? If they failed to make it, there was nothing he could do—he would just have to leave them. That was the chance they would have to take. He would do everything he could to get them to Houston, deliver the package for Bernie, and return for his reward. If he performed as expected, Bernie would forgive the debt and still make it worth the risk. He stopped as close to the park bench as possible.

In short order, Jimbob collected the one-half payment from Rafael, the family climbed aboard the crew cab pickup, and they were under way. When they reached Nuevo Laredo, Jimbob wondered how Bernie would react to the wife and two children. Maybe he wouldn't even know that they were his passengers. It shouldn't make any difference to Bernie. It was none of his business who he escorted across the border, as long as he delivered the package to Houston.

What could be in the package that was so much of a secret and so important to Chacón? Jimbob decided not to ask again; that was none of *his* business. *Just get it there,* Bernie would say. He checked his watch; he was well within his time frame to start the trip to Houston.

* * * *

Nuevo Laredo, Mexico—Wednesday, November 14, 2007

Jimbob parked in front of the Blue Eagle Men's Club. He turned to Rafael. "I'll only be gone a few minutes. All of you stay in the truck."

Rafael nodded that he understood.

"Glad to see you," said Beto after Jimbob climbed up on a barstool. "Your man has been in here every fifteen minutes looking for you. Here's the note he left. He said for you to hurry. Do you have time for a drink? You look like you need one."

"Not now," Jimbob answered as he glanced at the note. It said: Hotel Azteca bar. "Why was he upset?"

"I don't know ... something about you leaving on a trip to somewhere."

"I've got plenty of time to get there. I think all he's worried about is whether I have any money for him."

"He didn't say," said Beto. "All I know is that he is one mean-looking bastard. I wouldn't want to cross him."

"Yeah, I suppose so," said Jimbob. "I'll come by when I get back."

The Hotel Azteca, a couple of blocks from the Blue Eagle, was far from being a five-star luxury hotel—probably couldn't get a minus five rating. Jimbob remembered it as a sleazy campsite for hookers, drug dealers, and any other illegal activity that could be named. One small neon sign over the door marked its entrance. The "el" in the sign had burned out, leaving the name, Hot ... Azteca. Jimbob laughed thinking, *It's a "hot" place to be, more ways than one.* He pushed the buzzer switch and waited. Finally someone cracked the door open.

"Looking for Bernie Hefferman," Jimbob said. The man closed the door. A few minutes later he opened the door and motioned for Jimbob to enter. Bernie was standing close by to greet him.

"Tell your passengers to come in also," Bernie said.

"Why do you need to see them?"

"Goddamn you, Jimbob," yelled Bernie. "None of your fuckin' questions. Get them in here. I want to see who you're carrying ... make sure no one is going to rip you off."

Back at the truck, Jimbob told Rafael to bring everyone into the hotel. Reluctantly, Rafael's frightened wife and children followed him into the dark, hovel-like interior of the building.

Bernie was seated at a table by himself in a dimly lit room behind the bar. A small lamp on the table afforded the only light. Jimbob and his "passengers" stepped inside and stood by quietly waiting for Bernie to speak. At first Bernie ignored his visitors and continued scribbling notes on a sheet of paper. After a painfully long minute, he turned toward the group and scrutinized each member of the terrified family.

"What the shit, Jimbob?" said Bernie. "One man, a woman, and two kids? Are you out of your fuckin' mind?"

"I had to do it, Bernie. This man's friend in Houston sends me a lot of business. I didn't know Rafael was bringing his family. I thought I was picking up four men."

"This is a big job I'm asking you to do, man. You can't do it and escort this bunch all the way to Houston. How'll they get across? How'll they get around the checkpoints? You *are* out of your fuckin' mind! If you take all of these people, there'll be a slip-up somewhere."

"We can do it, Bernie," said a frantic Jimbob. "I know that getting the package to Houston is the most important thing. If they can't make it, I'll leave 'em behind."

"I don't like it, Jimbob. Chacón will never agree. These two kids and the woman will slow you down. Too much risk. Just forget it. I'll find another way."

"Look, I need the money, Bernie. I'll just put them on a bus and send them back home."

"I don't know," said Bernie as he turned and faced away again. After a few moments he turned back. He took a gun from his shoulder holster and laid it on the table in plain site of the group. The children and their mother cringed and moved closer to each other. Rafael stepped in front of them.

"*¿Qué pasa?*" said Rafael, staring fiercely at Jimbob.

"*Nada,*" Jimbob replied and then looked at Bernie. "Look, Bernie, we'll just leave. Here's the money this man paid me. I'll get the rest to you as soon as I have another job."

"Cool it, Jimbob," said Bernie as he glanced at the gun on the table. "I'll tell you when and if you can leave. We have a turn of events here. I have to call Chacón and get his approval before we go on. In the meantime, I want this man to know we mean business. Do any of them understand English?"

"I don't think so," said Jimbob.

"Take them out of the room anyway while I make the call."

In no longer than ten minutes, Bernie called everyone back into the room. The gun still rested on the table. Bernie seated himself at the table as before.

"Here's the deal," he said as he stared straight into Jimbob's eyes. "The package has to be taken to Houston as fast as you can get it there. You leave the girl behind. She would be the most likely one to give you trouble on the way. Chacón's sister is married to one of his bodyguards; they live here in Nuevo Laredo. The girl will stay with them. You take the other three now, deliver the package, then come back here, pick up the girl, and take her to Houston. Come back and you get paid."

"I can't do that, Bernie," said Jimbob. "If I force this man to leave his child behind, there's no telling what he'll do. If anything happens to the girl, he could claim that I sold her! I'd be in deep shit."

"Those are Chacón's orders. You speak Spanish better than I do, so explain the plan to these people and let's get on with it."

"This man is not gonna like this."

"What the shit can he do?" said Bernie as he placed his hand on the pistol. "Tell him, goddamn it! And get the hell out of here. And make sure everyone understands the importance of confidentiality here. They must never even mention anything about the delivery of the package."

* * * *

By now Rafael was wide-eyed with speculation, waiting for some explanation from Jimbob about the confusion that had arisen. Rosa edged closer to him, her face distorted into an expression of anxiety and fear. The children crowded together next to Rosa. Rafael kept glancing at the table and at the gun. What was going on? Something was not right. He still had half of the money for the trip that he had yet to surrender to Jimbob. Maybe they should just leave and go back home on the bus. But they had come so far and they were so near. He thought about going for the gun, but the man might have another. The children and Rosa would be in danger if there were a struggle. And this man called Bernie might have others around to help him.

Who was this Chacón they talked about? He was involved some way with the package that had to be delivered. Rafael gave Rosa a hug, tousled Ignacio's hair, and smiled at them with a look of reassurance. He figured they all must be as confused as he was.

* * * *

Jimbob motioned for Rafael and his family to join him in the corner of the room. He began explaining the quandary. When he came to the part about Esmeralda staying with a family in Nuevo Laredo until he could return for her, Rosa grabbed Esme and held her to her side.

"No, no ... no!" she screamed frantically. "Esme stays with us. Rafael ... no, we can't leave Esmeralda ... I won't leave her."

Rafael struggled with the predicament. He hadn't anticipated any problems like this. He couldn't stand by and see his family split. They would lose the money he had already given Jimbob if he resisted the proposal. And he might lose more that just money. *What if this man kidnaps both children?* he wondered, as he glanced again at the gun. He had heard of children being kidnapped and sold. *Why does he need a gun?* Rafael decided to try to buy some time.

"We can't do it, Señor Jimbob," he said. "We'll go back home. We can't leave Esmeralda."

"It'll only be for the day. I'll be back tomorrow night and pick her up," said Jimbob, speaking Spanish and looking anxiously toward Bernie—now impatiently drumming his fingers on the table top. "The man is forcing me to do this, Rafael, so he will know for sure that I will deliver the package. He knows that I won't get paid until I get the girl to Houston."

Esmeralda clung to her mother. Both she and Rosa sobbed convulsively. "Mamá ... Mamá, don't leave me. I'm so scared, I want to go back home. Papá ... let's go home ... please, Papá. Take us home ... please."

Ignacio, awestricken as the dilemma unfolded, held on to Rafael's hand with a firm grip. He tugged at his father's pant leg. "Papá, let me stay instead of Esme, so she can be with Mamá."

Rafael, eyebrows raised and a questioning look on his face, turned to Jimbob who looked at Bernie for an answer. Bernie shook his head. "We keep the girl ... easier to get rid of if you don't come back," he said in clear English. "Get on with it, Jim, we keep the girl. If you don't come back, I'll report you in both countries for child trafficking. I don't have to tell you what that will do to your business. Now stop this drivel and get going. We're running out of time. I'll give you five minutes to get moving."

Bernie leaned back in his chair, propped his feet on top of the table, and clasped his hands behind his neck. He glanced at the clock on the wall. "Five minutes ..."

Rafael, in the meantime, slowly moved away from the others and inched his way nearer the table. Bernie shifted his weight in the chair momentarily as he crossed his legs and allowed his eyelids to drop closed. As if waiting for this chance, Rafael dashed toward the table and grabbed the gun. With fire in his eyes, he kept the gun aimed at Bernie.

Bernie, startled, sat upright in his chair and yelled at Rafael, "You dumb son of a bitch! Do you know what you've done? Hand me that piece before someone gets hurt. Jim, come talk Mexican to this bastard."

"Nacio, take Esme and your Mamá out of the room … quick!" said Rafael. "Señor Jimbob, stand over by the table."

"Rafael, you are making a mistake," said Jimbob. "Put down the gun. You can trust me. We leave the girl now, but I'll be back to pick her up. She'll be safe. I have to come back for her, take her to Houston or I won't get paid the rest of your money … don't you see? Put the gun down."

"I have to be sure she will be safe before I leave her. I have to see where she will be and who she will be with. We're not leaving here until I'm sure."

"Goddamn, you Jimbob. How in the hell did this happen?" yelled Bernie. "Get the fuckin' gun away from him."

"He's just disturbed, Bernie. Can we show him where the girl will be? Just tell me where she'll be."

"I'll take you to the girl when you get back. Just get him to put the goddamn gun down. Chacón's sister will be here in a few minutes. These are nice people … he'll see. Don't let them see the *papá* waving a pistol. The whole deal will fall through. I never should have trusted you to carry out this project, Jimbob. I should have known that sure as hell something would happen."

"We'll get it done, Bernie. Let me talk to him some more. Can you reach the people by cell phone … see where they are?"

"I'm afraid to turn my back on these crazy people," said Bernie as he punched in a number in his cell phone.

Rafael called his family back in the room. He turned briefly to console Esme and Rosa but kept the gun pointed toward Bernie. After a brief phone call, Bernie called out: "Tell him Señora Carrillo will be here shortly and to put the pistol away, Jimbob. All of you wait outside for her to arrive. If they see him holding a gun, they won't stop."

Rafael glared at Bernie and at Jimbob, as if contemplating his next move. After a full minute, he said: "Señores, I will put the gun down. But if anything happens to my girl, I will come after you. I will kill both of you."

"It's all right, Rafael," said Jimbob. "Esmeralda will be safe."

Rafael kept his eyes fixed on Bernie as he placed the gun on the table. Bernie, shaking his head as if in disbelief, swung his chair around to turn his back on Rafael. Jimbob escorted the family out of the bar and into the street.

Soon a stretch limousine drove by, slowed for a second as it passed the Hotel Azteca, and then moved on to circle the block. On the next pass the limo halted in front of the hotel a few feet away from Rafael and his family. The driver and two uniformed attendants climbed out. The bulges in their jackets showed that they were armed. They looked up and down the street and waited a few seconds before opening the back door. Señora Carmen Carrillo, a shapely, well-groomed, heavily made-up, blonde woman of about forty years of age, stepped out.

"Where is Bernie," she asked, a pleasant smile on her face. "Someone tell him it's safe for him to come out." She laughed. "What is this about a child to stay with us … is this the girl?" she asked nodding toward Esmeralda. "Ah … what a beautiful señorita. And the boy … does he stay too?"

Bernie came out, trying to stay composed. Señora Carrillo met him with an embrace, stepped back, and frowned.

"What is this all about, Bernie?" she scolded. A coquettish expression crinkled her heavily made-up face. "You've been in Nuevo Laredo and you're staying in this dreadful place? Why didn't you come stay with me?"

"Business reasons, señora. Did you talk to Chacón?"

"Yes, my brother explained it all," she answered. "We need to get out of here, Bernie. You know it's not safe for us to stay around in this part of town very long."

"The girl and her mother are both sad about being separated," said Jimbob.

"Nonsense," she said as she stood in front of Esme and gently stroked her face. She turned to Rosa. "We'll get along fine, *Mamá*. I will take good care of her until Jimbob returns. She'll be smiling and laughing before you know it. I have no children and have always wanted a boy and a girl just like your two."

"Thank you, señora," said Rosa, clutching her rosary tightly with her hands. "I worry about my children."

"Of course you do. Now … we must hurry. My husband and brother have lots of enemies, but once we are in our home we will be safe." She took Esme's hand and walked toward the limo. Esme resisted at first, looked at her mother and father with tear-filled eyes, and started to climb into the limo. Rosa broke away from Raphael and ran to Esme for another hug before the limousine door closed.

"Don't cry, *mi hija*," said Rosa. "The man will come for you tomorrow."

"It's all right, Esme," said Rafael. "Señor Jimbob will be back for you later."

"Come visit me, Bernie," said Señora Carrillo as she rolled up the window and winked. "I always enjoy having you around." The limo sped away leaving Rafael, Rosa, and Ignacio huddled together, all with wet faces.

Chapter 9

▼

Nuevo Laredo, Mexico—Wednesday, November 14, 2007

The black limousine pulled away from the Hotel Azteca with the tires screeching and with Esmeralda's face plastered against the rear window. Tears streamed down her face, as she watched her mother, father, and brother fade into the distance. Señora Carrillo, her arm around Esme's shoulder, tried to comfort her, but the girl resisted her attempts and cowered in the corner of the backseat.

"You'll be fine, little lady," said the señora. "Once we get El Rancho Alegrón, you will get to know the other girls. They love living at El Rancho Alegrón and you will too; so many things to do and enjoy."

"How will Señor Jimbob know where I am when he comes back for me?"

"Now, don't worry your little head about that," she replied. "You might just decide to stay with me and my girls anyway. You'll have nice clothes, nice presents, and lots of fun things to do."

"I just want to be with Mamá and Papá ... and Ignacio. Nacio is little. He needs me to take care of him," she said between sobs. "I want to go home."

"Your home will be with me, sweet girl. I'll teach you many things while you grow up."

"But Señor Jimbob will come back for me tomorrow night. How will he know where I am?"

"He'll get the message, sweetie," she said. "Now you just relax a bit."

* * * *

The fragrance in the air from Carmen's heavy jasmine perfume thickened. Esmeralda felt as if she were suffocating from the heavy aroma. She kept rubbing her nose, at first not realizing the source of the odor.

"I can't breathe," she said, as she tried to open the door, but the safety locks controlled by the driver had been activated. The closer Carmen got to Esme, the stronger the smell became. Esme realized for the first time that it was coming from the señora. She had never been around anyone before where the smell was so repulsive. She had to get some fresh air. She kept trying to open the door while she held her nostrils together. Carmen finally understood what was bothering Esme.

"I see what's wrong, dear. You don't like my perfume. It's the most expensive I could find, but never mind. You'll learn to enjoy wearing perfume after I teach you how to live, little one."

"Can I open the door?"

"No, dear. I'll crack the window a little," she said as she signaled the driver to lower the glass a bit.

Esme placed her face to the opening for a breath of fresh air. *I have to get out of here some way,* she thought. *I have to get away from this woman. I don't want her to teach me anything. I just want to go to my mamá and papá. What is Nacio doing right now? Is he as miserable as I am? Papá should never have brought us to El Norte. I am so scared. I want to go home, back to Cuauhtémoc, back to my friends.*

The thirty-minute drive to El Rancho Alegrón seemed like a lifetime to Esmeralda. She was trapped. The only thing she could do was to go along with this woman and later find some way to escape.

* * * *

El Rancho Alegrón—Wednesday, November 14, 2007

At El Rancho Alegrón, on the ground floor, Señora Carrillo guided Esme through room after room of the elaborate mansion, pointing out all of the amenities, introducing her to a few of the girls along the way. Esme, her head drooped, avoided eye contact with anyone.

Every single girl they encountered scrutinized Esme from head to foot—snooty expressions on their painted faces. They were all heavily made up with bright red lipstick and heavy rouge. And they were dressed in sexually provocative attire. Some laughed at Esme's appearance and her sackcloth dress. They turned their heads and walked away without one kind word of welcome.

The señora and Esmeralda climbed the wide, curved, carpeted stairs to the second floor. Continuous music from the strategically placed speakers filled the air. From the top of the stairs, long corridors stretched in each direction. As they passed room after room, Esme could hear laughter and lively conversational sounds coming from each … words and phases she had never heard before.

"This is where the girls stay … where they entertain their guests," said the señora. She stopped and opened a door. "And this will be your room while you are here, sweetheart. I'm sure you are tired and need some sleep."

"I don't want to sleep … Señor Jimbob might come for me before I wake up."

"Now you just stop fretting, sweetie," she said as she escorted her around the room. "It will be a long time before he gets back. You just quit worrying about that."

"How will I know if he comes?"

"I'll let you know, dear. Right now you need to get out of those old clothes, take a good soaking bath to get that pretty body clean, and shampoo your hair," she said as she began filling the tub.

Esme looked on in astonishment. Señora Carrillo realized that Esmeralda probably had never seen a bathtub before. She brought out towels and a flimsy gown and draped them over a chair.

"While you bathe, I'm going to bring you some food. It'll help you get some sleep," she said. She motioned toward the commode and bidet. "When I come back I'll explain these to you. You have so much to learn, baby. Mamá Carrillo can teach you so many things. You'll enjoy this life."

"Do you think Nacio and my mamá and papá are all right?"

"They are fine. Now, I'll be back in a few minutes. Take your clothes off and get in the tub."

The señora returned with a plate of food and a full glass of wine. Esme was out of the tub and had donned the almost transparent gown. When Señora Carrillo came in, Esme grabbed the towel and wrapped it around her body.

"Don't be embarrassed by the way you look, sweetie," she said, trying unsuccessfully to remove the towel. "You have a beautiful body … you should be proud to show it. But never mind for now … you'll learn. Now drink this juice, eat your food, and climb into that bed so you can get some sleep."

"I don't want to sleep."

"You have a busy day tomorrow," she said. "I'll be back in the morning and wake you up. Now you just have a good night's sleep and dream pretty dreams," she added and bent over to give Esme a kiss.

Esme recoiled but didn't drop her towel. The señora smiled and turned to leave. "It'll take a little time, dear, but you'll learn. Mamá Carrillo will take good care of you."

* * * *

El Rancho Alegrón—Thursday, November 15, 2007

The night had passed, as had most of the day, before Señora Carrillo quietly opened the door to Esme's room and went to the bedside. Esme had slept on top of the bedspread, her towel still covering her body. *What a beautiful child,* thought the *señora. She will be a prize package.*

She kissed the girl on her forehead. Esme abruptly sat up, her eyes wide with terror.

"It's all right, dear. I'm right here. You had a good sleep, didn't you? You slept almost all day."

"Is Señor Jimbob here?"

"Not yet, my dear," she answered. "It looks like there will be a wait before he comes for you. In the meantime you are going on a little trip."

"I can't leave. He might come while I'm gone."

"We'll take care of it, sweetie," said the señora. "Right now, we have to get you spruced up before you go on your trip."

The señora left for a few minutes, soon to return. She was accompanied by a uniformed, middle-aged woman carrying a kit that contained what appeared to be grooming paraphernalia and an array of lotions and cologne. The woman placed a small metal container on the table, removed the lid, and lit something inside the dish with a match. Soon the room became saturated with the aroma of incense.

Before leaving the room, the señora motioned for the attendant to start the process that would change Esme's appearance.

"I don't want all of this; please leave me alone," said Esmeralda, trying to pull away.

"Now let's just do what Señora Carrillo wants for you," the lady said. "She wants you to look pretty for your trip. You'll be so pleased when I'm finished. Wait till you see yourself in the mirror."

Esme, hungry and appearing disconsolate from the emotional trauma she had experienced, submitted reluctantly to the grooming procedures.

A full hour later, Esme stood before the mirror. Her hair had been styled. She wore bright makeup, a flimsy, flashy pink tank top that exposed her midriff, a tight-fitting leather skirt, and knee-high boots to match,

"You look lovely … sexy," said the attendant, with arched eyebrows and a twisted smile on her face.

Esme sniffled. "This is not me. Please …" she said, sobbing. "I just want to be with my mamá, papá, and Nacio … I want my old clothes back."

"You'll get used to the way you look, dear. Now let's go show Mamá Carrillo, and you need to go into the dining room soon for dinner."

∗   ∗   ∗   ∗

Esme withdrew into a corner of the large, parlorlike room while she waited for Señora Carrillo to come after her. She sat with her legs tucked against her chest, her head resting on her knees and turned to the side, trying to avoid eye contact with any of the other girls in the room. Through the floor-to-ceiling windows that gave a panoramic view of the grounds surrounding the mansion, Esme could tell by the broadening shadows of the giant cypress trees that the day was ending. No one had come for her. Finally, the señora appeared and took one look at Esme, gasped, and opened her arms as if to give Esme a hug. Esme recoiled.

"You look gorgeous, my dear," she said. "When you walk into a room, everyone will turn and stare."

"Do you think Señor Jimbob might get here before I have to leave?"

"You must stop worrying about that, sweetie. Sometimes things happen that cause plans to change. Start enjoying your new life."

"I just want my mamá and papá," she said, staring out the window and making no attempt to blot her eyes.

"Come now, dear, tears can smear your pretty face," said the señora as she escorted Esme to the table. You must have a good dinner before you start on your trip. I'll come back for you after you've finished eating."

As hungry as she was, Esmeralda hardly touched her food. The other girls around the table at which she sat chattered like a bunch of magpies, uttering terms and phrases that she had never heard before.

She slowly eased out of her chair and retreated to a bench beside a window. She looked outside to see total darkness. No one had come for her as promised.

Whatever would happen to her now? She wanted desperately to get away from this house—from these weird girls and this weird woman.

She wished Nacio were here to help her. When they played hide-and-seek at the river he was always good at hiding and tricking his pursuers. But she was glad he hadn't been made a prisoner like she was. If she could just get rid of the horrible clothes and the paint on her face, she might feel more like herself. Just as she wondered what would happen next, she heard footsteps approach. Señora Carrillo entered.

"Your chariot is ready, sweetie," said the señora, trying to give Esmeralda a kiss. The girl turned her head. "Now be a good girl. You're a prize package for someone. You'll see. Now don't worry … Mamá Carrillo will take care of you."

"Where am I going?"

"To another El Rancho Alegrón. You'll like being there. Now quit worrying and have some fun. You are far too young to worry so much."

"But how will Señor Jimbob find me?"

"We'll take care of that. Now you just relax and let us take care of you."

Señora Carrillo took Esme by the arm and, against feeble resistance, escorted her to the limo. Only the driver was in the car. Once the door was shut, the señora went to the driver's side and motioned for the window to be lowered.

"You know where to go," she whispered. "Don't stop for anything. This little kitten is just waiting for a chance to escape."

Esmeralda stayed curled up in the corner of the backseat of the limousine. She covered herself with the lightweight blanket that the señora had given her, trying to hide her bare legs and bare midriff, which so embarrassed her. She had never seen anyone dressed like the girls at El Rancho Alegrón. Now she was dressed the same way. She hated the knee-high boots and the flimsy tank top that she had been forced to wear.

She glanced at her image in the mirror suspended from the ceiling of the limo: *Mamá and Papá won't even recognize me,* she thought while trying to rub off the heavy makeup and lipstick. *And Nacio will tease me. Where are they taking me? Señor Jimbob will never find me. I wish I were dead.*

She sat up and looked out the window. The limo seemed to be going faster. *What would happen if I just jumped out? There's bright moonlight outside. I could walk back to Nuevo Laredo and wait there for Señor Jimbob to come back. If he doesn't come for me, Papá will come.* She tried the door—the driver had left it unlocked! *Why not jump,* she thought. *I can roll into the ditch, run fast, and hide somewhere.* A line of cars ahead forced the driver to slow momentarily. It was her chance to jump. Esmeralda swung the door open and leaped. But she had not seen either the bridge ahead or the concrete barrier guardrails on either side. Instead of the grassy roadside, she hit the pavement, rolling and spinning uncontrollably until she crashed, headfirst, into the concrete bulkhead. Her body—rapidly becoming soaked in the blood spurting from her torn scalp—bounced once over the two-foot concrete wall and fell into the deep ditch below. Her torso and extremities jerked twice and then she remained still.

✳ ✳ ✳ ✳

The driver stopped alongside the road when he realized what had happened. He walked back to the bridge. He peered over the edge and, in the bright moonlight, looked down at the lifeless child, her head covered with blood. Should he climb down the slope and check on the young girl? If she were alive *or* dead, he would have to take her to a hospital to be examined. He would be in trouble for sure—bringing in an underage girl dressed like that. Someone would notify the *Agencia Federal de Investigación,* and he would be thrown in jail for human trafficking, never to be released. He looked around, saw no one in sight, and then hurriedly returned to the limousine and sped away.

Chapter 10

▼

Nuevo Laredo, Mexico—Wednesday, November 14, 2007

The limousine pulled away, leaving Rafael, Rosa, and Ignacio standing motionless on the curb staring at Esme's terror-stricken face against the back window. Bernie motioned for Jimbob to follow him back into the Hotel Azteca and into the room behind the bar. Bernie sat at the desk, Jimbob in an adjacent chair.

"Before the others come in, I want to make sure you understand the details of our plan," said Bernie, his eyes fixed on Jimbob's, his glare emanating ferocity. He recited again details of Jimbob's assignment. "Do you have any questions?"

"I know what to do, Bernie ... quit worrying," said Jimbob, grinning like a Cheshire cat. "Good plan, Bernie ... you're one smart son of a bitch."

"Yeah, you say that, but you have a way of fucking things up. You know you are to come straight back here after you drop the package, don't you? I'll be waiting for you, right here."

"Right," said Jimbob. "It's all clear, Bernie."

"Then we've got a deal?"

"Yeah, we've got a deal ... one hell of a deal."

"Then bring the others back in. I want to keep an eye on that wild son of a bitch. No telling what he might do next."

* * * *

"He just panicked, Bernie, when he grabbed the gun," said Jimbob, as he escorted the family back into the bar. "He was trying to protect his kid."

Rafael, Rosa, and Ignacio, retreated to a corner while Rafael continued to try to console and reassure his wife and son.

"I don't know," said Bernie. "He threatened me with the gun. What if he tries to steal the package?"

"He wouldn't dare … he knows that the package has to be delivered before he can recover the girl."

"You know what to do with the package, Jimbob. Just get it done, even if you have to lose this fuckin' bunch," said Bernie, waving his hand toward the family.

Bernie placed the book-size package—wrapped in thick vinyl and sealed with duct tape—into a heavy leather briefcase which he zipped shut.

"I'll get it there, Bernie," said Jimbob. "Is there an address on the side of the briefcase where I'm supposed to take it?"

"No … no. Now listen, Jimbob: All you have to do is go into the Galleria in Houston and walk through the mall. Someone will approach you and take the case from you. Whoever is there will ask you if it's from Chacón. If he doesn't ask that question, *don't* give up the briefcase. Once you are rid of the briefcase and the package, haul ass back here as quick as you can. Just hand it to him, don't say anything, and then get the hell out of there."

"What if the contact insists on checking the package?"

"Don't give him a chance. If he asks the right question, hand him the briefcase and beat the fuck away from there."

"Got it," said Jimbob.

"One more thing, Jim. While you're traveling on the road to Houston, keep the briefcase locked in the cargo toolbox. And when you're out of the truck, keep it by your side every minute"

"No problem," said Jimbob. "Do I bring anything back?"

"Nothing except yourself. Don't forget to call me as soon as you've delivered the package. Now, once again, are you clear on your instructions?"

"Yeah, all clear," he said.

"Then get the hell out of here, and get back as fast as you can make it. Don't screw it up."

"You worry too much, Bernie."

※　　※　　※　　※

Jimbob slowly drove along the river's edge until he spotted the tall poplar tree that towered above all of the other shrubs and trees along the river. He found his marker—a post with the top painted a fluorescent pink—set in the ground a few feet from the tree.

He told his passengers to stay in the truck until he was ready for them. He extracted a plastic inflatable raft, a paddle, and bottle of compressed air from the tool chest in the back of the truck. Next, he inflated the boat, pushed it into the water, and secured it with a short piece of rope before returning for his three passengers. All three appeared spellbound with apprehension of their next move. Rosa, rosary in hand, trembled as she clung to Rafael.

"Paddle across slowly so you don't make any noise, not even a ripple in the water," said Jimbob. "And don't talk to each other. Once you're across pull the boat out of the water, deflate it, and hide it under the brush. I'll pick you up in a few minutes. Remember, *don't make a sound.*"

* * * *

With Rafael paddling, they slowly and silently made their way toward the *El Norte* side, leaving Mexico behind. Rosa sat motionless behind Rafael, her face distorted by a look of anxiety. Her hands tightly grasped the sides of the raft.

Ignacio, seated in the rear of the raft, looked back and watched as Jimbob scurried around his truck. Ignacio saw him retrieve something from the toolbox but couldn't identify the object at first. Then he saw what it was—a shovel. It looked like Jimbob was digging a hole in the ground, next to the post with the pink-painted top.

As the distance that separated them increased, Ignacio's vision became blurred, but he could see that Jimbob had finished digging. He refilled the hole with dirt, tamped it down with his foot, and then tossed his gear into the back of his truck. The last object to go in was the shovel. The pole with the pink top was no longer standing.

* * * *

Jimbob gave a sigh of relief when the raft and "crew" neared the other side of the river. With the modern electronic surveillance tools the Border Patrol used, the actual crossing was one of several critical threat-periods of capture that they would face. Jimbob remembered a couple of times earlier when he had gotten his clients this far—only to have them picked up by the Border Patrol when they landed on the other side.

With the bright moonlight he could easily watch until he was sure they had made it across without incident. He climbed back into his truck. Within a few seconds he drove away rapidly from the launching site and headed toward Nuevo

Laredo and the gate for his own legal entry into the United States. At the gate the customs guard, a long-time acquaintance, made only a cursory inspection of the truck bed and waived him through.

✳   ✳   ✳   ✳

Jimbob found the family right where they were supposed to be. They were huddled together in the brush, wide-eyed with fright when he approached. They relaxed when they realized that their "guide" had arrived.

Back in the truck—Ignacio in the front with Jimbob, Rosa and Rafael in the back—they headed for Houston on Highway 59. Jimbob was careful to drive well within the speed limit and to observe all warning signs. Miles before the checkpoint, Jimbob stopped the truck alongside the highway and turned on the overhead light in order to give Rafael instructions for bypassing the border patrol station.

"Look closely at this compass," he said to Rafael, handing him the watch-size instrument. "Set the dial so it is pointing south by southeast. Now, when I let you out a few miles up the road, all of you scamper under that fence and walk in that direction—south by southeast—for exactly thirty minutes. Take my watch so you'll know when to turn. In exactly thirty minutes, change your direction and start walking to north by northwest.

"Keep going until you come to the highway again. When you get there, tie this yellow ribbon on the fence and stay in the brush. I'll stop close by the ribbon and honk two times. When you hear the honk, race to the fence. As soon as you see that no cars are coming from either direction, crawl under the fence, and I'll be there to pick you up. Don't come through to the highway until I am there in the truck. Do you understand, Rafael?"

"Yes, sir," he said.

"Good," said Jimbob. "Now, Rafael, repeat the instructions that I just gave you. I want to be *sure* you understand."

Rafael repeated the instructions perfectly. "Good," said Jimbob. "Just walk at a steady pace and don't stop to rest. With the bright moonlight you shouldn't have any problems."

✳   ✳   ✳   ✳

Right on target, Jimbob said to himself when he saw the yellow ribbon. He was proud of his system—he had used it for years. Every time he had passed a checkpoint, the passengers that he escorted, using his compass system to bypass the Border Patrol, had hit the highway close to where he had estimated. He had worried that the woman and boy might slow the trek, but it didn't happen. Once inside the truck, they resumed their voyage.

✳   ✳   ✳   ✳

Jimbob stopped in Freer for gasoline and picked up a few fast food items for his passengers. He glanced at his watch. Plenty of time to get there by eight o'clock. This was about a six-pack trip. He knew that beer made some people drowsy. It worked just the opposite for him. After one beer, he would relax while driving. *It makes the trip go faster.* He laughed at the thought as he popped the cap of the sixteen-ounce can. *That argument won't hold up in court if I'm stopped and get arrested for DWI.*

In spite of a weird feeling he was beginning to have—a sense of some impending danger ahead—just that one beer made him feel euphoric and confident of the plan: make Houston by 8:00 AM, be back to Laredo by 2:00 PM. *If I can just pull this deal off, my money worries will be over,* he thought. *I hope Bernie will be pleased when he gets my call from Houston, but why the fuck should I care? I need another beer.*

When he had stopped at the checkpoint before Freer and the patrolman had made him open his tool compartment, his heart had skipped a few beats, especially when the officer picked up the briefcase and held it down for the drug-sniffing dog to smell. The dog showed no interest, but Jimbob was afraid the officer would make him open it anyway. He had breathed a sigh of relief when he was waved through. Jimbob laughed when he remembered what Bernie had told him—just that the contents were valuable and to get the package to Houston by 8:00 AM.

Did anyone think the girl would still be in Nuevo Laredo when he returned? What a joke—he remembered the gleam in Carmen's eyes when she picked up the girl. Carmen would see to it that Esmeralda would be gone. He cringed at the thought of the problems he would have had getting her across the border. The old madam likely had other plans for a pretty girl like Esmeralda the minute she saw her.

So, why worry? He would never see any of them again—especially Rafael, the wife and the kid. It was the same as always—once they get a taste of the money they can make and spend in *El Norte,* they think of nothing else. In only a few months, Esmeralda's family would forget her entirely. He glanced at the clock on the dashboard: he was making good time. He'd make it to the Galleria by 8:00 AM easily, dump these passengers, and head back to Laredo.

Chapter 11

▼

Rosenberg, Texas—November 15, 2007

Jimbob gulped the last swallow of his sixth beer. They were already in Rosenberg, just minutes away from Houston. *A few beers sure make the trip go faster,* he thought. *And thank God the traffic has been light. Bernie will be pleased to hear from me when I call. When he gets the word about the delivery of the package, he'll be like a cat on a hot tin roof waiting on me to return. I wonder how much I'll get out of this.*

When I get this over with I need to think about what I'm gonna do next. I think it's about time for me to move somewhere else ... maybe to Arizona. I've heard there are a lot of crossings there—a lot easier than in Texas. Nah ... what the hell am I thinking? I'll just stick with Bernie. Even though he's hard to like, he'll always have something for me to do. He grinned, opened the window, and tossed the empty can.

All three of his passengers were asleep. He turned onto the next exit ramp and entered the parking lot of a convenience store and gas station. When the truck stopped and Jimbob opened the door to get out, the passengers awoke and stirred about, looks of bewilderment on their faces.

"It's all right," said Jimbob. "I'll be back in a minute. If you want to go to the bathroom, you can get out here." There was no response from any of the travelers.

Staggering as he walked toward the store, he stumbled at the entrance and would have fallen if the man walking behind had not grabbed him and pulled him upright.

"Thanks, buddy," Jimbob said. He glanced at the man's hard hat and blue work clothes. "Guess you're on the way to work."

"Yeah," he said. "Refinery. Looks like you've had a few."

Jimbob laughed. "A few beers will get you there faster. You ought to try it."

The refinery worker, a scowl on his face, shook his head as he walked away.

Jimbob paid for his gasoline, slipped the clerk ten dollars for a couple of beers, and returned to his truck. On the way he grabbed onto anything he could find to keep from falling. He again checked his watch to gauge his time; the sky was beginning to take on the pink hue of dawn. He barely had time to get to the Houston Galleria on time—maybe he ought to pick up his speed a bit.

With a maladroit effort, he struggled to open the door on the driver's side and climb into his truck. Once in his seat, he opened one of his newly acquired beers. *Surely I have time for one more beer,* he thought. *If I don't get there in time, whoever I'm supposed to meet will just have to wait.*

His vision—by now double-vision—became more and more blurred. *Must be gettin' foggy out there,* he thought, as he gazed across the parking lot. *I need to get moving … with this fog rolling in.* He shook the sixteen-ounce can … empty. *Already empty? How could that happen? Guess I must have spilled some.*

He tried to reconstruct how he had gotten to the convenience store in the first place. He remembered taking the exit ramp from the freeway, so he figured that in order to get back on the freeway he would have to find that ramp again. He opened his last beer. *Guess I better not drink this one too fast,* he told himself and laughed aloud. *And I sure as hell don't want to spill my last one. How the fuck do I get back on Highway 59? Only thirty minutes to get back on the freeway and get to the Galleria by 8:00 to meet my contact. What a weird place to meet someone anyway,* he thought.

In his haste to back out of his parking space, Jimbob cut the wheel too sharp and ran into the car adjacent to his truck. He looked at the sign on the side of the vehicle—looked like some company car. *I'd better get the hell out of here in a hurry. That car must belong to that hard-hat worker I just saw,* he thought. *I don't have time to argue with some fuckin' dude who parked too close to me.*

He raced out of the parking area and headed down the same frontage road that he had entered when he left the freeway. He would just reverse the path he had followed. That would take him to Highway 59. In his dazed state, he erroneously turned up the exit ramp that he had used to leave the freeway.

Jimbob blinked and shook his head a couple of times trying to clear the fuzziness from his vision. He could tell that he was going up an incline. *This ought to take me to the right highway,* he thought. He could just barely see the white stripes on the sides of the road. *Damn this fog; but all I need to do is to stay between them stripes until I reach the top.*

He could see a large colored sign glaring at him ahead. *Strange that the sign is red, but surely it will give me some direction.* As he got closer he could read the sign clearly: WRONG WAY! He shook his head again and rubbed both eyes. Surely not! He was headed toward Houston. It couldn't be the wrong way. He took another deep swig of beer, increased his speed, and kept going.

At the top of the exit ramp he thought he saw cars coming toward him. *What the hell? Couldn't be … must be my imagination.* The cars honked as they maneuvered past him. "Fuck you!" he yelled and gestured with his finger as each one passed. "You're going the wrong way!" he yelled.

Only seconds before it crashed into his vehicle did Jimbob see the eighteen-wheeler coming down the freeway toward him at a high rate of speed. His truck did a 180-degree spin, and then flew down the road over two hundred feet while parts and pieces flew through the air. Finally, Jimbob's truck, compressed into an almost indistinguishable ball of metal, erupted into flames, and finally came to rest at the crest of the overpass.

* * * *

Ignacio—ejected from the pickup during the spinning of the vehicle—landed on the grassy incline alongside the ramp and rolled all the way to the bottom. His torn, grass-stained clothing hung loosely from his body. His tote bag, however, remained intact, still secured to his body by the strap around his neck.

Dizzy from the flight down the incline, Ignacio lay still for a few seconds before regaining his sense of balance. He raised his head and looked around. Where was he? What had happened? Where were his mamá and papá?

He called out: "*¿Mamá … Papá … donde están? Vengan a ayudarme … Ayúdame!*" There was no answer. He stood, fell back again, pulled himself up, and stumbled about, trying to keep from falling. There was no one in sight. Jimbob's blazing truck lit up the sky and provided light for Ignacio to climb the incline. Not far from where he had come to rest, he saw the briefcase that contained the package that Señor Jimbob had to deliver.

Regardless of whatever had happened—despite his clouded senses—he knew that if he would ever see his sister Esme again, he needed to recover the package so it could be delivered. He unzipped the briefcase, took the package out, and placed it in his tote bag. He would take it up the hill to the truck, give it to Señor Jimbob, and find his mamá and papá.

On the way up the incline, he spotted his mother's rosary lying in the grass. He picked it up and dropped it in his bag also. *She surely will want her rosary,* he thought. He could see that people had gathered and traffic on the highway had come to a halt. In the distance, in the direction in which everyone was staring, he could see the raging fire that engulfed Señor Jimbob's truck.

By the time he reached the top, two police cars and a fire truck, all with gyrating red and blue lights, had arrived. He searched for his mother and father among the onlookers, going from one group to the other. In the distance he could barely make out the identity of Jimbob's truck. His mamá and papá must have been thrown out too. He had started making his way toward the vehicle when a uniformed officer, a constable badge on his shirt, approached him.

"What are you doing here, kid," he said in a gruff voice. Ignacio recoiled as the officer grabbed his arm. Then the officer saw the boy's disheveled appearance—torn, grass-stained clothes, bloody skin cuts on his head and face. "Were you in that truck?"

"Mi mamá, mi papá … en la camioneta," said Nacio, struggling to get away.

"Speak English, kid," he said. "I can't understand what the hell you're saying." He turned toward the gathering crowd. "Hey … anybody understand what this boy's saying?"

A man approached. "Let me try to talk to him," he said, taking Ignacio aside. After a few moments, a sad look on his face, he turned back to the constable. "Try to be a little kinder to this child, will you? Yeah, he was in the truck … must have been thrown out. He just lost his mother and father, and he doesn't know it. It's a miracle that he's alive."

Ignacio kept telling the man that he wanted to find his mamá and papá—that he needed to return the rosary to his mother and the package in his canvas bag to Señor Jimbob. The Spanish-speaking man patted his shoulder and walked away.

"Looks like they are all a bunch of goddamn wetbacks," said the constable with a sneer. "I'll take this kid on in … give him to the Border Patrol. Let them send him back to Mexico where he belongs. The highway troopers will handle everything else around here."

He grabbed Ignacio's arm and dragged him toward his patrol car. Ignacio tried to pull away from the constable, calling out as loud as his little voice would permit: *"Mamá, Papá … Ayúdanme!"*

Once in the constable's car, Ignacio pleaded with the man, *"¿Dónde está mi Mamá, mi Papá? ¿Dónde están ellos?"* He kept repeating his question.

"I don't speak Mexican, kid. I don't know what the shit you're saying."

As the constable drove his car away, siren howling, red and blue lights flashing, Ignacio struggled to open the door so he could jump out. When he was unsuccessful, he climbed up on the rear seat, leaned on the back ledge, and stared at the crowd milling around the accident site until they were no longer visible.

* * * *

By the time the third state trooper arrived on the scene, two-way traffic on Highway 59 had been reestablished, the crowd had begun to disperse, and the blazing inferno of a once-functional vehicle had been controlled enough that it could be inspected. Although it was impossible to identify the victims, the troopers could establish that three passengers—the driver plus two others—had been victims of the fatal accident.

"What's the story?" asked the last trooper to arrive.

"An eighteen-wheeler crashed into a pickup … looks like the pickup driver was drunk, came up the exit ramp, and was driving the wrong way when the eighteen-wheeler hit him." said one of the troopers. "The pickup driver and two of his passengers were killed instantly."

"What about the driver of the eighteen-wheeler?"

"He had only minor injuries but was taken on in to a nearby hospital."

"One of the worst freeway accidents I've seen in a long time," was another trooper's reply. "Can you believe it? The driver tried to access the freeway by going up the exit ramp … disregarded the Wrong Way sign."

"How could that happen?"

"Witnesses said he was on Highway 59, going to Houston, when he stopped for fuel. He bought two beers in the convenience store … started drinking one right away. One witness said the guy acted like he was already drunk when he stumbled into the store … must have been drinking before he got there. He ran into another vehicle when he backed out to leave … raced out of the parking lot with the other car chasing him."

"I heard some talk about a young boy that escaped without much injury."

"Yeah, looked to be ten or eleven, was thrown out of the pickup and rolled down the embankment. Apparently no serious injuries. A local constable took him in … said he was going to turn him over to the Border Patrol. The boy couldn't speak English."

"So you didn't get to talk to the kid … get any information?"

"Not a thing," he answered. "We'll need to get details from the constable. Another weird thing we heard from one witness—as soon as the boy could stand, he started climbing the incline, calling for his mother and father. He came across a briefcase that had been thrown from the vehicle. He took some object out of the briefcase and put it in a tote bag hanging around his neck."

"Did the boy say anything about the other occupants of the pickup?"

"Poor kid, he just kept walking through the crowd calling for his parents … in Spanish."

"Heartbreaking. Was he told that they didn't survive?"

"Apparently not … language barrier. But he had to know when he saw the raging fire."

"A sad, sad story. What can I do to help here?"

"Just help control the traffic till we get a cleanup crew. I've already written a report. The mystery remains: What did that kid pick up from the site?"

Chapter 12

Villa Hidalgo, Mexico—Thursday, November 15, 2007

Gilberto and Amalia Fuentes had set a routine for themselves. They started each day with an early, ten-mile bicycle ride before they headed off to work at the *maquiladora* plant in Villa Hidalgo. The heavily traveled Highway 2 was relatively safe for cyclists during the daybreak hour. It was a beautiful sight watching the day, and the river valley, come alive. Just ahead was the bridge with the wide concrete guardrail on each side where they always stopped to rest and enjoy their *pan dulce*—sweet bread—juice, and bottled water that they had packed in their saddle bags. This was their favorite time of day—just the two of them—without any interference from neighbors or family.

After leaning her bike against the concrete barrier, Amalia unfastened her saddle bags and pulled out their drinks and cakes. When she handed Gilberto his share, she noticed for the first time that her hand was covered with blood. Where had it come from? She had no cut or injury. She called to her husband.

"Gilberto, look at this ... are you bleeding from somewhere? Where could this have come from?"

He looked at the wall. There were heavy streaks of blood mixed with hair and congealed matter of some sort.

"A car must have struck some animal and knocked it against the bridge wall," he said. "Must have knocked it over the side."

He peered over the edge and yelled at Amalia. "Come look! Looks like a body in the bottom of the creek bed!"

Gilberto scampered down the embankment. "It's a girl!" he yelled up at Amalia. "I think she's dead. Ants are crawling all over her. You should see how she's dressed. She must have been thrown out of a moving car. What should we do?"

"Check her pulse … is her heart beating? Is she breathing?"

Gilberto felt for a pulse in her neck. "I can feel a faint heartbeat." Moving her only slightly brought a response of moaning as if she were in pain. "She's alive, Amalia! We've got get her out of here. Watch for a car passing and flag it down."

"Right … we need help," said Amalia.

Amalia stood by her bicycle and waved frantically at the first vehicle that came by. Instead of stopping, the car increased its speed and went on by. A second vehicle approached—a pickup truck. Amalia stood in the center of the bridge and waved both arms. The truck slowed and came to a stop only a few feet away. The driver cautiously got out of the vehicle, stood close to the car door as if appraising the scene—ready to drive away if necessary—before he called out to Amalia.

"Need some help?"

"There's an injured girl down there," she said, pointing to the creek bottom. "My husband is down there with her. She's alive but she needs to be taken to a hospital. We came across her accidentally when we stopped here to rest."

The man scrutinized Amalia for a few seconds. He glanced at the second bicycle, eased toward the barrier wall, and peered over the edge. When he saw Gilberto cleaning the blood off the girls face and sweeping away the insects he climbed down the slope to help.

"She's just barely alive," said Gilberto. "It looks like she was thrown or she jumped from a car and hit her head on the guardrail. She's lost a lot of blood."

"I have a phone in my truck. I'll call for an ambulance. We shouldn't try to move her ourselves."

Within a half hour an emergency crew appeared and the unconscious girl was brought out of the creek bed and placed in the ambulance.

"You'll need you to follow us to the hospital in Nuevo Laredo, since we can't get a story from her," said the EMS tech.

With the bicycles loaded into the back of the "Samaritan's" truck, and with Amalia and Gilberto in front with the driver, they took off following the ambulance. At the hospital, their new friend—after receiving many thanks from Amalia and Gilberto—helped them remove their bikes from his truck.

"Good luck. You did a good thing today," the driver said as he prepared to leave.

Once inside the hospital, after they parked their bikes in a guarded rack, they were approached by a hospital security guard.

"You brought this girl in?"

"Yes, sir," said Gilberto.

"The police are here. They will need to question you," he said as he walked away and motioned for the uniformed police officer to step into the room.

"Why do we need to be questioned? We have to get to work. We just found this poor girl in a ditch and managed to get her here."

"How do we know that you don't know more?" the officer asked.

"Look, we really need to get to work. If we miss work they will terminate us. Please, let us leave. We know nothing about this girl."

"We will call the company and let them know you are being held as witnesses."

"What can we do?"

"Just wait and see if they can get any history from the girl."

Amalia and Gilberto sat in the waiting area for almost three hours without any word about the patient. Finally a nurse came out. "You are wanted in the treatment room. The doctors want to question you about the patient."

"Why?" asked Gilberto. "We don't know who she is. We just accidentally found her in a ditch."

"The police want you in there. Follow me."

The young couple was escorted to the surgery recovery room. The girl they had rescued—now lying on a stretcher—appeared unconscious, with oxygen and IV lines attached. A heavy turbanlike bandage covered her head. She was unresponsive when any attempt by the nurse was made to arouse her.

"We need to know her name," said the police officer.

"Honestly, we have never seen her before."

"Do you live close to where you found her?"

"Yes, sir," said Gilberto.

"And you never remember seeing any girl like this before? Where do you think she came from?"

"From the way she was dressed ... probably from one of those houses."

"What do you mean?"

"You know ... a place where girls stay ... where men go to ..."

"I have to make a report of this. You will need to come with me and show me where you found her. And I need your names and where we can find you if we have more questions."

Gilberto and Amalia filled out a form giving their names and place of employment. "We really need to get to work. We don't get paid if we don't work."

"We'll take care of that after we release you. You won't lose pay since you're helping with an investigation."

"How is the girl?" asked Amalia. "Will she be all right?"

"The doctors say she has a severe head injury with bleeding into her brain. They will transfer her to Laredo or San Antonio, if she lives long enough, but they think it is a hopeless case. She probably won't make it … too much brain damage."

"Poor girl … I hope you find out who's responsible for this," said Amalia.

"We'll do our best. Thank you for your help."

Chapter 13

▼

Houston, Texas—Friday, November 16, 2007

"Did you leave the door unlocked when you left this morning?" asked Jeff as he, Megan, and Ignacio approached the entrance to their apartment.

"No, I definitely remember locking it," Megan answered.

"Maybe the maid forgot to lock it."

"This is not her day to do our place," said Megan. "It couldn't have been her."

Megan and Ignacio started toward the door. "Wait, don't go in yet," said Jeff. "Let me go first. Something doesn't seem right."

Jeff eased into the apartment, glanced around the place, and exclaimed, "What the hell?" Their home was in shambles: furniture turned upside down, every drawer left open, and contents strewn all over the floor in every single room. He turned back to Megan.

"Take Ignacio back down to the lobby while I look around. Someone's broken in. The place is a mess."

"Jeff, don't go in there alone. Whoever broke in might still be there."

"Send a security guard up here … I'll be all right. And tell the manager to call the police for us."

"I don't like the idea of leaving you, Jeff."

"Just take the boy on down to the lobby. He's been through enough trauma for one little kid."

Jeff explored each room and could find nothing missing. The refrigerator door had been left open. The food still felt cold, so the break-in must have occurred recently. He checked his watch: 6:30 PM. Maybe security could pick up something on the video in the elevator lobby. Everyone who entered the building would show on the tape.

Megan came through the door, the guard at her side. "Where is Ignacio?" asked Jeff.

"I left him in the manager's office. As you said, he shouldn't be exposed to any more turmoil right now. What happened?" she asked, looking around and picking up articles from the floor.

"I have no idea," he said. "I don't find anything missing."

"Don't touch anything," said the security guard. "The police may be able to get fingerprints."

"Look at all the things of value they left behind."

"Whoever did this was looking for something specific," said the guard. "What could it have been?"

"I don't know. How could they have gotten past the security in the lobby?"

"We'll look at the videotape … may give some clue."

Back in the manager's office, the guard loaded the video into the computer. "Do you have any idea when it happened?"

"I think it was within the last hour or so. The refrigerator door was left open; the food's still cold."

"The log shows someone from Cosmic Video signed in at 5:00 PM but doesn't show the apartment number. Did you call someone?"

"No, never heard of Cosmic Video."

"That's most likely the person. I'll look the video that was recorded a little before and after 5:00 PM."

The display on the monitor showed nothing before five o'clock except an occasional image of persons passing by or using the elevators. Just before five o'clock, a man dressed in a commercial-looking uniform entered, signed in, and walked toward the elevators. He glanced up at the elevator display screen briefly. A perfect picture of his facial features appeared on the monitor.

Ignacio watched with only casual interest until the man's image became clear when he looked up. Ignacio excitedly leaped from his chair, stood in front of the monitor, and started yelling, *"Allí está … allí está el hombre malo! Allí está!"* he repeated as he pointed to the man on the screen. *"El hombre malo … llamado Bernie … con el paquete. El hombre malo que dió Esme a esa mujer!"*

Megan went to his side, knelt down so she was at his level, and placed her arm around his shoulders. "It's all right, Ignacio. It's all right. Come with me," she said as she stood and led the terrified boy into the office. "Ignacio is ready to talk, Jeff. I don't want to miss this opportunity. Come along if you want to."

"Good idea ... take him into the lounge next to the workout room. It'll be private there," he said. "I'll stay here and see that someone gets our home cleaned up. Don't rush him, and try to take notes while he talks. I have a feeling we finally are going to have some answers."

*   *   *   *

Almost an hour later, Megan and Ignacio returned, both with wet cheeks.

"He told me the whole sordid story, Jeff. It will tear your heart out," said Megan, as she blotted tears from her face as well as Ignacio's.

"Can you tell me now?"

"We need to go somewhere else, she said. "It will take a while."

"Fine, the police are here. They're doing their fingerprint thing. They want to know if we have any idea who the thief might be."

"Wait until you hear Nacio's story. It might give us a lead, but I don't want anyone else to hear it right now."

"Not even the police?"

"Jeff, from what Nacio has told me, if he is ever to see his sister again, we've got to move fast ... I mean you and me. If we get the local police involved, we might be delayed and lose a chance to save Nacio's sister."

"You've got my attention," said Jeff. "Why are you calling him 'Nacio'?"

"That's what his family and friends called him in Mexico."

"Then Nacio it is," said Jeff. "Let's go somewhere while they clean up our apartment."

"Good idea. I'll try to summarize the boy's story after we get there. Right now I'm still stunned over what I learned from Nacio."

"We'll go to the club ... more private," he said. "The police printed the frame that shows this man's facial features so well. Do we need a copy?"

"I have a feeling we will."

*   *   *   *

Seated in a corner of the Trophy Room—one of the many conference rooms of the swank Houston Town Club—Jeff and Megan declined the menus and asked that the door remain closed.

Ignacio, an expression of wonderment on his face, walked around the elaborately decorated room inspecting the many trophies and commendation plaques. After a short interval, he retired to one of the chairs in the corner of the room and buried himself in one of the three books that Megan had purchased and brought along to keep him busy.

Megan glanced at Nacio and wondered: *What must he be thinking. He's been subjected to so much confusion in his young life—especially these last few days.*

Megan narrated for Jeff the sequence of events that had brought Nacio to Houston—his life in Mexico, his family's trip to Nuevo Laredo, the package incident with the *hombre malo*, his sister being left behind, and the crossing experiences with the *coyote*. Jeff, his forehead wrinkled in a frown, remained silent, and appeared awestruck while Megan related the sad saga.

"So ... that's the story, Jeff. The package and its contents are the key to this mystery. And the delivery of the package is the key to finding Nacio's sister," said Megan.

"And we have no idea what's in the package, and we don't have a clue as to where his sister might be," Jeff said as he stared out the window, a contemplative look on his face. "And we don't know why she was left behind."

"When you rub your forehead like that, I know your brain is filtering. Nacio seemed to think, from what he heard, that the man named Bernie was afraid that a girl like Esme would have trouble making the trip and would slow the *coyote*'s trip to Houston. What do you think?"

"We've got to find out what is in that package," said Jeff. "Whatever is there will explain why this guy would break into our apartment to get it back. Maybe explain the urgency to get it to Houston in the first place. At the same time I think we are in some danger and need to protect ourselves. The man ... did you get his name from talking to Nacio?"

"Yeah, Nacio says he was called Bernie," she answered. "He didn't hear any other name."

"What about the woman who took Nacio's sister?" asked Jeff.

"Nacio heard a name like Carmina or Carmen. He's not sure. Her last name is Carrillo. Nacio seemed to think Bernie and Señora Carrillo were friends. Oh … Nacio's sister's name is Esmeralda. She's called Esme."

"This Bernie is desperate to find the package. Would he go to such extremes if it only contained coke or heroin … or some other illicit drug?" said Jeff. "I don't think so. It's not likely to be cash, but the package must be of great value. We have no idea what's inside but we have to know. Will Nacio let us look now?"

"Yes, if it will help us find his sister."

"Maybe something inside the package will tell us where it was supposed to be taken. Maybe it just contains some legal documents that have to be hand delivered. But why didn't Bernie just bring it here himself? More mystery, Megan."

"Bernie must not be a U.S. citizen—or maybe he is wanted for some reason in this country," said Megan.

"Sure ... that's it. He couldn't risk being apprehended and losing the package by crossing the border himself to make the delivery," said Jeff. "So he hired the *coyote* to do it. He probably promised the *coyote* an attractive bonus, contingent on his completing the job."

"And according to Nacio, his father would not pay the remainder of what he owed the *coyote* until Esme was picked up and brought to Houston," said Megan. "But we can't be sure why Bernie insisted on keeping Esme."

"Probably threatened to report the *coyote* with human trafficking if he didn't complete the job and return for the girl," said Jeff. "I'm sure that a successful *coyote* has to keep his record clean in order to travel back and forth across the border."

"So Bernie's holding Esme captive as leverage to get the *coyote* to perform."

"Hopefully Bernie hasn't already taken steps to market Esmeralda," said Jeff. "Of course, now that we know Bernie is here, there's no telling what has happened to the girl."

"Don't even think that way," said Megan. "What do we do now?"

"Whatever is in the package has to be some sort of contraband being smuggled into the country," said Jeff after a long pause. "Which means that ICE would have turned the package over to the FBI, if they had discovered it first. We shouldn't open it ourselves, Megan. My firm has several contacts in the local FBI office. I can contact someone there to help us. If there's a chance that it might be related to a smuggling operation, we shouldn't tamper with the evidence."

"Good thinking. I think Nacio is convinced that we want to find Esme, so he will agree to turn the package over to an FBI agent, if we explain the reason to him."

Jeff became contemplative again. He stood and paced the floor, all the while brushing back his hair from his forehead.

"We're involved in this in a big way, Megan," he said. "Right now we may be obstructing justice by not reporting what we know and what we possess. On the other hand, we have to move fast if we're going to find Esme."

"Let's get realistic, here," she said in a tone of determination. "The FBI will do a detailed examination of the package. Their forensic lab will test for everything from fingerprints to saliva to fragments of cigarette ashes ... it will take days. We can't wait if we are going to find Esmeralda."

"Yeah," said Jeff. "For one thing, Bernie knows who we are now and where we live. Bernie is here in Houston and we are his only link to finding the package. Every minute we stay here we are in danger."

"What do you mean?"

"We need to turn the investigation of the package over to the FBI and quietly disappear with Ignacio. We'll leave Bernie here and go to Nuevo Laredo without anyone knowing. That's where we'll find information and, right now, where we'll be safer."

"Good idea. I agree. Can you get off? I'll tell the chief some story to explain why I can't come in … like taking Nacio to the clinic."

"Yeah, I'll get off," he said, and then laughed. "I'll just say someone is threatening to kill me and I have to go in hiding."

"And you might not be far from the truth."

Chapter 14

Back in the condominium, all appeared quiet. The police had finished their work and the place had been put back in order, reasonably well.

"Do you think it will be safe to stay here tonight?" asked Megan.

"Yeah, the guy's going to look for the package somewhere else," said Jeff. "I don't think he'll risk coming back here. I imagine he'll find some way to search the demolished truck more thoroughly … maybe the accident site again."

"That will give us time to get out of Houston early tomorrow morning," said Megan. "Let's take the picture to Jaime before we leave and confirm that the man who was so curious about Ignacio was Bernie."

"Good idea," Jeff replied. "I'll get the names of the FBI contacts in my office, and then we'll head for Laredo. Should you notify your parents?"

"It would only disturb them right now," she answered. "They'll have to know the story eventually. My father might be able to help us locate the mysterious señora."

"Just to be safe, explain to Nacio what we're doing and that we think the package should be placed in the safe in the security guard's station."

"He probably knows we're up to something," said Megan. "When I tell him we're going to Laredo to find Esme, he'll agree to give it to us."

* * * *

Even with the package stored away in the safe in the security guard's office, the door to their home locked, and the dead bolt engaged, Megan still slept fitfully. She awakened, walked about for a while, and sneaked a quick look at Nacio in the spare room. He looked so angelic: sound asleep and dressed in his new blue pajamas. Jeff had managed to show him how to shower and shampoo—much to Nacio's delight, according to Jeff's interpretation of what Nacio gleefully tried to say. She grinned when she thought of Jeff's story that Nacio had not wanted to turn the shower off.

Megan quietly shut the door to Nacio's room and glanced at Jeff, who couldn't be aroused by anything short of a fire alarm. She sat at her desk and tried to read for a while, but to no avail. Something was not right. They couldn't be any safer; they had taken care of every possible threat to their safety. She wished daylight would arrive faster so they could hit the road. She was anxious to see her mom and dad, especially her father. He would come up with some solid advice for sure.

She returned to the bedroom and started to turn off the small lamp on her dresser when it struck her—none of her jewelry had been disturbed, but in the bottom of her jewelry box were extra keys to her car, Jeff's car, and to their condo. Her hand trembled as she rummaged through the box. No keys!

The thought had no sooner crossed her mind than she heard noise at the front door. Thank God for the dead bolt. She quickly went to the door and looked through the peek-hole. No question about it: Although their visitor was wearing a security guard shirt, the face she saw matched that shown on the video strip. It was Bernie! Before she could wake Jeff there was a tapping on the door. She raced to the bedroom, shook Jeff awake, and returned to the door. The dead bolt was holding solid. The knock continued, louder.

"Who is it?" she called out.

"Security … Just checking to see if everything is all right. I need to come in and check," was the answer. *What a strange accent,* thought Megan.

Jeff came to her side. As drowsy as he was, he still had presence of mind to grasp what was happening. He put his finger to his lips, pulled her away from the door, and grabbed a full-size hammer from the tool drawer in the kitchen.

"Call the security station. He has probably disabled the guard some way," Jeff whispered. "If no answer, call the police. I don't think the guy can get in, but if he does he's gonna be met with hammer blow to his head."

✻   ✻   ✻   ✻

Within minutes another knock on the door was followed by a loud: "Police Officers! Open the door please." Jeff confirmed that two policemen were in the corridor and cautiously cracked the door but kept the safety chain in place. He kept his hammer raised.

"You're safe now," said the officer. "We've searched the building, and there's no sign of the intruder."

"Well, he *was* here," said Megan in a tenor of indignation.

"We know that," he answered. "The guard below was bound, his mouth taped, his shirt ripped off, and he was thrown in a closet. No one seems to know why you have been targeted by this man."

"We have no idea. Do you have any identity of this person?" asked Jeff.

"None yet. His picture and prints have been put online … no response yet."

"When he was here earlier, he took the spare keys to this apartment," said Megan. "He also took our spare car keys."

"We checked the garage and saw one car parked in your numbered slots, but only one."

"Yeah, there is only one here now. And it won't be here long. We're gonna pack and leave as soon as we can."

"If you're sure of that, we'll stay until you drive away."

"We're sure," said Jeff. Megan nodded.

* * * *

Jeff and Megan hastily packed suitcases before they awakened Ignacio. Then, accompanied by the police officers, the three of them—Nacio drowsy and still in his pajamas—made their way to the parking garage. They loaded into Jeff's car and exited the multistoried garage, wary of every dark corner they passed until they were well away from the building.

"What did you do about the package?" asked Megan.

"While you were packing, I had the guard open the safe. I put the package in the trunk of the car," Jeff answered, his eyes roving the rearview mirrors as though looking for a pursuer. "It's safe right now; but I don't believe we're safe."

"We're fortunate that Bernie didn't force the guard to open the safe."

"He probably didn't see it or he would have. We couldn't leave it. If we should run into Bernie, the package is our bargaining tool to find Esme."

Miles clicked by as they raced down the highway. At that early hour there was little traffic to contend with so Jeff could maintain a good speed. Ignacio slept soundly, curled up in a blanket in the backseat. Megan reclined the front seat and, within minutes, the drone of the car cruising along the long stretch of highway toward Laredo lulled her asleep.

✳   ✳   ✳   ✳

"Megan, we're stopping in the next town for gas. Do you need anything?" asked Jeff as he reached across the seat and gently shook her awake.

"How far to Laredo?" asked Megan. She sat up straight and looked around to see the sky coming alive with a golden glow. "I must have been in a deep sleep. We're starting a new day."

"Yeah … maybe in more ways than one," he said. "What lies ahead?"

"I see you've been thinking while driving."

"Trying to sort out the pieces to the puzzle and to make some plans."

"Any ideas?"

"Let's get fuel and food and hit the restrooms before we go farther. We'll be in Laredo soon."

"Yeah, Freer is just ahead. I'll need to call my mom and dad. They go to the shop early every day, but I can talk to Celi and let her know we're coming in."

"Who is Celi?"

"Araceli Talamantes. She's our housekeeper. Been with us as long as I can remember. She lives with us. She's a part of the family."

"Where will we stay?"

"We have two guesthouses behind the main house. Celi lives in one and we can stay in the other. Mom and Dad will be so pleased that we are coming."

"Even after they know why we're here?"

"They might be able to help us with our plans. They know almost everyone in Nuevo Laredo and Laredo. The two Laredos are close-knit communities."

"Both of your parents work in the store?"

"They've worked together every day ever since they started … about thirty years ago, I think. They started in a small hole-in-the-wall space on the main thoroughfare just across the border."

"They're still in the same location?"

"No, you'll see how they've expanded … still in Nuevo Laredo, though."

"Doesn't your dad worry about all of the crime and killings in Nuevo Laredo that we read about?"

"Not as much as I worry about it. Mom and Dad have been in Nuevo Laredo so long they know everyone. Dad hires armed, off-duty police officers to stay in the store during business hours, and he has a high-tech security system. There has never been even as much as a shoplifting incident."

"I guess they get a lot of their clientele from Laredo."

"From Laredo, yes. And customers also come from all over the country. They have built quite a reputation over the years. They managed to get several exclusive dealership franchises, like Rolex watches and Bernard Passman jewelry."

"Did you ever work in the store?"

"Hard to call it work. Even though they both worked, Mom and Dad have always been there for me, and for Andy, when we needed them. You know, school stuff, athletic events, and parties. They were attentive, caring parents. When I was growing up, they would take me to the store with them sometimes. They'd always find something for me to do so I'd think I was working. But it was fun. I think my dad always hoped I'd come back and take over the business."

"So he was disappointed when you went to law school?"

"No, he thought a law degree would be an asset in running a business."

"Any regrets?"

"None. Everything happens for a reason, Jeff. Look at us now," she said with a chuckle. "If I had buried myself in the jewelry store, we wouldn't be having all this intriguing fun right now!"

"And we have no idea what we're in for ... how much danger. And, for sure, we don't know how much success we'll have in finding Esme."

"We have to be optimistic," Megan replied and looked in the backseat where Nacio was sleeping soundly. "We owe it to this poor, lonely waif to try as hard as we can."

"I agree. I may have seemed skeptical at first but, with the way events have unfolded, I know we have an obligation here. Tell me about your mom and dad. What are they like?"

"You'll like them both," she replied. "You'll feel relaxed around them. They are both hard workers. Mom is the archetypical, subservient Hispanic wife ... very bright—could have had a great career as an accountant. But she's happy just being my dad's partner at the store."

"What about your dad?"

"I think he's the most wonderful father ever ... kind, gentle, caring. Everyone he works with worships him, and he has countless friends on both sides of the border. At my *Quinceañera*—my fifteen-year-old celebration—in addition to the many, many family members, Mom and Dad invited hundreds of people that I'd never seen before. It was an elaborate affair."

"So they are well respected in both Laredos?"

"Very much so," she said. "My dad is so law-abiding. I don't think he has even had a parking ticket. When I had my own car and traveled back and forth to college, he refused to buy me a radar detector—said it was just a gimmick to help me break the law."

Jeff chuckled. "What a difference from my dad. He taught me the advantage of a radar detector when I was sixteen years old."

"My mom was always protective of Dad," said Megan. "As I was growing up—teen years and college days—I remember Mom getting upset when some of Dad's out-of-town friends would appear in the store and Dad would leave with them and be gone for hours. I think they were business associates from Tampico. I can still see Mom scolding him and telling him to stay away from them. I never knew why, but I know Dad would never get into any trouble.

"Dad never talks about his personal life, past or present. Mom says he was in Vietnam, but Dad never talks about it. Also, I think Mom gets disturbed when he goes off on buying trips by himself and stays longer than she thinks necessary. Of course, she has full responsibility for the store while he's gone."

"I imagine all of you had problems when your brother died."

"You wouldn't believe it … every one of us, including Celi," she said. "Mom stayed in her room and cried for a week, Dad just disappeared for three days, and I stayed with Celi most of every day and most of every night. It took us months to get back to near normalcy."

"I just can't imagine what it would be like to lose a brother … or a sister," said Jeff, his eyes glued to the road, sometimes struggling to control the car against the wind blast from an eighteen-wheeler passing at a high speed. "Sure are a lot of heavy trucks on this highway," he added.

"Always have been," she said. "These are trucks that come across the border and are headed for Houston and the East Coast." She gazed out the window for a while and then turned back to Jeff. "Why are you asking all these questions about my parents?"

"Just want to know what to expect … what they will think about our dilemma."

"Dad will help us. He's like you in a lot of ways—very analytical, comes to decisions only after careful deliberation."

"Sometimes I think I'm too analytical when it comes to arriving at decisions," he said.

Megan grinned, thinking back on their conversation in the deli. "Maybe you are, but I'm not going to try to change you."

Chapter 15

Freer, Texas, had come alive by the time they turned down the one wide thoroughfare that was lined with most of the businesses in town. From the myriad trucks and pickups packed in the parking areas, they decided that the local Dairy Queen and the two *taquerias* in town must be the places where the oil field workers and ranchers began their days with a country breakfast.

Jeff pulled into a convenience store and stopped by a gas pump. Megan leaned over the seat and gently shook Ignacio. He opened his eyes, smiled at Megan, and sat erect in his seat.

"Good morning, Nacio. We're close to Laredo. When we get there, we'll go to my parents' home first, and then we'll plan how we are going to find Esme. Are you hungry?"

"S, señora."

"We'll get some food for breakfast after we all go to the restrooms. Jeff will take you."

"*Bueno,*" he said, rubbing his eyes, struggling to waken. He looked out the window as though curious as to where they were.

On the way back from the restroom, Jeff picked up a sack full of *taquitos* and containers of juice and coffee. Ignacio clung to him as closely as possible. While Jeff and Ignacio were inside the store, Megan used her cell phone to call Celi.

"A lot of activity in this little town," said Jeff as he handed the sack to Megan. "The people are friendly and curious at the same time. What in the hell is the Rattlesnake Round-up?"

Megan laughed. "You've just been exposed to brush-country culture. There's nothing like it anywhere else. It's an annual event, has been going on for years.

They spend the day hunting and capturing rattlesnakes, give prizes for the largest. Then they barbecue the snakes and serve them along with all the other trimmings for a festival."

Jeff grimaced. "Somehow that just doesn't sound appealing. But, it looks like a beautiful day ahead." He turned onto Highway 59 and headed away from Freer and toward Laredo. "This is interesting country. It looks dry, brown, and desolate, but it still has an inexplicable beauty."

"I'm glad you think so. I've always thought that. In fact, I resent people describing it otherwise. It's this way from here on to Laredo … no towns or stops."

"While I was driving, the thought kept coming to mind: How do those immigrants manage to trek across these vast miles of brush land? They go without food or water, and I'm sure there's a snake behind every bush."

"Unbelievable, isn't it? You wonder what drives them to take such chances."

"What did Celi say when you called?"

"She was excited. She loves me. When I'm home she treats me like the spoiled child that I've always been. I told her not to call Mom and Dad until we arrive."

Jeff laughed. "I guess it's a toss-up then, between which one of us was spoiled the most."

"I would win the contest," she replied. "After Andy died, I couldn't have made it without Celi. Sometimes I would get up in the morning before daylight, go to Celi's quarters, crawl in bed with her, and cry."

"That must have been an emotionally traumatic experience for you."

"I've never been able to talk about it before," she said. "Oh … that reminds me, I didn't thank you for listening."

"Being with Nacio must have triggered a lot of those memories."

"I'm anxious for you to see the pictures we have of Andy. You'll see how much Nacio resembles him."

"It's good that you could finally tell me the story, but I worry about another thing."

"What do you mean?"

"Look, Megan, you suffered a loss then. Some day soon you're going to lose Nacio."

Megan turned her head and stared out the window at the passing scenery of scrub brush and dry prairie grass. She was silent and didn't move for a long while. She finally turned back toward Jeff.

"I'll fix juice and a *taquito* for you," she said as she opened the sack of food. "Be careful that you don't spill food on your clothes while you drive."

"You didn't respond to my concern, Megan," said Jeff.

"I can handle it," she said.

Her abrupt response told Jeff that she didn't want to talk about it.

"I see some familiar landmarks on the horizon. We'll be there within an hour. I'll tell you where to turn," said Megan as she handed Jeff some food. Then she focused her attention on Ignacio. She handed him juice and a *taquito*. "The lady you will meet at my parents' home is named Araceli. We call her Celi. She took care of me when I was a small child. You'll like her, Nacio."

Nacio nodded as he munched on his *taquito*.

"He's more relaxed with us now, Jeff."

"I think so too," he said. "Do you think we'll be able to take him across the border? He might be able to recall something that would help us reconstruct the events leading up to his crossing with the *coyote*."

"We'd be taking a risk," she said. "He's still considered an undocumented immigrant—even though we have custody. If he goes into Mexico now, it's the same as being deported. We could have a problem bringing him back across."

"Of course … you're right," said Jeff. "There has to be a way. We'll talk to your father. Maybe he'll have some idea how it can be done."

"The first thing you are going to do—after we meet Celi—is to get a couple of hours of sleep. Then we start our search."

* * * *

Laredo, Texas

They drove through the open gate and up the driveway to the expansive, Spanish-style, adobe home set on a five-acre tract. A gardener was busily trimming hedges in front of the house. Colorful, flowering plants adorned both the front flower beds and those alongside the driveway.

"This is the first time you have invited me to your home to visit your mother and father," said Jeff.

"I'm sorry. I should have long ago," she said. "I guess we've been too busy with other obligations to spend time visiting. You met my mom and dad at our graduation. You probably don't remember."

"Sure I do. I just didn't have time to get to know them," he replied as he glanced around the spacious yard. "The grounds are beautiful."

"José works daylight to dark, every day, keeping the yard this way."

Araceli Talamantes ran out of the house with open arms to greet them. She appeared to be in her early sixties—lean with a small frame. Her gray hair was neatly pulled back into a bun.

"Meggie! Meggie!" she yelled as she grabbed and embraced Megan. "How I have missed you."

Ignacio climbed out of the backseat and stood slightly behind Megan. When he stepped out from behind her, Celi looked at Nacio, put her hand over her eyes, and gasped. *"Madre de Dios!"*

"I know what you're thinking, Celi," said Megan. "Isn't it remarkable? This is Ignacio, Celi. Jeff and I are taking care of him for a while. And this is Jeff Harrison. You've heard me speak of him."

"S, s, Megan. I'm still in shock. Your mom and dad will drop in a faint," she said as she turned to greet Jeff, trying to avoid looking at Nacio. "It's the eyes, Megan. Does he have dimples when he smiles?"

"Be ready for that too, Celi."

"Dios mío!" she replied, shaking her head in disbelief. "How are you, *mi hija*?"

"I'm fine, Celi. I've missed you too. Jeff and I have a story to tell you, Mom, and Dad … why we're here."

Celi glanced at Jeff, then back at Megan. "Uh …?"

"No, not yet, Celi. It's about Ignacio. We have a big problem here," said Megan as she pulled Ignacio and Jeff to her side. Jeff remained silent.

"First, let me fix you something to eat."

"We picked up food on the way, Celi."

"Nonsense," she said as she ushered everyone into the house. "I need to call Isaac and Margarita. They'll be furious if I don't let them know you've arrived. And I know Ignacio would like some of the *pan dulce* that I just made. Wait until your parents get here to tell me the story. I'm getting curious, the way all of you are acting."

* * * *

At Andrade Jewelry, Isaac Andrade stood behind the glass counter that displayed dozens of glittering diamond necklaces and matching diamond earrings. While he conversed with the customer who was seated on the opposite side of the counter, he unlocked the cabinet and placed tray after tray of jewelry on the surface for the client to inspect. Isaac tried to ignore the intrusive ringing in the office behind him.

Finally, he looked around to see Margarita, phone to her ear, motion for to him to come take the call. He frowned. *She knows not to interrupt me when I have a potential buyer,* he thought. *Must be important.* He motioned for one of his sales assistants to take over, and he joined his wife in her glassed-in business office.

"What is it, Margie?" he asked, an exasperated tone to his voice.

"Stop frowning," she replied. She put her special computer glasses aside, grabbed her purse, and retrieved her mirror and her lipstick. "It was Celi. Megan is here. Her friend Jeff is with her. I knew I should have had my hair done. Now we have visitors and I look tacky."

"You look fine. Good news!" he replied. "Let's turn the store over to the girls for a few hours and go home. What's the occasion?"

"First, go look at yourself in the mirror," said Margarita as she scampered toward the break room. "You've been running your fingers through your hair again. It's all ruffled. And brush the bangs off your forehead. We have to look nice for Megan and her boyfriend. Isaac, I believe you have more gray streaks in your hair today than ever. Maybe you should blacken it."

"Margie ... forget my hair. Why are Megan and Jeff visiting?"

"Celi was very vague about why Megan is here ... said Megan needed to talk with us. She and Jeff have a young boy are with them."

"Who is the boy?"

"She didn't say ... just said they were taking care of him."

"Maybe they're going to make an announcement."

"I asked Celi. She said it was about the boy."

"Why bring him here?"

"We'll find out," said Margarita. "You need to brush your hair back and straighten your tie. Oh ... why didn't I put on a different dress? I had planned to work in the office all day. Megan's friend will think we're Nuevo Laredo lowlife."

"Stop worrying and let's go."

"You do remember that Jeff's parents live in the most prestigious part of Houston. What will Jeff think ... seeing me looking like this?"

"Margie ... will you please stop it and come on. We have no idea why they are here or why they have brought the boy."

"Celi seemed a little apprehensive," she said. "I hope it's not bad news."

Isaac stood in the rear doorway, waiting. He shook his head. "I'll get the car."

* * * *

Driving out of Nuevo Laredo, they paused at Mexican customs and were waived on by an officer who recognized Isaac and Margarita. Once over the International Bridge that separates the two Laredos, they stopped at the gate into Laredo. A smiling border patrolman came to the open window on the driver's side.

"Hi, Mr. Andrade … a little early for you to be going home."

"Good morning, Tom," said Isaac. "Our daughter from Houston just arrived at our home."

"Oh … Megan is home? Tell her hello for me. You remember … we graduated from high school in the same class."

"Sure … I remember. I'll tell her you're on duty."

"She's with ICE, I hear."

"Yes, she is. She is on your team instead of mine."

"That's not fair to Megan," said Margarita and turned to the Border Patrol officer. "He wanted her to stay in Laredo, Tom."

"Wish she had," he answered as he motioned for them to go through the entry lane to the United States.

* * * *

Isaac and Margarita entered through the electronically controlled gate at the beginning of the driveway to their home and waived to José, who was busy working in the flower beds as they passed. They parked behind Jeff's Lexus GS430. José leaped to the passenger side and opened the door for Margarita.

"Jeff must be doing well in Houston," said Isaac motioning toward Jeff's vehicle.

"He's a lawyer, Isaac," Margarita replied. "Now don't comment on his expensive car."

"Megan and Jeff need to stop thinking of themselves and start a family," said Isaac.

"Thank you, José," said Margarita. "The flower beds look nice. Isaac, if you say one word to embarrass those kids, you'll catch it from me."

"I'll be careful."

Celi, wide-eyed and flashing a subtle smile, met them at the door. "They are in your study, Isaac. They won't tell me why they came until we're all together. I don't know what it's about. It has something to do with the boy. And brace yourselves when you see the boy. I thought I was going to pass out when I saw him."

"Calm down, Celi," said Isaac. "What in the world could be going on that you're acting this way?"

"Just trust me. You'll see."

Celi led them to Isaac's study where Jeff was seated in a chair reading the *Laredo Morning Times*. Megan and Ignacio were hovered in front of the computer. Megan was busily trying to teach him the basics of accessing some of the game programs. Jeff jumped to his feet when Megan's parents entered.

"They're here, Megan," said Celi.

Megan and Ignacio both turned at the same time. Margarita grabbed her husband. "Isaac, Isaac ... I don't believe it. Hold me Isaac," she said as tears, which she made no attempt to blot, washed over her face.

Isaac held her close for a few moments and looked away to hide his own misty eyes. "I know what you're thinking, Margie," said Isaac as he moved her toward a nearby chair. Celi immediately came to her side.

"I know how you feel, Margarita," she said, "I had the same reaction."

"I'm sorry, Megan," said Margarita as she embraced her daughter. "Not a very hospitable greeting. How are you, dear? You look great. And Jeff ... nice to see you again."

"Mom, Dad, I want you to meet Ignacio," said Megan. "His home was in Cuauhtémoc in Mexico. He will live with Jeff and me for a while."

Greetings were exchanged and everyone seemed to have gained composure—enough that Celi, Isaac, and Margarita could calmly gaze at Ignacio, study his features, and observe his mannerisms without uttering exclamations. Without saying a word they would occasionally look at each other and slowly shake their heads in disbelief.

Ignacio—seemingly oblivious to what had made him the center of attention—relaxed and occasionally conversed with the others in Spanish. Many times, however, he was unable to answer questions, and would turn to Megan or Jeff with a questioning look on his face. Megan then would repeat the question using a dialect more familiar to Ignacio.

"Celi, Mom, I want to show Jeff pictures of Andy so he'll understand everyone's reaction to Ignacio—seeing how much he resembles Andy."

"Megan ..." said Margarita. "You haven't been able to even talk about Andy, let alone look at any old pictures."

"That's changed, Mom," she stoically replied, her head held high, "thanks to Jeff and to Ignacio."

"I'll find the pictures," said Celi "We still have them but, at your request, we've kept them stored away."

"First, now that we are all together, you need to hear the story about Ignacio and the story behind why we are here," said Megan. "I know you both need to get back to the store, but this won't take too long. Help me Jeff … don't let me leave out anything."

Megan began her narration with how she learned about Ignacio's pitiable plight. She then described all that had happened prior to their arrival in Laredo. When she came to the part about the package and Bernie's break into their apartment, Isaac jerked his head toward Megan momentarily. He stood and briefly paced around the room—a contemplative expression on his face—before sitting down again.

"Dad … you're disturbed about something."

"Just the thought that you were threatened," he said, as he struck the palm of his hand with the clenched fist of the other. "I don't like it, Megan."

Megan finished her story. There was not a sound from any of her audience for an agonizingly long time. Finally, she turned to Jeff.

"Jeff, do you have anything to add?"

"No, you've covered it thoroughly," Jeff replied. He paused for a few seconds before saying more, and then faced the family with a look of solemnity, as though trying to read the response of each to what they had just heard.

"All of you need to know this: We are well aware of the dangers we face, but we are determined to protect this child. Also, we are here to find his sister. We don't know what will come afterward, but we are both committed to going forward. We'd like to have your support while we dig our way out of this quagmire."

Isaac started to speak but stopped himself and retreated into a pensive state.

Chapter 16

The silence seemed to thicken by the minute. Finally, Margarita turned to Megan.

"Megan, how long will you be able to keep Ignacio?" she asked.

After a long pause Megan answered. "I really don't want to think about it," she said as she glanced at Nacio and at Jeff. "We're going to keep him until we know he is safe somewhere."

"I agree," said Jeff. "Our first task right now is to find Nacio's sister. We have to locate the lady that he identifies as Señora Carrillo. Surely we can find someone in Nuevo Laredo who can tell us where she might be."

Margarita looked first at Megan and then scowled at Isaac as she said, "Your father can tell you how to find Señora Carrillo, can't you, Isaac?"

"Now, Margie, cut it out! Don't bring that up in front of Megan and Jeff," said Isaac as he glared at Margarita with a puckered brow.

"What are you saying?" asked Jeff. He looked at Isaac. "Do you know where we can find this woman?"

Isaac paused before answering. "Señora Carrillo has been a good customer of ours for years. When she comes in I know she'll spend no less than ten to twenty thousand dollars, sometimes more. Margie thinks she flirts with me when she comes to the store."

Megan grinned. "What is this, Mom … you think she hits on Dad when she comes in?"

"I don't know what you mean by 'hits' on him," she said, "but her demeanor when she's around your father is deplorable … and he loves it."

"Margie, this is no time for us to go there." He turned to Jeff and Megan. "I think I can answer some questions for you about the mysterious package and also about the character named Bernie. First, let me tell you about Señora Carrillo … and clear the air about her." He glared at Margarita for a moment. "She has one of the most fashionable bordellos in all of south Texas and northern Mexico—El Rancho Alegrón. Her client list includes hundreds of the most prestigious and reputable individuals in the country—professionals, politicians, wealthy executives. I could name countless that you wouldn't believe."

"Ask him if he's on the list, Megan," said Margarita, still glaring at Isaac. Megan and Jeff tried to conceal their amusement at Margarita's accusations.

"I am *not* on that list, Margie, and you know it," said Isaac. "I've told you that before."

"All right, all right," she said. "Now, what can you do to help Megan and Jeff?"

"I think I know what's in the package that the *coyote* was supposed to deliver," he said. Megan and Jeff sat straight in their chairs, waiting on his explanation. "You need to know something of the background. Much of what I'm going to tell you comes from what I hear from some of the law enforcement officers in Nuevo Laredo."

Isaac made himself comfortable in a chair and continued, "It's well-known that Carlos Chacón heads the drug cartel in northern Mexico … has for years. Recently, however, he has been threatened by competitors in drug trafficking as well as from law enforcement agencies in Mexico and the United States. That's what is behind all the killings you've heard about—pressure on Chacón from law enforcement officers on one hand, and from his competitors on the other. There's no question about it, there is a fierce war going on."

"How does that tie in with Señora Carrillo's activities?" asked Jeff, listening intently to Isaac's every word.

"She is Chacón's sister. She lives in Nuevo Laredo, in a mansion-sized residence located in a large fenced-in compound on the edge of town. It's known as El Rancho Alegrón. Her husband, Horacio 'Horse' Carrillo, is one of Chacón's henchmen … one of his bodyguards. I'm reasonably sure that Bernie is also one of Chacon's gang. They use El Rancho Alegrón as a headquarters of sorts when they are active in the area."

"So that's how Bernie and Señora Carrillo are linked," said Jeff.

"Exactly," said Isaac. "When Bernie—I'm sure on Chacón's advice—decided to hold the girl hostage, they had her placed with Chacón's sister. From what I know about the señora, she probably looked upon Esmeralda as potentially becoming one of her 'girls.' If the señora has her, it will be difficult getting her back—or ever finding her."

"Which makes it more imperative that we find Esme as soon as possible," said Megan.

"Right," said Isaac. "Señora Carrillo pampers her girls to the point of brainwashing. She has brought them in the store on occasion to adorn them with jewelry. You can tell … she leads them around like puppies on a leash. She keeps them laughing and giggling. They worship her."

"So you think the package contains illegal drugs?" asked Jeff. "You know I have that package locked in the trunk of my car."

"No, it does not contain drugs," said Isaac, "I should have reported my suspicions to the AFI long ago but I had no proof. The AFI in Mexico is the equivalent of our FBI. Here's what happened: Bernie Hefferman came to me a few weeks ago with a proposal. Bernie represented himself to be an importer of diamonds from Tel Aviv. He offered me a dealership in imported diamonds, already cut and polished. I would broker them to other retailers over the country and realize a nice profit."

"How did you answer him?"

"Simple answer: sure, I would do that as long as the diamonds carried a Kimberly Certificate. Of course they didn't … which meant that they were mined in Africa by slave labor and political prisoners. I was well aware of what he was doing: He wanted me to assist him in smuggling illegal diamonds into the United States."

"What's a Kimberly Certificate?" asked Jeff.

"The very finest diamonds in the world are found in Africa—the Congo, Zimbabwe, Angola, and Sierra Leone. For years, before the mining and marketing of the diamonds became regulated, the bloody civil wars between political factions in those countries in Africa were financed by funds received from diamonds imported into Europe and the United States—into the metropolitan areas where the market is the strongest. The mining was done by political prisoners and by the destitute masses who worked for nothing more than food."

"So that's where the terms 'blood diamonds' and 'conflict diamonds' originated," said Jeff. "I've read about that."

"Exactly," said Isaac. "Then, a few years ago, strict regulations were enforced internationally. All diamonds imported into and through the United States had to be validated by a Kimberly Certificate. The certificate guaranteed that the mining was done ethically, and that money from the sales was used for the economic well-being of the people of those countries—not to finance civil wars.

"Consequently, without funds from the sale of diamonds, the civil wars quieted down. The warring factions in Africa were brought to a standstill after the international adoption of the Kimberly Process Certification System, the KPCS.

"But recently the wars have flared up again, especially in Sierra Leone. So now diamonds once again are being smuggled out of Africa into the United States and the money from the sales is being used to finance new civil war conflicts just as before ... used for weapons, ammunition, and payoffs."

"So the Kimberly system is no longer effective?" asked Jeff.

"It has become too easy to circumvent," said Isaac. "No, it's not working, and the wars are raging again. The diamonds in the package that Bernie sent with the *coyote* were conflict diamonds—they carry no certificate. Bernie is working for Chacón. With the pressures on his drug trafficking, Chacón is again turning to diamond smuggling."

Jeff winced. "So that's why the package is so important to Bernie," he said. "And we have the package in the trunk of my car."

"That's the danger, Jeff. That package is worth millions ... Bernie will stop at nothing to recover it. For one thing, if he doesn't, Chacón will take him out in a heartbeat. So, if Bernie gets curious and does a little sleuthing, he'll find that the Megan Andrade who lives at your Houston address is the same Megan Andrade whose father is Isaac Andrade, and that her home in earlier years was this address. He will put it all together, and he will be visiting Laredo soon in search of the package. None of us is safe right now."

"That's so frightening, Dad. What should we do?" asked Megan. "I know that Jeff and I are taking a risk here, but we never meant to endanger all of you. Do you want us to abandon our plans? We can go back to Houston and turn the package over to the FBI."

Isaac leaned back in his chair, his chin resting on his clasped hands. After a prolonged thirty seconds, he finally spoke.

"Whatever you do, all of us will still be in some danger," he said. "Even if you leave, return to Houston, and contact the FBI, you will still be at risk for another attack by Bernie. I suggest that you stay here and continue toward your objective to find Ignacio's sister. There might be another way out of this mess. Let me think for a while."

* * * *

Celi retired to the kitchen to put together lunch for the group whenever they reconvened. Megan took Ignacio by the hand and, along with Margarita, led him outside for a walk. Jeff stayed in the study with Isaac. Both were quiet and appeared deep in thought. Isaac finally spoke, a serious tone to his voice. He spoke barely above a whisper, as though taking advantage of the others being out of the room.

"Jeff, how did we get to this point?" said Isaac. "It would have been so easy for you and Megan to have turned over the package to the FBI and turned Ignacio over to ICE for deportation. Why has all this come about?"

"I know what you're thinking, Mr. Andrade," said Jeff, after a long pause. "Let me tell you this: I am very much in love with Megan. I want to marry her and build a life together … with children. But we have both been so career minded that we haven't even talked about long-range plans … until Ignacio came into our lives."

"I suspected that," said Isaac.

"Being with him has changed both of us," Jeff continued. "I see how Megan has bonded with Nacio, and, honestly, being around this kid has made me stop and do some soul-searching. I have known Megan for four years. Just yesterday she told me about her brother for the first time. She's been in pain ever since her brother died, and never before has she talked to me about it. Nacio coming into her life has been a giant step toward healing that turbulence in her mind … it has helped her bring closure to the loss of her brother.

"I don't think either of us will be willing to abandon our plans to pursue the recovery of Nacio's sister and to see that Nacio is placed in a safe environment. And, what's frightening, I don't see how either of us could ever give him up."

"I knew that would be your answer before I even asked," said Isaac. "It's the right thing to do, and what you've said describes Megan ever since she was a child."

Isaac turned his head away from Jeff for a moment as if searching for the right words. He turned back, "Jeff, I have some suggestions. I'll wait until the others return. There is danger whatever path you take, but there may be a way that the problem can be resolved with minimum risk. Thank you, Jeff, for your honesty. I admire both of you for the stance you've taken."

"Thank you, sir."

"One of the first things you need to do is get that package out of your car and place it in the safe here at the house. Later, we'll transfer it to the safe at the store."

✳   ✳   ✳   ✳

Celi laid a tray full of sandwiches, drinks, nuts, and sweets on the coffee table. Everyone gathered around Isaac, anxiously awaiting his opinion of the quandary that Jeff and Megan were up against. The food Celi had put before them looked delectable, but no one seemed to have much of an appetite.

"What do you think, Dad?" asked Megan. She sat upright on the couch, one hand on Nacio's shoulder and the other nervously brushing back her hair.

"All of us must look at this problem realistically," he said. "First, we must recognize that we all *are* in danger; that includes all of us in this room. Here's why: Bernie knows by now who you two are, where you live, and that you probably know what he looks like—maybe even his name. He'll link Megan's name with Andrade Jewelry, and his criminal mind will make him suspicious that I have something to do with the disappearance of the package."

"What do you think he will he do, Mr. Andrade?" asked Jeff. "Will he try to attack here?"

"Not likely. I am going to arrange for guards to stay around the house. We don't need to worry right now, but after Bernie has given up trying to find the package in Houston, the thought will hit him that maybe you are in Laredo … looking for the girl. Bernie is likely getting rather desperate about now. He knows Nacio picked up the package and that he's with you. And he will figure out that you are here. We just have to be ready for whatever he might do."

"Mom, Dad, Celi, I feel so bad about getting you involved," said Megan.

"Look … I'm glad you came and that we know what's transpired," said Isaac. "Bernie would likely strike, even if you had never come to Laredo."

"We'll do whatever you suggest, Mr. Andrade," said Jeff. "I think you're probably going to agree that we need to move fast."

"Absolutely," he answered. "Bernie probably is frantic by now. The package's value to him is his life. He has to recover it or face Chacón. Having said that, here's what I suggest: if we can make contact with Bernie, we might be able to exchange the package for Nacio's sister."

"Wouldn't that be dangerous?" asked Jeff.

"Not as dangerous as *not* dealing with him. After we're sure the girl's all right and is with us, we'll hand him the package. The next thing we'll do is tell the story to our customs people. After we give up the package, we'll notify the FBI and the Mexican AFI and let them deal with Bernie."

"Isaac, are Megan and Jeff violating any law by negotiating with this criminal and surrendering the package to him?" asked Margarita, her hands clasped as she sat on the edge of the couch.

"Good question, Margarita," Isaac replied. He looked at Jeff and grinned. He turned back to Margarita and put his arm around her shoulder. "We have two attorneys here, Margie," he added. "Let's get their opinion."

"I see what you mean," said Jeff. "Here's my opinion: We don't know what's in that package. What you've told us, Mr. Andrade, is your assumption of what it contains. We can't be concealing evidence when charges haven't been filed and there's no investigation underway to determine the contents of the package. We're not obstructing justice or interfering with a criminal investigation. We don't know for sure what's in the package."

"Well said, Jeff. That has been my thinking," said Isaac. "Margie, stay here with the kids. I'm going to the store to check on a couple of things and arrange for guards to stay here on the premises day and night until we resolve this problem."

"Will we be safe, Isaac, while you're gone?" asked Margarita.

"For today ... yes. But we want guards here as soon as possible."

"We've talked about taking Ignacio across to see if he might be able to identify some familiar landmarks from the night of the crossing," said Jeff. "Megan said it was too risky—that we might have trouble bringing him back."

"She's right," said Isaac. "There would likely be no problem if the officers were ones we knew, but I don't think you should take a chance."

"Also, I thought we might leave word somewhere that we are looking for Bernie, and where he can find us," said Jeff.

"That would be unwise, Jeff," said Isaac. "Ignacio has mentioned the Blue Eagle and the Azteca Hotel, from what you tell me. I know where they are located. I'll go by and leave messages for Bernie and leave my cell phone number ... not yours or Megan's."

Isaac turned to Margarita, sitting on the couch, a scowl on her face and her arms folded across her chest. "Don't look at me like that, Margie," he said. "I have been in Nuevo Laredo long enough to know where just about everything is ... doesn't mean I've ever been there."

"Watch him squirm, Megan," said Margarita. "He *has* been to the Blue Eagle and has bet on the horses. One of the girls at the beauty parlor told me he was seen there."

"Mom ... leave him alone!" said Megan. "He's trying to help us."

"Celi, make sure the entrance gate lock is engaged," said Isaac. "And tell José a sketch of what's going on without scaring him, and ask him to stay around until we have the guards posted."

"No problem, Isaac," she said as she headed for the door to find José. Isaac followed her and, so the others could not see, motioned for her to follow him into the adjacent room.

"Celi, do you still have that Glock 19 that I gave you a couple of years ago?" He had thought the gun might make Celi feel safer in the guesthouse where she lived, somewhat removed from the main house.

"Yes, I do," she replied. A look of anxiety swept over her face. "But I don't know much about guns. When you gave it to me, I put it in a drawer in my bedside table. It's been there ever since."

"Bring it into the house, Celi, please. Put it in my study … in my top desk drawer."

"Sure, Isaac," she said. "You're really concerned about this mess, aren't you?"

"Yes, I am," he said. "But I don't want to upset the others."

"Be careful, Isaac."

Chapter 17

Isaac went straight toward the border and the bridge. He needed to have Chief Pedro López-Guerra place police officers at the house as soon as possible. He'd make the call as soon as he got to the store. There was no telling what that dumb-ass Bernie would do next. He had to stop him.

Chacón should never have depended on Bernie in the first place to carry out a job with that much responsibility. Chacón had been insistent on it—against Isaac's advice—but Chacón was worried that there would have been a tip-off from some snitch in the Tampico Syndicate organization to customs about the shipment of the package across the border.

All of Chacón's men were on the ICE watch lists at the border gates, so if anyone was to be caught, Chacón must have decided to let it be Bernie. Bernie had taken a big chance going across when he went to retrieve the lost package. Isaac wondered how Bernie ever got across; he probably just swam the river.

Isaac had heard that Bernie and his friend, the *coyote* ... what was his name? ... Jimbob something, had botched another deal just a few weeks earlier—a shipment of high-grade snow. The dumb-ass *coyote* even pocketed five grand of the payoff. Then, Chacón let Bernie send Jimbob to Houston with a twelve-million-dollar package ... stupid! He would tell Carlos in a nice way when he talked to him next.

At the International Bridge, customs officers on both sides recognized Isaac and waved him through as they did every day. Isaac crept through the heavy traffic on the crowded streets in Nuevo Laredo, filled with visitors, hawkers, and begging urchins. The pace gave him time to think about Megan and Jeff's determination to find the boy's sister. A commendable effort, and he didn't want to interfere. Except he would have to intervene if it appeared that they were getting too close to some unpleasant truths in their explorations.

If his plan worked out, the problem could be unraveled without exposure of his relationship with Chacón. It was an adverse turn of events that Megan had become involved, but it should go well if everything worked according to plan.

The boy *did* resemble Andrew. What a shocker it had been to walk in and see him! It opened painful old wounds that Isaac thought he had buried ages ago. He could see what having the boy by her side had done for Megan. Of course, that's the only reason he was embarking on this new plan to find Bernie and work out a trade with him for Nacio's sister.

The easiest thing to do would be to tell Chacón to bring Bernie in, tell Megan and Jeff that the girl had disappeared, convince them to leave the package at Andrade Jewelry for safekeeping, and send the two of them packing back to Houston. In all these years during his business ventures with Chacón, knowledge of his secret life had never been so close to discovery by his family. No matter what the outcome of his plan to negotiate with Bernie, he would do everything he could to protect Megan from embarrassment over her father. He couldn't let Megan go through the pain of learning the truth.

Isaac could see the Andrade Jewelry sign ahead and turned to enter the ramp to his private parking garage above the store. He spoke to his employees and went directly to his office, sat at his desk, and dialed Chacón's phone number.

✳ ✳ ✳ ✳

"Carlos, this is Isaac," he said. "What the hell is going on?"

"You tell me, Isaac," he replied. "How did Megan get in the picture?"

"She works for ICE … you know that, Carlos. Just by coincidence she was asked to help interview the boy. And she and her friend, Jeff Harrison, now have taken protective custody of the boy."

"The boy picked up the package at the accident scene," said Chacón. "Does he still have it?"

"Jeff has it locked in the trunk of his car. I'm going to put it in my safe at the office," said Isaac. "Look, Bernie has made two attempts to get the package—broke into Megan's apartment once. If he harms her at all, I'll kill the son of a bitch."

Chacón chuckled. "You'd do me a favor. I know the story. I told him not to touch Megan … that he might have to take out the boyfriend."

"Back off, Carlos, we've recovered the package," said Isaac. "Megan wants the girl back. I told her she could make a trade with Bernie—the package for the girl—and keep it quiet from ICE and the FBI."

"Might pose quite a problem," he said. "I think Carmen plans to move her to El Rancho Alegrón in Piedras Negras. She needs her there ... already too many girls in Nuevo Laredo. Since the *coyote* didn't return, she decided to ship her."

"Could you call Carmen and see if she can be returned? Megan's worried about her safety."

"You call Carmen, Isaac. You know she'd do anything for you," he said with a chuckle. "Never mind ... *I'll* call her. She'll have a dozen questions. The girl's safe for now and will be for a few weeks."

"What do you mean?"

"I've heard Carmen say that it takes a while for the new girls to go through 'orientation.'"

"Megan wants her back, Chacón," said Isaac in a tenor that spelled sternness.

"I'll see what I can do," he said. "What about the package?"

"It's in my safe at home for now; I'll move it to the store. Bernie needs to think that he is responsible for its recovery and the return of the girl."

"Will your house be guarded?"

"Yeah, I have asked Chief López-Guerra to place two of his best officers on the compound. They'll have to waste Bernie if he tries to take the package before we have the girl."

"All right with me. I'd like to keep Bernie; he's needed. I know he's impetuous, Isaac, so be careful how you pull this off. Once you get the girl, give the package to Bernie. He'll get with me and we'll start over on getting it delivered."

"Will your guy in Houston be patient?"

"He'll wait. We're talking about *mucho dinero* here. He'll wait."

"Let's get the girl back here, Carlos."

"I'll see what I can do," said Chacón. "Same as always ... huh, Isaac? What Megan wants, Megan gets."

"Yeah, I'm still spoiling her, I guess. And I sure don't want her to delve into our affairs too deeply."

"What about the boyfriend? Are they serious?"

"Yeah, and I don't want him bruised either."

"Fine ... unless he starts getting too inquisitive," said Chacón.

"Your call, Carlos," said Isaac. "So, here's the plan: You'll bring Bernie in, get Carmen to bring Esmeralda back—wherever she is. As soon as we know that the girl is safe, Bernie gets the package—his neck is then out of the noose. He delivers it to you, and the process of sending it to the Houston contact starts over. Megan and Jeff return to Houston. Carlos, please don't give Bernie another assignment like this one.

"I'll have to agree, Isaac. And please don't let Bernie know the dollar value of the package. I'm afraid he'll get some unhealthy ideas. I'll want you to appraise the merchandise again, Isaac."

"Good idea. You mean Bernie doesn't know what the merchandise he's going after is worth on the market today?" asked Isaac. "Why has he been so fuckin' intense?"

"He just knows the consequences if he doesn't recover the package, regardless of the content."

"Then we have work to do. I need to get back home. I'll tell Megan and Jeff that I left my cell phone number at the Blue Eagle and the Azteca and that we will wait for a return call from Bernie. Call me when you know something."

"Isaac, we need to get this cleaned up quickly … whatever it takes. I want to protect Megan, help her find the boy's sister, but we have another shipment coming later this week. We can't let anyone get in our way."

"I hear you. Call me on your secure cell. I don't want these calls traceable."

"Will you ever stop worrying about what Megan knows and doesn't know?"

* * * *

Megan and Jeff retreated to a corner of the large den while Celi busied herself in the kitchen and Margarita used the time to straighten objects throughout the house—trinkets that Celi had not replaced in their proper place when she cleaned. Megan laughed as she watched her mother.

"Mom's constantly cleaning and rearranging things," she said to Jeff. "She carries a dust cloth with her everywhere she goes."

"And *that's* where you get your obsessive-compulsive streak. I'm learning a lot about you."

"Dad and I joke about her dust cloth. Dad says he's going to hang it on her tombstone."

"Your dad surprises me," said Jeff. "He appears so much younger than he really is. He is thin, has a muscular build. It doesn't match his graying hair."

"Oh … I didn't tell you—Dad is an exercise freak. Even at his age he runs and works out at the gym every day."

"So that's what got you started running every day?"

"Yeah, I guess so," she said. "Even when I was just a child, my dad took me with him to the gym ... almost every day."

"Nothing wrong with that."

"And he used to be a diet faddist ... read health food magazines and always watched closely what the family ate. I can remember as a child being chastised about some food that I wanted because all my friends raved about it. He would take it away from me. Hey ... you're like that in some ways."

"I guess so. I try to avoid certain foods that the magazines say are harmful," said Jeff. "And I know that I've been negligent about exercise lately."

"Yeah ... ever since we graduated. When we were in law school, you were very diligent about exercising. You need to get back to that."

"You're right," said Jeff. "When I think about the situation we're in right now, I realize that I might be called on to muster every ounce of strength and endurance possible before it's over."

"Then you need some sleep to prepare yourself for whatever we might have to face."

"How about this couch?" he said, as he began to stretch out. Megan quickly removed his shoes before he put his feet on the couch.

"See what I mean ... just like your mother," he said as he placed his hands across his chest, closed his eyes, and fell asleep in seconds.

*   *   *   *

Isaac dropped by the Blue Eagle and the bar in the Hotel Azteca just to check and see if anyone had seen Bernie. The replies were all negative. He left his cell phone number for Bernie to call if he put in an appearance. He then turned toward the bridge and home. He dreaded facing Megan again. How could he continue hiding his secret from her?

Of course, it was a streak of bad luck that the *coyote* had wrecked his vehicle and had failed to deliver the package. And it was pure coincidence that Megan had gotten involved with the boy. Still, he could see why Megan had attached herself to Ignacio—he was so much like Andrew. If Ignacio filled a void in Megan's life right now, all of these attempts to conceal his past history from Megan were worth the effort, but it was going to have to come to an end some day.

He had asked himself over and over again lately why he had allowed himself to become so involved with Chacón. He had always said that he could get out any time he wanted. Why hadn't he just done it? He didn't need the money any more. How long could he continue living this double life and deceiving his wife and daughter?

And now he had just concocted a story to try to explain to Jeff how he knew the package contained the diamonds. That was a worry—Jeff was no dummy. He would find out the truth. Maybe it would be just as well if he did … reaching Megan through Jeff might be a good idea.

But *could* he get out? Chacón would be concerned, of course, considering all Isaac knew about Chacón's activities. The AFI would love to hear him sing about Chacón, but he would never rat on Chacón. Not because he was afraid of reprisal, but simply out of loyalty to his friend. Isaac's train of thought was rerouted for a few seconds as he realized that it was his friendship with Chacón that kept him "in."

He thought about the years past when he had welcomed additional income from Carlos in the form of funds to expand the store and to upgrade his inventory. It had been so easy—carry "merchandise" across, and transfer it from his car to a courier at a prearranged drop point. And channeling funds to an off-shore account for Chacón through Andrade Jewelry was an easy way to make a lot of money. The transactions were almost impossible to detect since his store was such a high-volume cash operation.

How had it all begun? It had to have begun when Andy died. Andy was Isaac's prince … his heir apparent. After he was gone, life seemed to have no meaning. In his mind, Isaac had forgiven Megan, but there was always that lingering resentment that she had survived and Andy hadn't. After all these years, he now realized that he alone had made the choice to take this path into questionable illegal activity with Chacón. No one had coerced him into his dealings with the cartel, and now there was no easy way to get out. As long as Carlos needed him, he had to deal with it.

CHAPTER 18

Usually, on his way home, Isaac activated the electronic gate that guarded his home when he was half a block away. Today, however, he waited until he was close to the gate before he pressed the button. He didn't want to take any chances that someone could break through while the gate was open. He crept through slowly, eased into the semicircular driveway, and parked in front of his home. His first chore would be to face his anxiously waiting family. Next, he would need to get Jeff to open the trunk of his car and transfer the package to the safe in his study.

Isaac paused for a moment before getting out of the car and feasted his eyes on the beauty of José's flower garden creation. José, smiling as usual, looked up from kneeling over one of the flowerbeds just long enough to wave. Isaac climbed out of his car and stopped by to commend José on his work.

"Muy bonitas, José," he said pointing to the colorful plants.

"Gracias," José replied, and then nodded his head toward the driveway that coursed alongside the house. *"Mire, señor ... el muchacho y Meggie,"* a grin creased his face, but at the same time he wiped away a tear with the back of his soil-stained hand.

Isaac, appearing puzzled at José's comment and show of emotion, started walking down the driveway and stopped in his tracks at what he saw. He stepped behind a tall plant at the corner of the house and watched. His throat tightened, and he fought back tears.

"Faster, Meggie, faster!" cried Ignacio. Megan raced alongside the bike, holding onto the boy as he peddled. Then Nacio yelled: "I can do it, Meggie, turn loose." He traveled on his own for a few feet before he fell. But he jumped up as

Megan ran to his side. A scraped knee but not a whimper from Nacio. He grinned as he said: "One more time, Meggie! One more time, please." Megan gave him a hug, kissed his forehead, and helped him back on the bike.

Events from years past swept through the memory neurons of Isaac's brain. The scene was as vivid as if he were witnessing it at that very moment: Megan was six years old. Teaching her how to keep her balance on her new bicycle—her birthday present—Isaac had run alongside her and had held her on the bike seat, much as Megan was doing with Nacio right then. "I can do it now, Papá!" Megan had said. "Turn me loose, Papá. I can do it!" Minutes later the bicycle had gone down, and she had been thrown off. He remembered running to her side and picking her up … kissing her bruised knees and watching in wonderment as she'd grinned and insisted on trying again. They had both laughed as he'd helped her back on the bike.

Had he taught her to deal with adversity and to rise to fight again any time she was knocked down? Now she was teaching this boy to ride a bicycle—the very same bicycle on which he had taught Megan. He remembered her saying, "I'll teach Andy some day, Papá."

Isaac shook his head to clear the reverie. That had been one of many memorable experiences that had been responsible for the close bond with Megan that he had enjoyed for so many years. Now that bond might be threatened. He had to shake this demon off his back some way and preserve the respect that his daughter had for him. *I wonder if Megan remembers when I taught her to ride a bicycle when she was a child,* thought Isaac.

"Muy bien, Nacio," Isaac called out as he walked down the driveway toward the pair. He placed his hand on the boy's shoulder and pulled him close. "You're learning fast."

"Una buena maestra," Nacio replied as he looked at Megan. His dimples deepened from his wide grin.

Isaac sat on the curb that bordered the wide driveway and watched. After one more lesson, Megan sat beside him while Nacio devoted his attention solely to the bicycle, spinning the pedals, gripping the handlebars, rubbing the leather seat.

"Where's Jeff?" asked Isaac.

"I made him get some sleep. He drove all night while Nacio and I slept," she said. "Thanks for saving my old bicycle, Dad."

"I never could bear the thought of getting rid of it," he said.

"That's the sentimental dad that I will always remember. Do you bring any news?"

"I'm afraid not," he answered. "I went to the Blue Eagle and to the bar at the Hotel Azteca and left word that I needed to get in touch with Bernie. Now we wait for his call ... or his appearance. We will have two off-duty police officers on the premises beginning late tonight."

"Dad, does any of this mess have any meaning to it? Where is it going?"

"Sure it does ... everything has meaning, Meggie," he said. "Yes, this quandary we're facing right now has meaning, deep meaning. It could mean changes in all of our lives—yours, mine, your mother's, and Jeff's ... as well as Nacio's."

"I'm feeling guilty again, Dad, for dumping this on you. You and Mom don't deserve this sort of dilemma."

"Don't even mention it," he said. "We didn't plan it this way, but I welcome this opportunity to visit with you and get to know Jeff better."

Megan turned her head away and was silent for a few moments before speaking. "We *are* in real danger, aren't we, Dad?"

"We never know when we might be facing danger, do we?" said Isaac. He looked straight into Megan's eyes with a solemn, pensive look as he spoke. "Sometimes I think we need situations like this to remind us to look inward and examine ourselves and our lives—our values, our goals, our very purpose of existence."

"Dad, you're getting philosophical," she said. "Has seeing Nacio, with his resemblance to Andy, brought all this on?"

"I don't know, Meggie ... maybe so. Let's not try to analyze it for now. Let's just find a way to deal with it."

"I'm for that," she answered.

Ignacio wheeled the bike to where they sat and tugged at Megan's slacks. He wanted another lesson. She blew a kiss to her dad as she moved away with the boy.

* * * *

Jeff stirred for a moment, raised his head, and looked around trying to bring into focus exactly where he was. The fuzziness finally cleared, and he realized that he had slept for probably a good two hours. Where was Megan? And Ignacio? He stood beside the couch, which had been his arms of Morpheus during his nap. He wandered into the anteroom adjacent to Isaac's study. Drowsy to a state of near-stupor, he collapsed into the first comfortable chair that he found, closed his eyes for a moment, and promptly dropped back into a light sleep state.

He was startled at first, before he realized that the voice of Isaac in his private office next door had awakened him. Isaac was speaking to someone on the phone.

I should leave, he thought. *Mr. Andrade doesn't know I'm in here listening to everything he says. It might be a private conversation.*

He started to stand. No one else was in the room, so he could ease out without being seen. He stood beside the chair and turned to leave when a couple of words caught his attention—words like "the package" and "Bernie." He stepped behind the door to the den, out of Isaac's sight, and listened.

✻   ✻   ✻   ✻

Isaac stood with his back to the door—his cell phone flipped open and held against his ear.

"This is Isaac."

"Isaac … Bernie here." *He didn't have to identify himself,* thought Isaac. *I know no one else with a German accent like that.* "I got a message from Beto on my cell phone to call you."

"Yeah, Bernie," he replied. "Did you talk to Chacón?"

"Haven't yet. What's up?"

"A change in plans," he said. "I'm sure you're still looking for the package, aren't you? Where are you?"

"I'm almost to Laredo," he answered. "Have you seen your daughter?"

"Yeah, she's here with me," said Isaac. "She and her friend Jeff are with me in Laredo. You're in deep shit, Bernie. What the fuck did you think you were doing, breaking into their home, scaring the hell out of them?"

"Goddamn it, Isaac," he yelled. "I'm looking for the fuckin' package. If I don't find it, you know what Chacón will do to me. Either that kid or your daughter has the package."

"Cool it, Bernie," he said. "I have the package … it's safe."

"What the shit? Why hasn't someone told me? I'm out here bustin' my fuckin' ass and you have it?"

"Right. Now listen to me, Bernie," he said. "Get the girl and bring her to my house and don't fuck around."

"Shit, I can't do that, Isaac," he yelled, a frantic tone to his voice. "Carmen has already shipped that girl."

"Get the girl, Bernie," he said. "Find the girl and bring her here … or you have me to deal with."

"I need to talk to Chacón."

"Fine ... talk to Chacón," said Isaac. "But bring the goddamn girl here or I'll ice you, Bernie. You won't have to worry what Chacón would do to you. I'll give you twenty-four hours."

"Damn, damn, damn," Bernie said and clicked his phone off.

* * * *

Jeff slowly slipped away from the door as quietly as he could but, still a bit groggy, he bumped into a table and a vase wobbled noisily. Maybe Isaac didn't hear. Jeff went outdoors to find Megan. He couldn't believe what he had heard. There must be some explanation—Megan's father conversing with Bernie, a common gangster ... the very person who had broken into their home and later terrorized them? And the language he'd used! He had to have been familiar with the guy.

Jeff couldn't say anything to Megan about what he had discovered until he was sure. But how could Mr. Andrade's familiarity with a representative of the Mexican underworld be explained? Jeff wondered what he should do. He needed a plan, but it couldn't include Megan. He would just to have to wait for an opportunity to seek some answers.

Jeff found Megan and Nacio in the playroom that was part of Celi's guesthouse quarters. They were hovered over what looked like a toy box, dragging out toys that Megan must have played with as a child. They were so deeply involved in chatter that they didn't hear him arrive on the scene.

"Having fun?" asked Jeff.

Megan and Nacio, both smiling, looked up. "Jeff ... yeah, I'm showing Nacio some of the old toys I used to spend hours playing with. Everything is so new to him. Did you sleep?"

"Solid like a rock, at least two hours," he said. "Any news from your dad?"

"He's back. We didn't talk much."

"So, the world could be on fire and you and Nacio haven't let anything interrupt your play?" said an unsmiling Jeff.

"What's wrong with you?" said Megan, eyes on fire. "I'm just trying to teach Ignacio a few things. He's missed so much in his life."

"Megan, have you forgotten why we're here ... has Nacio forgotten his sister already?"

"Jeff ... stop it! The sound of your voice is upsetting to Nacio ... and to me."

"I'm sorry. I guess it must be just-woke-up irritability," he said, as he sat on the floor and tousled Nacio's hair. "What's this?" he said, pointing to a bright pink radio/tape player.

"I found this in my old toy box. It still works," she said. "You should see Nacio keep time with the rock music."

"You'll have him rapping before long," said Jeff, laughing and then becoming pensive.

"All right, out with it," said Megan. "Something is bothering you."

Jeff paused before answering. "Let's go in and see if your dad has anything to tell us."

"Don't keep anything from me, Jeff," she said, her eyes fixed on his.

"You should have been a *prosecuting* attorney," he said with a chuckle. He stood and pulled Megan to her feet. "We'll talk later."

"We'll leave Nacio out here for a while. He's having too much fun with the contents of this toy chest. You should see him build with the Legos. I think he's going to be an architect."

Megan turned to Nacio to explain that they were going inside, and he could stay in the playroom while they talked with Isaac.

"If you need anything, Nacio," she said as they prepared to leave, "Celi will help you. We won't be gone long."

Nacio, totally preoccupied with the Legos and with the loud music from the tape deck, barely acknowledged that they were leaving.

"Will he be all right out here?" asked Jeff.

"He'll be fine … he's so fascinated with all the gadgets. I'll tell Celi to look in on him every few minutes."

Chapter 19

With the family gathered in the den once again, Jeff carefully studied Isaac's demeanor to see if there was any indication that he had been aware of Jeff's presence within earshot of his conversation with Bernie. Isaac appeared to treat Jeff exactly the same as he had before. Could he be sly enough to show no signs of knowing that Jeff might be suspicious of his relationship with Chacón and Bernie? Still, Jeff needed to tread cautiously.

What should he do if he were asked to open the trunk of his car and give up the package? He was sure Isaac would ask him to do so. Isaac had told Bernie that he already had the package. *If I turn it over to Isaac, knowing that he might be connected in some way to a criminal organization, could I be charged with participating in an illegal activity? Maybe I'm just thinking like a lawyer,* he thought.

He needed to put these thoughts aside for now and not jump to conclusions. After all, he had to keep in mind that the impact of exposing any wrongdoing by Isaac would be devastating to Megan. That was his foremost concern. He decided to go along with any plan that Isaac suggested that seemed reasonable. He would remain quiet, and stay observant.

* * * *

"Where is Ignacio?" asked Margarita.

"He's busy in the playroom, Mom," said Megan. She chuckled. "I wish you could see him with the old toys. And he is either watching the TV or playing the radio—sometimes both. He is fascinated by it all."

Margarita frowned. "You need to get him some good books ... keep him away from that TV," she said.

"It helps him learn English, Mom. Also, there are a lot of books in the toy box," said Megan as she laughed and turned to Jeff. "Mom's convinced that television is going to be the ruination of civilization."

"She's probably right," said Jeff. His face wrinkled into a grin. He cut his eyes toward Isaac, studying his reactions to the dialogue, only to find Isaac staring back intently. An uncomfortable chill swept over him: *He knows I was eavesdropping. What other reason would he have for watching me so closely?* Jeff decided it was time for a poignant inquiry about Nacio. He would watch Isaac's reaction closely.

"Do you think it is safe for Nacio to be left out in the playroom, Mr. Andrade?" Jeff said, keeping his eyes glued on Isaac.

Isaac showed no change in demeanor. He remained as calm and relaxed as if he had just finished an evening dinner. He turned his attention to Megan.

"I don't think there is any risk now, leaving him there. The police guards will be here later tonight. Does Celi know he's alone?"

"I asked her to look in on him," Megan said. Then her face briefly reflected fright. "Should I bring him in with us?"

"He'll be all right. You know Celi will watch him," Isaac said and then grinned. "She's probably already in the playroom with him."

* * * *

The sun slipped below the brush-covered hills as Bernie neared Laredo. It would be getting dark soon, especially this time of year. Bernie thought he knew about where Isaac lived, but he was not sure. Since Megan and her boyfriend were there, he would drive around until he found Jeff's car. They likely would have traveled in his car since they were bringing the kid. Bernie knew what that car looked like; he had checked it out at the condo parking garage.

He felt in his pocket to confirm that he had the keys to both Megan's and her friend's car. It had been a stroke of luck that, when he'd lifted the keys to their apartment, he'd found the car keys.

He thought about his last conversation with Isaac. *The bastard threatened me,* he said to himself. *Who in the hell does he think he is? Just because he has been a long-time friend with Chacón, he thinks he runs the show. I'm not so sure he's so tight with Chacón. The business would run without Isaac. Chacón needs me more than he needs Isaac. The first task is to find the package. I know what will happen to me if I don't. What if I tell Chacón that Isaac had planned all along to rip him off—that he planned to keep the diamonds? I can make up some story about how I found out what Isaac had planned.*

Now within the city limits, he continued into the center of Laredo, entered the freeway, I-35 north, and turned on Del Mar, the street that lead to the part of town where he thought Isaac lived. He was not sure what he was going to do, but first he needed to confirm that Megan Andrade was at Isaac's house.

He drove through the winding roads past one elaborate estate after another. Ahead, in one of the circular driveways, he saw a car that looked like the vehicle that he remembered seeing in Megan's condominium parking garage. He slowed his car to get a better look ... definitely that was the car that he remembered seeing. He passed on by, circled the block until he was back on the same street, and parked a block away. *It's dark enough that I can stroll around without stirring suspicion,* he thought. *I need to get a clear picture of what I'm facing.*

He approached Isaac's house and walked past it while cutting his eyes over the premises. No sign of any activity, but he saw lights beginning to flash on in the windows. He stayed close to the tall hedges that bordered the house and the driveway, and cautiously worked his way to the back. Through windows into the den he could see Isaac and his family gathered together. He moved on further back. He could hear loud music coming from one of the guesthouses—loud enough to rattle the windows. When he peered through one of the windows he could see Ignacio playing with toys on the floor. No one else was in the room.

* * * *

Nacio poured through one book after another while he listened to the tape player. He was fascinated by the pictures in the books on every page, showing characters in action. Meggie had told him that some day he would be able to read the writing in the books.

He thought he heard a tap on the door. *Maybe I should turn the music volume down,* he thought. *But why would Celi or Meggie knock before coming in? Besides, the door is open.* With the next tap he turned off the player and jumped to his feet. The door opened and Bernie stepped in. He put his finger to his lips to signal Nacio to remain silent.

Nacio froze. He recognized Bernie instantly. His first reaction was to yell for Megan and Jeff, but he was so startled that he couldn't move. He just stood still, his mouth dropped open, and his eyes widened. What should he do? Bernie blocked the door so he couldn't run. All he could think of was the terror in Esmeralda's eyes when Bernie had forced her to go with the señora.

"Don't be afraid, *hijo*. I will take you to Esmeralda," said Bernie, using as many Spanish words and phrases as he could recall in getting his message across. "Esmeralda needs you. She sent me here to find you."

"I need to tell Meggie," said Nacio, retreating away from Bernie and edging toward the door.

"No … we don't have time," said Bernie. He held out his cell phone. "We'll call from the car. Esmeralda said to come now. Hurry!"

"Is Esme all right?" said Nacio.

"She's been hurt … can't come here. You need to go to her. She doesn't know about your mama and papa. You must tell her."

"I need to let Meggie and Jeff know. They'll want to go too."

"No, no," he said. "Hurry, we don't have much time."

In spite of the fragmented picture of urgency painted by Bernie with his attempt at communication with Nacio in Spanish, Nacio was hesitant to go with him without talking to Meggie and Jeff first. Surely they would understand. What should he do? The man said he needed to hurry and that he would call Meggie while they were on their way.

Bernie held out his hand, Nacio hesitated a while longer before he grasped it and kept looking around Bernie, hoping to see Meggie or Jeff or Celi coming to his rescue. Bernie held Nacio's hand and led him out of the playroom. Within minutes Nacio was in the front seat of Bernie's car.

* * * *

"What can we do now, Dad?" Megan asked. "It's beginning to get dark. Do we just wait? Is there some way we might be able to find Esmeralda?"

"It wouldn't be wise to try," he answered. "If we haven't heard anything by tomorrow, our only hope is to contact the police in Nuevo Laredo and see if they can help. I thought we would have heard from Bernie by now."

"You've heard nothing from the messages you left in the bars?" asked Megan.

"Nothing yet," he said. He avoided looking straight at Jeff as he talked. "But he'll get the word, you can count on that. The Blue Eagle is a sort of message center for people like Bernie."

"For Nacio's sake, I hope she's all right," said Megan.

"I worry that she has been sent to another brothel," said Isaac. "That's the business that Señora Carrillo is in, underage-girl trafficking. You'd be surprised at what goes on like that just across the border. It's staggering."

"How do you know so much, Isaac?" said Margarita. "You don't get out that much."

"Talk to some of the officers that we hire as guards ... they'll tell you. It's horrible."

"What do we do if we can't find Esmeralda? I dread telling Nacio," said Megan.

"You probably should start preparing him for that eventuality," said Isaac. "I think for now we should stay with the same plan—tell Bernie to find the girl and then give him the package in exchange for her."

"Should we leave the package in the trunk of my car?" asked Jeff. He continued studying Isaac while he waited for the answer to his question—an answer that he already knew would be coming.

"You really should bring it in and place it in the safe here. If we don't hear from Bernie tonight, it should go into the master safe at the store."

Everyone was quiet for almost a full minute. The silence was broken by the shrill cry from Celi as she crashed through the door: "Ignacio is gone! Megan, he's not in the playroom! I can't find him."

Chapter 20

"*Se fue, Meggie … se fue … Nacio!*" Celi yelled. "*Hice pan dulce fresco y le llevé un plato. Dios mío … le ha pasado algo?* He wasn't there; he has just disappeared. He was there when I checked earlier. Where could he be, Meggie? He's gone! *Madre de Dios … dónde podría estar?* He's not in here, is he? I looked everywhere … outdoors, in the garage. The other buildings are locked—he couldn't be there. Where could he be, Meggie? Did someone take him? We've got to find him before he gets hurt."

Meggie and Jeff both leaped to their feet. "Calm down, Celi … he can't be far," said Megan. They raced outdoors, Isaac was close behind. Megan turned to Isaac. "Could he have been taken, Dad?"

Isaac, slowed his pace. His wrinkled forehead and sphinxlike facial muscles reflected not only concern but intense anger as though he suspected what had happened. He looked past Megan as he spoke.

"I need to alert Chief López-Guerra that the boy is missing. His men will scout the neighborhood," he said. "Ignacio hasn't been missing very long. You and Jeff keep looking. Look for your bike, Megan. Maybe he decided to take a ride by himself."

* * * *

Isaac retreated back toward the house, searching his PDA for a number as he walked. Instead of going into the house, he walked around to the front, away from the others, with his cell phone to his ear.

"Bernie, you son of a bitch, did you pick up that boy?"

"It's a new game, Isaac," said Bernie. "I'll bet Megan will do most anything for the kid's safety. She has protective custody, doesn't she? I found that out when I was in Houston. What will ICE do to her if she loses the boy? I've already crossed the bridge with him. They waved the 'father and son' in the car right through. You want him back? Give me the package. It's a different game, Isaac … different stakes."

"What about the girl?"

"You find her. I couldn't," said Bernie. "The message I got from Carmen's driver is that she jumped out of the car while they were speeding toward Piedras Negras and that she's dead. The driver got scared and ran away. Carmen made him go back and check on her the next day, but he found that someone had removed the body."

"You've managed to screw up everything again, haven't you, Bernie?"

"Call it that if you want. But … Isaac, don't threaten me again. I imagine you'd pay a pretty price to get Megan back."

"Goddamn it, Bernie, you're already in deep shit, you know. If you even think about doing harm to Megan, or kidnapping her, I'll slit your goddamn throat. My next call right now will be to Chacón."

"Don't be surprised at what you find, smart ass. He thinks you're behind a scheme to steal the package."

"Who do you think he'll believe, you or me?"

"Chacón wants the package back. He depends on me to retrieve it … any way I can. If you get in the way, I don't have to tell you what will happen."

"You're not scaring me, Bernie."

Bernie laughed. "Who you got on your side, Isaac?"

"Come after me—or anyone in my family—and you'll find out."

"But I have the boy, Isaac. Call me when you're ready to deal."

"Bring him back within the hour or I'm coming after him."

"You and who else?"

"Are you brave enough to wait and see?"

"Fuck you, Isaac," Bernie replied and the line went dead.

✳ ✳ ✳ ✳

Isaac pocketed his phone and returned to his distraught family. Megan was curled up in one of the overstuffed chairs, holding her wet face with cupped hands. Jeff sat on the edge of the chair, his arm around her shoulders trying to console her. Celi and Margarita sat on the couch, both with vacant stares on their faces. When Isaac entered, Megan jumped to her feet and ran to him. He met her with open arms and pulled her close.

"It's all right, Meggie," he said. "We'll find him."

"I shouldn't have left him, Papá," she said between sobs. "I failed him, Papá … I failed again."

Memories of the day that Andrew drowned flashed through Isaac's mind. Megan had uttered those identical words. This was the first time since her childhood that she had called him "Papá." *She is suffering a flashback of the emotional trauma that she endured years ago,* he thought, *when she felt guilty that she had not been able to save Andy. God knows I understand flashbacks.*

"It's all right, Megan," he said. "You couldn't have prevented this. We now know that Bernie kidnapped him."

"But why, Dad?" she asked. "Have you heard from Bernie?"

"Yeah, he called, gloating over having Nacio. It's not good news. All of you need to hear this. When Bernie returned from Houston, he came straight here, found Nacio alone in the playroom, and somehow convinced Nacio to go with him. I'm sure Bernie thought that having Nacio would give him more leverage to gain possession of the package.

"With Nacio in hand, he crossed into Nuevo Laredo and went to El Rancho Alegrón, hoping he might be able to find Esmeralda so he could make the trade for the package. But he was faced with the news that Señora Carrillo had already shipped her to another brothel."

"Shipped to another brothel? How could anyone be so cruel?" asked Megan.

"Young girls Esmeralda's age are a commodity," said Isaac. "It's human trafficking … young girls *and* boys, traded like merchandise. Many of them are exploited, end up in pornography studios. I agree it's cruel, but it's happening big-time right here."

"Where do you think Esme was taken?"

"There's more to the bad news," said Isaac, a downcast look covered his face. He paused before continuing: "They loaded Esmeralda into a limousine, and on the way somewhere, she managed to get the door open and to jump out while the car was traveling at a fast rate of speed. Bernie said that she was killed instantly."

"Oh … no, no, no," said Megan. For a full minute the only sound in the room was sobbing. Margarita and Celi both crossed themselves. "How can Nacio stand another emotional blow? We have to find a way to tell him when and if we find him. That poor child … how can I tell him his sister's dead?"

"We'll find him. Don't say 'if,'"

"What can we do?"

"I'll go across and start searching for Ignacio," said Isaac. "I talked to Bernie. Of course, he can't deliver Esmeralda to us, but he now has Nacio and is holding him to exchange for the package."

"Let's give him the package," said Jeff, in a tenor of anger. "Our plan was to exchange it for Esmeralda anyway. Just think of that poor child, losing his mother and father and now his sister. He needs us right now … he needs his Meggie for sure."

"I don't think it will be simple," said Isaac. "Bernie is now aware of the arrangement with ICE—that Megan has protective custody of Nacio. He found that out while he was snooping around Houston. His evil mind tells him that we would pay generously to get Nacio back so Megan won't be in trouble with ICE. Bernie will try to extract more from us than just the package."

"You mean you believe he'll try to hold Nacio for ransom?" asked Megan.

"Exactly," said Isaac. "The other risk is that he might try to manipulate us in a way that he gets the package and ends up with Nacio anyway. He would then turn him over to Señora Carrillo. She would reward him handsomely for a young boy like Ignacio."

"No … no … no …," cried Megan. "We've got to do something, Papá."

"I'll go across," said Isaac. "I'm not sure what I'll do when I get there, but we have to start somewhere. I have friends in the Nuevo Laredo police force. If I can find someone who is brave enough to help me go after one of Chacon's men, there's a chance we'll find the boy and make a deal with Bernie."

"You're not going alone, Isaac," said Margarita. "I'll go with you."

"That's foolish," he replied.

"Let me go," said Jeff.

Isaac looked at Jeff with narrowed eyes and studied him as though seeing him for the first time. He was silent for what seemed an eternity, as if he were contemplating Jeff's offer. He turned and gazed out the window. *If anything happened to Jeff it would be another blow to Megan*, he thought. *And I would be responsible. Still, at some time Megan and Jeff need to know about my relationship with Chacón. Maybe this will be a good time to make a clean break from Chacón. Jeff might be able to help me … help me pull it off. I'm sure he heard me talk to Bernie, and I can tell by his demeanor that he suspects something.*

"Are you serious about going with me?"

"Very much so," said Jeff. "We can't let you go alone, and I'm the most logical person to go."

Isaac glanced at Margarita and Celi and then at Megan. "What do you say, Meggie?"

"Just take care of him, Dad. We don't need any more scares."

"When we get to the office, I'll call Señora Carrillo ... see if she will let us interview her," said Isaac. "That will be a start. If she has Nacio, and if she will admit that she has him, we may be able to talk her into releasing him. I don't predict that she will be unreasonable. She might want money ... I can handle that." He looked at Margarita with a sly grin. "We'll get it back the next time she comes shopping."

"Just remember, you said you were going to *interview* her," said Margarita. "Nothing else, Isaac."

"Mom ... be quiet!" said Megan. "This is no time for innuendos. Remember, Jeff will be with him."

"Let's go, Jeff," said Isaac. "Are you sure you want to do this?"

Jeff laughed. "Do I have a choice? What would Megan think of me if I said I was afraid to go?"

"Then we're out of here," he said and tossed the keys to his car to Jeff. "Get the package and put it in the trunk of my car. We'll transfer it to the large safe in the store."

While Jeff hastened through the back door, Isaac went into his office. He glanced back to confirm that no one was watching and removed the Glock from the top desk drawer where Celi had placed it. After checking the magazine to confirm that it was filled, he seated it into the Glock and placed the gun in a heavy leather briefcase.

Isaac paused for a moment before leaving his office and reminisced about how he had acquired the Glock 19 in the first place. His friend, Moshe Rosen from Tampico, had given it to him years ago, during one of his visits. "Keep this close by, Isaac," he had said. "Learn how to use it. It could save your life some day."

Isaac wondered if this would be the day. He laughed, thinking, *Moshe had no idea, when he said that, how well I knew firearms; but this gun was so different from any firearm I had ever used in the past.* Unbeknownst to Margarita, he had practiced hour after hour until drawing the gun and hitting a target was as familiar to him as his daily shaving routine.

He thought about all of the life-threatening crises that he had faced years ago. Somehow they didn't seem so worrisome to him at the time—not as much as going against Bernie, finding Nacio, and getting Jeff back to Meggie safely.

Chapter 21

They crossed the bridge into Nuevo Laredo without incident. Isaac waved to the customs officers in a way that told Jeff that there was mutual familiarity. Their first stop was Andrade Jewelry. Once inside, Isaac entered the code into the keypad and unlocked the heavy, steel door to the safe room. Jeff waited outside until Isaac returned, briefcase in hand.

They headed out across the city and turned right on the highway leading toward Piedras Negras. During the entire journey, from the time they had left the house in Laredo, there had been little conversation between the two. Both seemed contemplative and in deep thought.

Jeff wondered what they might be facing. Mr. Andrade seemed so confident—not a hint of fear was noticeable. How were they going to approach Bernie, if indeed they found him? Any encounter likely would not be a friendly one. Was he up to the violence that might follow?

Isaac had kept the briefcase close by his side ever since they had been on the road. Jeff noticed that it was unlocked and unzipped. Jeff wondered what Isaac had in the briefcase. Maybe he had taken some cash out of the safe after he had deposited the package ... but why had he left it unlocked and why did he keep it so close to his side?

No more than twenty minutes away from Nuevo Laredo, Isaac turned onto an unmarked road that appeared to traverse across an expanse of brush country. To Jeff, Isaac seemed quite familiar with where to turn and where he was headed. *He may not be a frequent visitor, but he has been here before,* Jeff thought.

Jeff estimated that they had traveled about a mile when they came upon an eight-foot, net-wire fence that crossed the road. A closed gate, apparently controlled electronically, blocked their way. Beyond the gate, the entrance road ahead was lined with indirect lights that were placed low along its borders. In the distance Jeff could make out a mansionlike structure surrounded by well-lighted, landscaped grounds. Strategically placed flood lights along the eight-foot brick fence marked the enclosure borders of the compound.

Just outside the gate, Isaac stopped alongside a concrete post on which was mounted a receptacle that would accommodate a coded card. Below the slot was a button next to a speaker. Isaac punched the button and waited. A throaty voice came on the speaker and, in Spanish, inquired of the identity of the caller.

"Isaac Andrade," he said. "Here to see Señora Carrillo."

"*Un momento,* Señor Andrade," was the response. After an uncomfortably long wait, the same voice returned. "Do you have your card, señor?"

"Yes, I have it," said Isaac. "Thanks, Victor."

Jeff, with raised eyebrows, jerked his head toward Isaac in time to see him reach into the briefcase and retrieve a bar-coded plastic card that he inserted in the slot. The gate slid open. When Isaac reached inside the briefcase for the card, Jeff caught a glimpse of light reflected off metal. *My God! He has a gun in there,* he thought. *We need to talk.*

"What's the plan, Mr. Andrade?"

"We're going in, Jeff," he replied with a tenor of determination that made him sound like a military officer leading a platoon into battle. "When we get to the house, there will be at least two guards to meet us. You can stay in the car if you wish. Carmen will have warned the guards by the time we get there so they won't challenge us."

"Look, I'm here to help you. I'll stay with you unless you say otherwise."

With narrowed eyes, Isaac studied Jeff again for a moment and then drove through the gate. As they neared the mansion, Jeff could see that the place was teaming with activity. A few cars and two stretch limousines were parked outside the entrance. Before they reached the house, two uniformed, armed guards came toward them and went to the driver's side of the car. Isaac lowered the window.

"Good evening, Mr. Andrade," one of the guards said.

"Hi, Sergio, Victor," he replied. "Nice to see you again."

"Will you need us?" the other guard asked.

"I don't think so … thanks. Of course, I'll need you at the store next week."

"We'll be there … already marked on the calendar," was the reply from one of the guards as he opened his cell phone. "Señora said to call her when you arrived."

Isaac drove the short way to the mansion. As soon as the car stopped completely, two smiling female attendants opened both front doors. Loud music from the inside the house had been piped to the outside—so loud that every sensory receptor in Jeff's inner ears vibrated from the rhythm.

"*¡Bienvenidos al Rancho Alegrón!*" the two attendants said in unison and then stepped aside while Isaac and Jeff exited the vehicle.

No sooner were they on their feet than the two front doors to the house flew open and Señora Carrillo rushed out. She grabbed Isaac, threw her arms around him and shouted, "Isaac, my Isaac, you've come to visit me. I have wished that you would come again. Why have you waited so long?"

"Carmen, we are here on a serious matter," said Isaac, as he turned his back to Jeff. A faint blush blossomed as he awkwardly tried to return the embrace while still holding onto the briefcase. Jeff struggled to suppress a smile as he imagined the embarrassment that Isaac must be enduring.

"Oh ... Isaac, Isaac," she said with pouted lips, slowly shaking her head. "Always the same. That's your problem, Isaac ... always business, always serious. You've got to learn to have some fun."

She hadn't taken her eyes off Isaac since they had arrived. Finally she turned and glanced at Jeff.

"Well, well," she said, in a lilting voice. "Who do we have here?"

"Carmen, this is Jeff Harrison. He is a friend of my daughter's. We need to talk to you."

"Certainly," she said, her eyes glued to Jeff, studying his every feature from top to bottom. "I think maybe he needs to have some fun too. Now both of you just come into my private parlor. We'll have a drink. You still like your Scotch don't you, Isaac?"

"Just one measure, Carmen. We really need your help," he replied. Carmen, still preoccupied with Jeff, pretended not to hear him.

"And I'll bet you would like a glass of merlot, wouldn't you, Jeff," she said with a twinkle in her eyes. "All young men like their red wine, don't they? Increases your virility, doesn't it?"

"Wine will be fine, thank you."

They sat in overstuffed, satin-upholstered chairs in a sitting room elaborately decorated in a color motif of red and gold. An aroma of strong incense saturated the room. Carmen, in some furtive manner, without raising a finger, summoned an attendant. A voluptuous, scantily dressed girl took their orders, and within minutes she reappeared with drinks and a plate of hors d'oeuvres.

Jeff could see that Isaac was becoming impatient. While they sipped their drinks, Carmen engaged Jeff in idle talk, as if she were deliberately delaying any meaningful conversation.

After a minute or so, Isaac started to speak. Carmen raised her hand to stop him. As though she were trying to signal Isaac, she repeatedly glanced across the room toward a door behind Isaac's chair that was slightly ajar.

"Tell me how you have been, Isaac," she said with a wink and another glance at the door. "I think it's about time for me to come and upgrade my jewelry, don't you think, Isaac?"

"If you wish, Carmen … always glad to see you," he said. "Carmen, we need to find …"

Carmen stopped him. "I know why you're here, Isaac," she said, speaking almost inaudibly. In spite of her coquettish smile, her demeanor changed abruptly to one bordering on anger. "I won't stand for violence in my home, Isaac. I am not at all happy with the scenario that's developing here. Now whatever you want here, let's get it over with. Sure, I want to help you, but Bernie is standing behind that door right now, watching us."

"Is the boy here, Carmen?"

"He's here and he's safe," she answered in an almost whisper. "But you and Jeff are not. I'm leaving the room on some pretense. While I'm out, you and Bernie work this out peacefully. I'll go after the boy."

"How many are there, Carmen?" asked Isaac in a whisper.

"Just Bernie and one other—a wannabe, minor player named Tony, but he's dangerous. Be careful, Isaac." She leaned over and kissed Isaac on the forehead. "I must take this call, sweetie," she said aloud.

Carmen stood to leave, her cell phone to her ear pretending to have a call. Isaac held his briefcase in his lap with his right hand inside and remained seated. Jeff stood and watched, wondering what the next move would be. *Isaac must be expecting the worst,* he thought. *His hand is actually clutching the gun now. I can see a silencer attached.* Jeff surprised himself that he felt so calm. He tried to envision how he would be able to help Isaac if a serious conflict developed.

As soon as Carmen had stepped out of the room, Bernie quietly entered and took a seat across the round glass coffee table, his eyes fixed on Isaac.

"Are you here to deal, Isaac?" said Bernie.

"I'm here to take the boy back where he belongs," said Isaac.

"And what do you have to offer?"

"You want the package, don't you, Bernie?"

"Do you have it?" he asked, in a tone that betrayed his eagerness.

"In this briefcase, Bernie. Where is Ignacio?"

"It will take more than the package now, Isaac. What's your offer?"

"Let me put it to you straight," said Isaac. "I'm not a patient person, Bernie. Get the boy and bring him in here … now. Then we all walk out to my car. Once Ignacio is in the car with Jeff, I will hand you the briefcase." Isaac pulled the Glock 19 out of the brief case and aimed it at Bernie. "So, it's your move. Bring out the boy, or I waste you right now and I'll tear this place apart until I find him. I'll count to ten."

Bernie cringed at the sight of the gun. Obviously he had not expected this. His face turned pallid and sweat broke out on his forehead. He paused for a few moments as if contemplating his next move.

"So we play this way … huh, Isaac?" said Bernie. He glanced toward the door behind Isaac, hit the floor, and yelled: "Take 'em out, Tony!"

Tony, a young, small-framed, punk-looking kid with greased-down hair and a small goatee, stepped out of the shadows, his gun aimed at Isaac's back. Jeff saw what was happening. He slid to the floor, screaming at Isaac, "Behind you!"

Isaac kicked the table out of the way and dove head first to the floor just as Tony fired. The shot missed. Isaac quickly rolled across the floor. Tony's second bullet missed him also. Isaac halted his roll in a prone position, the Glock still in his hand. He quickly raised himself to rest on his elbows, took careful aim, and fired one shot. The gun flew out of his assailant's hand and scooted across the tile floor. Tony yelled out in pain and grabbed his hand. Blood flowed from his wound in a steady stream. By good fortune, the expensive scatter rugs were not soiled.

Isaac leaped to his feet, the gun still aimed at Tony. "On the floor, Tony. Arms above your head. You do the same, Bernie. If either of you moves a muscle, I'll fire another shot. I won't be as kind with the next bullet. It will be through your head instead of your hand. Take their guns, Jeff. One more time, your final chance, Bernie. Where is the boy?" Isaac held the muzzle of the gun under Bernie's chin.

"He … he … he's here, Isaac," he said, his voice cracking. "Carmen will bring him out. Just put that gun down."

"I don't think so, Bernie. If Ignacio is not here, I will need the gun. Where in this house is he?"

"He's here, Isaac. Carmen will bring him to you."

"How did you convince the boy to go with you, you sleazy bastard?" said Isaac. He held the Glock under Bernie's chin. "What did you do to him?"

"Just told him I'd take him to his sister. I didn't touch him, Isaac. The boy's all right."

"You son of a bitch. Killing is too good for you. Get your ass off the floor and in that chair. I don't want Ignacio to see me with a gun. Tony ... out of here. Chacón will take care of you later. My condolences to your family."

* * * *

Isaac and Jeff wasted no time getting out of the house and into the driveway, Isaac leading the way and Jeff—holding Nacio's hand—following close behind. They were met by the valet attendants, who were standing alongside their car as though waiting for a tip. The two armed guards approached as Isaac, still tightly clutching the briefcase, entered the driver's side of the car. *What's next?* Jeff wondered. *It will be interesting to see how Mr. Andrade handles this confrontation, especially if the officers have questioned Bernie's accomplice, Tony—I know he left the house just before we did.*

"Is everything all right, Mr. Andrade?" asked one of the guards. Jeff saw Isaac glance at the officer's name tag.

"Fine, Sergio ... fine," said Isaac, climbing into the car, as cool as if he had just left a friendly business conference. Jeff guided Ignacio into the backseat and then climbed into the front beside Isaac.

"Everything all right out here?" Isaac asked as he passed generous gratuities to both guards and both attendants.

"Someone with an injured hand, wrapped in a bloody towel, just rushed out of here. He wouldn't stop long enough for us to speak to him. I don't know what happened to him."

"Oh ... yeah, that was one of Chacón's new recruits. He was showing us his piece and it accidentally went off while he was attaching the silencer. Didn't look like anything serious."

"Sounds like he needs some training."

"I think he's learned his first lesson," Isaac replied, laughing. "I imagine he's got more lessons coming."

"I wouldn't want to be in his shoes when Chacón learns about his stupidity," said Sergio. He waved them on as Isaac drove off.

* * * *

They were well on their way to Nuevo Laredo before either spoke. Jeff finally broke the silence:

"Anytime you want to talk, I'm ready to listen," he said.

"I know you have a lot of questions, Jeff. It hasn't been fair to you for me to keep you in the dark," said Isaac.

"That's putting it mildly. My imagination is running wild."

"I really hadn't planned on this happening," Isaac said. He kept his eyes on the road and on the rearview mirror while they raced down the highway. He looked at Jeff momentarily as though studying his reaction. "I have known that a time would come when my family would have to be told about some of my sub-rosa activities of the past, but this is not a good time."

"I marveled at your agility and especially your calm manner back there," said Jeff. "Megan told me that you kept yourself in top physical shape, but you were under life-threatening stress and never showed it. I think you've been there before."

"All I can tell you, Jeff, is this: Yes, I've been there before. I'll have to let all of you know the whole story some day … not now."

"Then you don't want me to say anything to Megan and Mrs. Andrade about our close call today?"

"I hope you don't. If you do, I'll simply say that … how did you put it? That your imagination was running wild."

Jeff chuckled. "I'm glad I wasn't dating your daughter as a teenager."

Isaac joined him in laughter. "The next sensitive issue we face right now is how to tell Ignacio about his sister."

"I agree. It's not going to be easy."

"We can't escape it … so let's head for Laredo and get ready for Margarita, Megan, and Celi's emotional reunion with Nacio."

"Don't you have to go by the store and put the package back in the safe?" asked Jeff.

"The package is still in the safe at the store, Jeff," he said, flashing a sly grin. "Right now, just worry about that car that seems to be following us."

"What?" said Jeff, his eyes glued to the rearview mirror. "Haven't we had enough excitement for one night?"

Chapter 22

They turned onto the street that led to Isaac's house. On the way, ever since the bridge crossing, Isaac had been unusually quiet. He had watched the rearview mirror as often as he had looked ahead. Jeff could sense that he was tense.

"Someone is following us, Jeff. We'll need to pull a diversionary tactic. I want to find out who it is. Just hold on. It won't take more than a couple of minutes."

Isaac whirled the car into a convenience store parking lot, alongside a gasoline pump. A few seconds later a medium-sized black sedan slowly passed by. Isaac opened his door and pretended to step out. As soon as their pursuer had passed, Isaac jumped back in the car, slammed his door shut, took off with tires spinning, and tailgated the vehicle.

"Jeff … quick! Memorize the license plate number and then get down as low as you can."

Isaac, in Spanish, called out to Ignacio: "Nacio, lie down on the seat so you are out of sight. We can't let anyone know you and Jeff are in the car."

Jeff watched as Nacio dutifully obeyed without questioning. He seemed to think it was some kind of game when he saw Jeff drop down also. As they neared the next intersection, Isaac whipped around the car ahead, passed it, and then turned in front of it, blocking its path. *My God! What is he doing?* Jeff wondered, as he got down even lower. *What if they have guns?* Isaac grabbed his briefcase, retrieved his Glock, threw his door open, and jumped out.

"Stay down, Jeff," he cried as he ran behind his own car and then along side the pursuer's vehicle to the driver's side. With his gun aimed through the window, he motioned for the driver to get out. A startled driver quickly exited the car holding up his identification badge. His partner, from the passenger seat, did the same.

"FBI!" the driver said. "Put down your weapon."

"Both of you!" yelled Isaac. "On this side of the car! Place your hands on top of your vehicle!"

"Do you know what you're doing, sir?" said the man. "Do you know the penalty for assaulting federal law enforcement agents?"

"Look … maybe you're FBI and maybe you're not. This is Laredo, man! Criminals masquerade as law enforcement officers every day to take out anyone on their hit list. Now, each of you, slowly use one hand to show me identification other than your badges—badges can be bought across the border for a dollar a dozen. Then you can tell me why you've been following me ever since we left El Rancho Alegrón."

The two men at first hesitated, and then complied with Isaac's orders. Jeff, in the meantime, had raised his head enough to witness the scene. He decided it was time to come to Isaac's aid. Motioning for Nacio to remain hidden, he got out of the car and approached Isaac.

"Jeff, take their ID badges and cards and hold them in front of me so I can see if they look authentic."

"Their IDs appear valid as far as I can tell, Mr. Andrade," said Jeff.

"Good. Now check for concealed weapons, Jeff."

"Mr. Andrade … uh … I'm a little reluctant to go to that extreme."

"Jeff, the last person I knew who said that can be found in the Garden Rest Cemetery. As I have said, this is Laredo and we're in the middle of a war between law enforcement and cartel people."

Jeff patted down both agents. "There's no sign of a weapon, Mr. Andrade."

"Come on, you guys," said the driver. "You're digging the hole deeper for yourselves. The charges against you are piling up. We've had enough of this."

Isaac ignored the threat. "One more thing, Jeff. Look on the ID cards. You'll see a phone number. Dial that on your cell phone. If a live person answers, hang up. That means that the card is a fake. If you are given a five-digit number, I'll ask these guys to repeat it."

Jeff dialed. A recording answered and recited a number. Jeff punched the digits into his cell phone and held it up for Isaac to see. The agent who appeared to be the leader of the two called out the numbers accurately.

Isaac dropped his gun and turned to replace it in his briefcase. "My name is Isaac Andrade. This is Jeff Harrison, a family friend. Sorry for the inconvenience. Obviously you are new to the border."

"I know who you are, Mr. Andrade. Agent Ralph Walton here," he said, his rancor still glowing like a bright light. "This is my partner, Wes Perkins. Yes, we are new, but we never expected anything like this."

"Mr. Walton, you stay alive around here by being suspicious of everything and everybody," said Isaac, his demeanor as congenial as though nothing had ever happened. "One question still not answered: Why were you following us?"

"I'll ask the questions, Mr. Andrade. Retreat to your car … both of you, while we make a few calls," said Ralph, ignoring Isaac's question. "Don't even think of trying to drive away. As you say, 'we have to be suspicious of everyone.'"

Agent Walton turned his back to make his call while Wes escorted Jeff and Isaac to their car. Ignacio, still lying in the backseat, raised his head. Isaac smiled and motioned for him to sit up. A full two minutes passed before Agent Walton returned.

"Mr. Andrade," said Ralph Walton, assuming an authoritative posture after completing his phone call, "we will want to confer with you at length, privately, sometime tomorrow if you will give me a time and place."

"Any time you say," said Isaac. "Do you want to talk to Jeff also?"

"No, that won't be necessary. Where can we find you in the morning?"

"Either at home or at my store. Do you need addresses and phone numbers?"

"No, we have everything we need. We will contact you between nine and ten o'clock."

"Fine, I'll be expecting your call," he replied. "Good evening, gentlemen."

Isaac and Jeff climbed into their car. Ignacio, now sitting upright in the backseat, a frightened look on his face, rolled his eyes toward the two men without moving his head.

"It's all right, Nacio," said Isaac. "You have nothing to be afraid of. We're on our way home."

✳   ✳   ✳   ✳

As they drove into the driveway to the Andrade residence, Jeff again broke a long period of silence. "Mr. Andrade …" he began, and then paused. He tried again. "Mr. Andrade, could you give me just a hint of an explanation of your 'other life.' When you think of all we've been through tonight—all I have been subjected to—I think I am entitled to some clarification."

"I know how you must feel," he said. "I plead with you to give me a little time and to say nothing to Megan or her mother … or Celi. It will all unfold in due time."

"I'll go along with that as long as I know it will be coming."

"I promise, Jeff. The picture is very complex, and the wrong word uttered or misinterpreted could lead to a wrong impression," said Isaac. "Actually, I feel more at ease discussing this with you than with either Megan or her mother."

"You will meet with Mr. Walton tomorrow? Where?"

"Yes, tomorrow. He'll call first. I'm not sure where would be the best place. I really don't want to be seen with the FBI."

"Do you think I should be with you?"

"Thanks, Jeff. He said it wouldn't be necessary. But he didn't say no. Yes, I'd like for you to be along. I'd like you to listen to what these guys say. I can use your support right now."

"Then it's agreed. You can introduce me as your lawyer," said Jeff with a chuckle. "From what I've witnessed so far, I suspect you need one."

"You don't have to get involved, Jeff, if it makes you uncomfortable."

Jeff laughed. "Look, 'discomfort' lost its chance to infiltrate my sense of well-being tonight, with all we went through."

"You're pretty tough. I must say I worried about how you'd hold up. But, as you say, I lost my chance to worry."

"I have an idea about meeting the FBI guys tomorrow. There's an attorney here in Laredo whom my firm has used in the past. I'm sure that he'll let us use a conference room or a private office. We can be assured of confidentiality if he'll agree."

"Good idea, Jeff. Call in the morning and see if that's a possibility. Of course, you'll have to answer to Megan when she asks where you're going and why."

"She'll understand when I tell her I called my office in Houston for messages."

"Let's go in and face a trio of anxious, worried—maybe angry—women," said Isaac.

"Probably be more difficult than facing two underworld thugs, followed by facing two FBI agents," said Jeff, his face creased with a grin. "I think I'll let you do the talking."

"You know, some day we won't be able to talk like this in front of Ignacio," said Isaac.

"Megan's already started teaching him English," said Jeff.

"Thank God the boy has Megan to lean on right now. Imagine the emotional trauma that boy will have to deal with the rest of his life."

"He'll have some good stories to tell when he grows up." Jeff laughed. "Except, no one will believe him."

* * * *

Ignacio gripped Jeff's hand tightly as they followed Isaac through the front door. Jeff thought, *Imagine the emotions this child has endured in the last few hours, trusting Bernie to take him to his sister, only to become disappointed and frightened. And he must have been totally confused over the sequence of events that followed. And now he has to be told that Esmeralda is not alive. He needs his Meggie.*

"We're back!" Isaac called out to the others. "Look what we brought back!" They found Megan, Margarita, and Celi seated in separate chairs, all appearing despondent, dabbing at their wet cheeks with tissues. As soon as Megan saw Nacio, she leaped to her feet. Ignacio released Jeff's hand and ran to her open arms. Worried looks were replaced by smiles, but the wet cheeks didn't go away. *Why do women cry when they're happy?* Jeff wondered. *How am I going to keep the details of our adventure from Megan? And now she has the task of explaining to Nacio the tragic story about Esme.*

Chapter 23

Isaac, awake and dressed, sat in his home office trying to concentrate on the morning paper while awaiting the call that he dreaded to take but knew would be coming—the call from Agent Walton to arrange a meeting. That's all he could think about. Why were the FBI agents here right now anyway? It wasn't time for him to report in. Surely it had nothing to do with the package delivery. But maybe it did. It was just another reason that he needed to let Carlos know that he didn't want to have a part in the organization any longer.

Jeff was going to arrange for the meeting in the lawyer's office. Maybe the call would come from Agent Walton soon, and they could leave without awakening Megan and Margarita. Then they wouldn't have to explain where and why they were going.

Celi kept popping in and out and finally "ordered" Isaac to the breakfast room. She brought him coffee and a plate of eggs and chorizo. Jeff arrived, clean shaven, hair groomed, and dressed in coat and tie.

"Better prepare the same for Jeff, Celi. We have a busy day ahead," said Isaac.

"Good morning, Mr. Andrade," said Jeff, cheerily as if he had not a worry in the world.

"You look like a lawyer," said Isaac, grinning. "Ready for this day?"

"I called my company's referral law firm here in Laredo. We have the use of one of their conference rooms any time between now and two o'clock."

"Good work, Jeff. Now, what do we tell Megan and Margie?"

Jeff grinned. "How does this sound: Megan, I called my office this morning to check for calls. Just by coincidence, when my group learned that I was in Laredo, they asked me to call on the law firm of Berman, Hutchinson, and Chavez," said

Jeff, trying to keep a straight face. "And your father has been kind enough to offer to guide me to their offices." He paused. "Do you think we can expect a look of skepticism from Megan when she hears the story?"

Isaac chuckled. "She's just like her mother. It's hard to hide anything from either of them. You've already discovered the problem."

"Have you heard from Agent Walton?"

"Not a word. You have time for breakfast. Celi puts on a real performance when we have guests."

Isaac had no sooner uttered those words than his cell phone vibrated in his pocket. He gave Agent Walton the address and confirmed that nine-thirty, sharp, would be acceptable.

"We need to get moving," said Isaac as he glanced at his watch and called for Celi. "First, you need breakfast. Who knows what we'll face with the FBI snooping around?"

"You seem so calm about it, Mr. Andrade. What do you think they want?"

"Who knows? They'll play a cat and mouse game at first. I imagine they are on a fishing expedition. Be sure and bring a briefcase."

* * * *

The prestigious offices of Berman, Hutchinson, and Chavez filled over half of the top floor of the Executive Office Tower. Jeff assumed the lead role as they entered and approached the receptionist.

"I'm Jeff Harrison from Houston. I spoke to Mr. Berman about using one of your conference rooms this morning."

"Oh, yes, Mr. Harrison. We've been expecting you. Please follow me."

Jeff checked his watch. "We're a little early. There will be two others attending our meeting."

"I'll watch for them. There's fresh coffee and bottled water at the bar. If you need anything else, just touch the button on the teleconference instrument. My name is Lupita."

"Thank you, Lupita. Oh … one more thing," said Jeff, pointing to the electronic device anchored in the center of the table. "Is the recording mode deactivated?"

"Yes, sir," she answered with a smile. "No recorder and no cameras. Why do lawyers always ask those questions?"

Jeff chuckled. "I think you know."

After Lupita left the room, Isaac turned to Jeff. "Well done. Uh … don't be surprised at anything that's said in here, Jeff."

"Still no Q-A hour?"

"Not yet," said Isaac. "Let's just get this over with."

* * * *

With a tap on the door, Ralph Walton and Wes Perkins entered, unsmiling and sober faced. They sat across the table from Jeff and Isaac, both of whom had remained in their chairs when the pair came into the room. Isaac, his chin resting on the palm of his cupped left hand, the fingers of his right hand drumming on the table, stared at Agent Walton with an impatient glare.

Jeff had his head buried in a document he had picked up from the conference room bookcase. He barely glanced at the visitors. Struggling to suppress a smile while he watched Isaac put on his act, Jeff thought, *I'm learning some lessons from this man. He is remarkable. The agents are defensive before we even start this session.*

"Are we late? Had trouble finding the office." Neither Jeff nor Isaac answered. Jeff put down the document he'd been studying and extracted a legal pad from his briefcase. Isaac sat upright in his chair and waited for the agents to speak.

"I'm sure you are wondering why we're here. I see you decided to bring Mr. Harrison along. It's all right, but I don't think you'll need a lawyer." *How did he know that I am an attorney? Looks like he's done his homework.* Jeff thought.

"Mr. Harrison is my attorney. I prefer that he listen to whatever you have to say."

"Fine … fine," said Ralph. "As I said, I'm sure you're wondering why we are here."

"Yes … and I'm wondering why *we* are here. What do you want from us? All I want from you is an answer to why you were following us last night."

"We were sent here from the Dallas office on a confidential mission, Mr. Andrade, and we were told to contact you. We've been watching you for the last three days."

"So it was you … rather amateurish. I would have expected better from the FBI."

My God! Jeff thought. *You don't go around insulting the FBI. What the hell is he up to?*

"What do you mean, Mr. Andrade?" asked a startled Ralph Walton.

"Look, I told you once: You stay alive around here by being suspicious and keeping your eyes open. This is Laredo … across the border is Nuevo Laredo.

The cartel works both sides. Three days here? You are lucky to still be alive. You come here looking and acting like FBI, AFI, ICE, or DEA—all on the cartel's hit list. I'm surprised you haven't already been taken out. You might as well have had FBI in yellow letters on the backs of your coats. If they can identify you, you get iced."

Isaac stood and paced around the table without speaking. He stopped, turned his back to the others, and looked out the eighth-story window toward Nuevo Laredo.

"You're in a war zone, Mr. Walton," he said, turning around to face the table again. "Do you know why we're meeting here … under the pretense of conducting some legal business?"

"I don't understand," said Ralph.

Isaac approached the agent and locked eyes with him. "Because I don't want to be seen with you! You are hazardous to my health … to Jeff's well-being. In this part of the country mobsters shoot first and don't care a damn whether or not they made a mistake."

"We need your help, Mr. Andrade."

"The government needs my help … hah! You want me to put my life on the line again for my country? Is that what you're saying? What do you know about me?"

"We know everything about you—and about Mr. Harrison."

"Well, you don't know this—I'm *not* going to do it anymore. Go back and tell whoever sent you that I'm through."

"I was told that you would say that. We need your help, sir."

Isaac couldn't stop pacing, except for a brief pause when he looked at Jeff for a moment and then walked away, shaking his head. After a few minutes of total silence in the room, Isaac finally settled down and sat at the table again.

"All right," he said to Ralph. "Brief me on your mission, and make it short. Why in the hell are you here and what do you want from me?"

A faint smile crossed Ralph's aquiline facial features. He reached into his briefcase and brought out a stack of documents.

"Here's the pitch: The Mexican government has agreed to collaborate with United States agencies in a joint effort to interrupt the flow of contraband through Mexico and into the United States. There is concern over the ability of the Mexican Federal Investigation Agency to handle this problem alone. There is evidence and belief that you can be of assistance in correlating the coalition of the AFI with the U.S. agencies; namely, the FBI and ICE."

"Why me?" asked Isaac.

"I think you know why, Mr. Andrade."

An awestricken Jeff sat back and listened to every word. He had long since stopped being surprised at anything he heard or learned about Megan's father. How could Megan have grown up in a home with her father all those years and be oblivious to the fact that Isaac was not just your stereotypical businessman who owned a jewelry store? *Or does she know more than she's telling me?* he wondered.

Just the few sketches that he had heard of Isaac's past told Jeff that this man had lived in a colorful world. He would wait for more to unfold. Isaac seemed to trust him. Maybe he thought that dropping hints of his past on Jeff might be a way of reaching Megan and Margarita—help him reveal the truth some day about their father and husband, assuming they didn't already know.

"What's the proposal, Mr. Walton?" said Isaac. "And back it up with real facts."

"I'll lay it out the way it was given to me, Mr. Andrade. Your attorney can take notes as I narrate, if you wish, and he should feel free to ask questions."

"Fine. Okay with you, Jeff?" said Isaac, as he turned to Jeff. He looked Jeff squarely in the eye as if to ask, *Are you ready for this?*

"Before we go any further, Mr. Andrade," said Jeff. I would like to ask these gentlemen a couple of questions. First, is our conversation being recorded?"

"No, it will not be recorded," said Walton. "Unless you request that we do so."

"From what I have heard so far, this seems to be an exploratory meeting," said Jeff. "If you are asking my client to agree to some request by the government, I would like for our discussions to be recorded … and a copy of the tape provided to me for the record. You are carrying an agency-issued briefcase, I see. I'm sure it contains a hidden recorder."

Agent Walton, taken aback momentarily, his face covered with a faint blush, motioned to his partner to place the briefcase on the table.

"Turn on the recorder, Wes," said Walton. "I'll want you to dictate your mailing address into the recorder, Mr. Harrison."

"Sure," said Jeff. "Next, are you empowered to speak for the government regarding any proposal you are going to present to my client?"

"That isn't necessary, Mr. Harrison," he said. "Likely you are not fully aware of Mr. Andrade's existing commitment to the government. I am here merely to deliver a message."

Jeff glanced at Isaac who avoided eye contact with Jeff but made an almost imperceptible negative gesture by a quick movement of his head. Isaac stared with a look of contempt at Agent Walton as though he objected to the agent's statement. Jeff turned to the agent, eyes blazing, with an assumed posture that said he resented being challenged regarding his relationship with his client.

"To the contrary, Mr. Walton! I have been given ample information by Mr. Andrade to enable me to represent him competently. I think it is time for you to deliver your message."

Isaac smiled an all-knowing smile and sat back in his chair. "Well put, Jeff. Now, Mr. Walton, please proceed with your narration of the issues at hand."

The room was eerily quiet as Agent Walton, with Wes's assistance, arranged the documents in organized stacks on the table. After they had finished, the agent sat back in his chair, his elbows on the armrests. He locked eyes with Isaac.

"The civil wars in South Africa have been rekindled," Agent Walton said, as if making a media announcement. "The legitimate flow of diamonds to reputable dealers in the United States and Canada has been jeopardized. The demand is still present, but the supply has been seriously disrupted. Consequently, the smuggling of diamonds—none carrying the appropriate certificates—into the United States has been escalated. We have valid information that the major port of entry for the contraband into North America will once again be Nuevo Laredo."

The atmosphere in the room once again thickened into silence. Out of the corner of his eye, Jeff could see Isaac's cheek muscles tighten. *Where is this going?* he wondered. *How could Isaac be of help to the agencies in controlling illegal contraband traffic?* The question had no sooner entered his mind than Isaac stood and again started his pacing around the conference table. He finally stopped, looked across the table, and pointed his finger at Agent Walton.

"So, you have good evidence that the supply path will be through Nuevo Laredo?" said Isaac.

"Yes, sir," said Walton, pointing to the papers on the table. "I was told you might want to see the report on the escalation of diamond smuggling. These are your copies."

Jeff, after a nod from Isaac, scanned the documents for a few moments.

"Keep your reports," said Isaac. "I am well aware of the increased traffic."

"We need your help, Mr. Andrade … we need to know the estimated value of the merchandize."

"And who is the only diamontaire in the Laredos … in all of northern Mexico or in all of southern Texas, Mr. Walton?" said Isaac, still standing, his eyes blazing. "Do you know?"

"Yes, sir," said Agent Walton. "And so do you."

"Jeff, I think it's time we brought this meeting to a close."

"Yes, sir," said Jeff as he began gathering papers and packing his briefcase.

"Can we count on you, sir?" asked Ralph Walton.

"What can I say?" said Isaac. "We'll talk later."

"Before you leave, tell me about the boy you had in the car with you," said Agent Walton, a smirk on his face.

"Why do you ask?"

"Is he documented?"

"He's in the custody of my daughter. She works for ICE."

"I am aware of that. Is he documented? Is this customary … allowing an undocumented immigrant, in the custody of an employee of ICE, to pass back and forth across the border? And to be taken to a brothel that is known, among other despicable activities, for sexually exploiting underage children?"

"We rescued him from the brothel, Walton," said Isaac. "Surely you are not trying to make a case against me, my daughter, and Jeff based on what you've witnessed or what you have surmised."

"It certainly appears to be incriminating, Mr. Andrade."

"Don't even think about making a case here," said Isaac with fire in his eyes. "I'll tear you apart, Walton, if you try. It will get the agency nowhere with me in forcing me to assist you with this contraband trafficking."

"When can we talk again, Mr. Andrade?"

"Call me at the store," he said. "And in the meantime, get rid of those black suits. Buy some *guayaberas*—Mexican shirts—they'll hide your side arms. Wear *huaraches* with no socks, let your hair grow longer, grow a moustache. If you want to stay alive, try to look native, and don't hang out together."

Isaac paused. "I meet people in the back barroom at the Blue Eagle in Nuevo Laredo. The bartender is Beto. He'll handle messages. We're leaving, Mr. Walton. Please wait a few minutes so it doesn't appear we've been meeting together."

Chapter 24

On the way home, Isaac's first words hit Jeff broadside: "Jeff, welcome to the world of FBI subterfuge and clandestine behavior," he said, his face pleated by a furtive grin.

"What are you saying, Mr. Andrade?" asked a quizzical Jeff. "I thought they seemed sincere."

"It was all an act, Jeff," he replied. "They know that I know about the illegal diamond smuggling and that I know that the pace has picked up to the level it was at a few years ago. They also found out that I will work with government agencies again, just as I always have and just as I did with the package that we are now concerned about."

"You mean that you deduced all that from this meeting. Then you also must have been …"

"Faking my behavior, Jeff?"

"Yeah, you led them to believe that you weren't sure you wanted to work with the government in any capacity … you were abrasive and outright rude."

"All part of the act," he replied. "Much of it was for your benefit. They were not sure of your role in the picture. But they left with the information they were looking for. Likely we will not see or hear from them again."

"So they'll leave here knowing that you'll do what they want you to do and that you'll continue doing what you have been doing … and just what is that, Mr. Andrade?"

"I'll tell you later, Jeff," he replied as they approached the driveway to his home.

"What is a diamontaire?" said Jeff. "I've never heard that term."

"A diamond cutter. I spent some time in Sarat, India, years ago, learning the craft. I had decided that the best way to give a completely accurate evaluation of a diamond's value was to learn as much as possible about the skills of a diamontaire."

"So you learned how to cut a rough diamond?" said Jeff.

"No ... I learned that only experienced cutters know how. But I learned what to look for," said Isaac.

"Just tell me one more thing right now, Mr. Andrade," said Jeff, a tone of irritability surfacing. "Is Megan aware of what you've been doing?"

"No," he said. "I see what you've been worrying about. Megan will always be honest with you, Jeff."

"Thank you, sir," said Jeff. He grinned as he looked straight into Isaac's eyes. "Just one more thing—since I am now your professed attorney, charged with the duty to preserve confidentially, are you guilty of any unlawful activity?"

Isaac paused before answering. "None, Jeff, other than that necessary to fulfill my role as an informant for the government."

Jeff looked at Isaac for a few moments without speaking. He smiled to himself. "Again, I thank you," he said, finally. "The picture is beginning to come into focus," said Jeff. "Now ... how are we going to handle the inquisition we are about to face when we go in the house?"

Isaac laughed. "Just field the questions as you wish. You can handle it."

* * * *

Jeff and Isaac were met with skeptical glares. Celi ducked into the kitchen to avoid what appeared to be some type of confrontation. Megan pulled Jeff aside.

"I'm worried about Ignacio," she said. "He slept very little last night. He awakened this morning but wouldn't get out of bed. He said his stomach hurt. I need you to go with me to check on him. And you can tell me what you and Dad have been up to for so long," she added with wrinkled brow.

"Sure, let's go see about Nacio," he said, avoiding response to her last statement. "It's probably related in some way to the grief reaction he's going through. How did he deal with the sad news about Esme?"

"Not very well. The pain started while he was trying to keep from crying. He just wanted to be held close. How much more can this poor child take?"

"I'm just glad he has you to care for him."

"Jeffrey, you are avoiding discussing something with me. I can always tell. Whatever it is, you can't keep it from me. What have you and Dad been up to?"

"We'll talk later. Let's check on Nacio."

Ignacio, his eyelids swollen from uncontrolled sobbing, lay on his side with his knees drawn up. He looked up at Jeff and smiled briefly before turning his head away.

"Hey, Nacio, time to get up and ride the bike … right?" said Jeff, with Megan translating. Nacio showed no response to Jeff's cheerfulness. "Want me to run alongside … maybe I can outrun you." Jeff paused but still Nacio didn't move. "I'll bet you haven't eaten anything this morning, have you? Want to come with me … see if Celi can fix something for us to eat?"

"Something's wrong, Jeff. He's acting just like he did after the accident. What could it be?"

"Ask him again about his stomachache," said Jeff. "Let's see if we can get him to roll over on his back."

"Does it still hurt, Nacio?" asked Megan. "Here, let's turn on your back and let Meggie and Jeff see about your stomach."

Nacio attempted to turn over, but the least movement caused him to grimace and brought tears to his eyes. When he attempted to straighten his legs he grabbed his lower abdomen and cried out in pain.

"It's all right, Nacio," said Megan as she held his hand. "You don't have to move. We'll find a way to make it stop hurting."

"One thing for sure—the pain is real," said Jeff.

Megan felt Nacio's forehead. "He has a little fever. And he looks sick. What should we do?"

"We need to get him to a doctor. I'll talk to your father. We probably should take him to an emergency room."

Jeff found Isaac in his office. From the tenor of the conversation he was having with Margarita, Jeff assumed that Isaac was probably going through the same grilling that he himself had just experienced with Megan, but to a greater extent. When they realized that he was coming in, the talking ceased abruptly and Margarita stormed out with only a nod at Jeff when she passed by him.

"I imagine you've been going through the same thing," said Isaac. "Celi's enjoying every minute of it. She's having difficulty controlling her laughter."

Jeff grinned. "Yeah … you predicted all this admonishment accurately," said Jeff. "Mr. Andrade, I'm worried about Nacio. Something's wrong. He seems to be having a great deal of pain in his abdomen. I think he needs to see a doctor."

"We may have a problem, Jeff. The doctors don't like to take illegal immigrants as patients."

"Why?" said Jeff. "Because they can't pay?"

"Yes, that's one reason. The other is that the hospital gives them a hard time about admitting an indigent patient."

"My God, Mr. Andrade," said Jeff. "I can't believe it. What can we do?"

"Let's try the emergency room. Maybe we'll get lucky. Doctors Regional Hospital is the closest."

*   *   *   *

Nacio wrapped his arms around Jeff's neck as Jeff carried him into the emergency room entrance of Doctors Hospital. *He is so frail,* thought Jeff as he carried him through the ER doors. *He must not weigh more than fifty pounds.* Nacio winced from pain with each step Jeff took. Megan walked close by their side. Isaac and Margarita followed behind.

"It's all right, Nacio," said Megan. "The doctor will make you better ... make the pain go away."

Once inside, the admitting nurse, as soon as she realized the severity of the pain that Nacio was enduring, took him directly into an examining room. She allowed Megan to stay in the room but asked the others to leave.

"Only one person allowed in the room," she said. "Are you the mother?" she asked in a condescending tone while she performed her routine evaluation of the so-called 'vital signs.'

"No, I'm his custodian."

"We'll need the consent of his next of kin before we can examine him."

"I understand your concern," said Megan, struggling to control her growing irritability. "I am his legal custodian and guardian. Could you please have him examined by a doctor? He is in severe pain."

"I can see that. Do you have his insurance information with you?"

"He has no insurance. He is a young orphaned Mexican immigrant who is in distress. Can you help us?"

"I'm sorry, miss," she said without looking up. "These are my instructions. We must have proof of ability to pay before we can admit him to the emergency room."

"But we are *in* the emergency room."

"Technically, you are not. This is the triage room. We have not accepted him as a patient yet."

"What will it take for you to 'accept' him, as you say?"

"We will need a deposit in advance. Otherwise you will need to go to another hospital."

"Okay, how much do you need?"

"Just a minute, let me see," she said as she pulled out a folder and scanned through it. "Let's see … abdominal pain, undiagnosed: five thousand dollars in advance and a signature on a note for an undisclosed amount pending the extent of the diagnostic workup and treatment. Are you prepared to comply with these provisions?"

"What?" cried Megan. "You're telling me that you will not take care of this child unless we come up with a deposit of five thousand dollars and guarantee you an undisclosed amount for his total care?"

"Well, you have summarized it very well, miss."

"I need to confer with my father and friend. Will you excuse me for a moment? In the meantime, please do something for this boy … now!"

"I'm sorry, miss," she replied. "We have to follow protocol."

Megan left the room and went in search of Jeff and her father. Once she found them, she virtually collapsed in their arms. She pulled them both together.

"You've got to help me," she said. "They won't do anything for Nacio until we pay them five thousand dollars in advance."

"Let me go back in there with you," said Isaac. "And Jeff will accompany us. I think we can make a difference."

"They won't let you in there, Dad."

"Let us take care of that, Meggie," said Jeff.

They approached the treatment room and were immediately intercepted by the nurse who had been with Megan and Nacio earlier.

"I'm sorry, there can only be one of you in here."

"Sure, Miss.… uh … what is your name?" said Isaac, honey dripping from his every word. "Oh, I see it now … you are Angie Ruiz. Please, Miss Ruiz, would you call administration and ask if someone in the department could speak with us? If they are too busy to come here, we can go there."

"I suppose you would like to speak to one of our financial advisors."

"Uh … no," said Isaac. "I really want to speak to someone in administration."

"I'll have to ask my supervisor. I can't call administration."

"That will be fine, Miss Ruiz. But please hurry, our boy is very sick. Does he have a fever?"

"I'm not allowed to tell you anything about his condition."

"Of course," said Isaac. "So let's find your supervisor."

Jeff looked on in amazement. Once again he was seeing Isaac in a new light. He smiled thinking: *I've never heard such a silky voice.* He wondered how any hospital ER could refuse treatment to a patient. He remembered from law school days about the EMTALA law. Hospitals had to treat emergencies regardless of the patient's ability to pay. Also they couldn't ask for money in advance. *I have a feeling that Mr. Andrade is getting ready to attack,* he thought.

Within minutes, a stocky, middle-aged nurse appeared on the scene, clipboard in hand, obviously irritated that she had been pulled away from some other task.

"What can I do for you?" she asked, her attention focused on Isaac. Her tone reflected both authority and agitation as she scanned the scanty notes written by the admitting nurse.

"Thank you for giving us a couple of minutes of your time. What is your name?" asked Isaac. The nurse pointed to her name tag clipped to her scrubs. "Oh, I see now ... Beverly. Uh ... Beverly, we brought Ignacio Narváez in a little while ago with fever and abdominal pain. It appears that it is an emergency. We would like to have him examined and cared for. There seems to be a delay for some reason."

"From what I see here, the reason is that you have not paid the deposit that we require—an amount based on his complaint."

"I understand your concern. Ignacio is a Mexican immigrant. But he is ill. Could you please let us speak with someone in administration?"

"That won't be necessary. The issue here is simple. You must pay a deposit. If we don't use all of it, you will get a refund."

"Beverly, I really want to verify that demand with someone in administration. I'm sure they are too busy to come here, so I'll go there. While I'm gone, will you please get a physician to check Ignacio? We need to know what's wrong."

"Are you a relative?"

"No, but he is a visitor in my home. I am responsible for him."

"I can't give you any information. And we can't do anything until you comply with our rules."

Isaac turned to Jeff. "Uh ... Jeff, you do have your recorder turned on, do you not?"

Jeff fought against appearing startled. "Of course, Mr. Andrade."

"Good. We'll return as soon as we have visited with your administrator. In the meantime, let's get started on examining and treating our patient, shall we?"

Nurse Beverly, nose in the air, her cell phone to her ear, whirled and waddled off into another part of the ER.

Chapter 25

Like a predator stalking its prey, Isaac marched off toward the suite of administration offices, portraying a posture of determination. Jeff followed, trying to keep up with Isaac's rapid pace. They entered the waiting area that was signed Executive Offices. The receptionist, busy filing her fingernails, looked up at them with a silent, questioning, vacant stare.

"We would like to see your chief executive officer, please," said Isaac.

"Do you have an appointment?"

"No, miss, we do not. You have already been warned that we were on our way. Now, kindly tell your CEO that Mr. Isaac Andrade and his attorney are here to see him about a pressing issue in his ER. And that time is of the essence. We'll wait here while you notify your executive." Isaac glanced at the clock on the wall. "Please make a note of the time, Jeff," said Isaac, loud enough for the girl to hear as she hurried through the door to the inner offices.

In less than a minute, the inner door flew open and the receptionist motioned for Isaac and Jeff to follow her. A tanned, tall, stately individual, streaks of gray showing through his close-cut black hair, met them at the door with a deadpan expression, and ushered them into his office.

"I'm Harmon Fulbright, CEO of this hospital. I'm told you have demanded to see me," he said, without offering his visitors the option of being seated.

"That's absolutely right, Mr. Fulbright," said Isaac. "I'm Isaac Andrade and this is my attorney, Jeff Harrison. I think we have a problem here, Mr. Fulbright."

"And just what is the problem?"

"We'll be brief, Mr. Fulbright. Your emergency room and your hospital system are in violation of a federal statutory regulation. The regulation, with which I'm sure you are familiar, is the EMTALA law."

"Impossible. We have a policy in place to stem the abuse of the ER by illegal immigrants crossing the border and swamping our facility. Our attorneys have assured us that we are on solid ground here."

"Let me put it this way, Mr. Fulbright: Mr. Harrison represents me in this case—as well as Megan Andrade, an agent for Immigration and Customs Enforcement. We have brought a very ill young lad into your ER. Now you have two choices: inform your emergency room personnel to treat the boy, or tell us that you will not.

"In the event that you elect not to take care of the boy, we will be forced to seek help elsewhere, and you can expect two events to occur: Agents from the Office of the Inspector General, representing of the Department of Health and Human Services, will be at your door in the morning. The fine for the violation is fifty thousand dollars, I believe. And you can expect to be served with civil suit litigation subpoenas that will be initiated by Mr. Harrison. We are concerned about the consequences of delayed treatment for this child, Mr. Fulbright, so please give us your decision in the next few seconds."

Harmon Fulbright unblinkingly stood his ground for a few moments as if he were analyzing the validity behind Isaac's accusations.

"Jeff, do you have anything to add?"

"No, sir," he said. "You have explained the situation very well to Mr. Fulbright. I'm sure he is aware that there could be other cases that an unscrupulous plaintiff attorney could uncover. Of course, each violation carries the same fifty-thousand-dollar fine, and there appears to be a strong incentive for someone to initiate a whistleblower case ... just from what we've seen already."

"We'll return to the ER, Mr. Fulbright. I apologize for taking up so much of your time," said Isaac. "I do hope you make the right decision."

*   *   *   *

When they returned to the waiting area in the ER, Margarita met them with tears streaming down her face.

"What is it?" asked Isaac.

"Megan came out," she said between sobs. "All at once everyone started scurrying about. They are taking Nacio to the operating room for emergency surgery."

"What's wrong?" said Jeff.

"Something about his ... what do you call it? Oh, what else can happen to this poor boy?"

"What happened to him, Margarita?" Isaac demanded.

Before she could answer, Megan appeared. The two women fell into a weeping embrace. Isaac and Jeff looked on in wonder.

"Tell us what's wrong, dammit," said Isaac. "Stop crying long enough to enlighten us on what the hell you're crying about."

Megan dashed at her tears and looked at Jeff first and then at her father, her hardened eyes flashing daggers at both. "Do you even care? Do you? He's just a little orphaned, illegal Mexican alien. He has no one else except those of us in this room to care about him. How would you feel if you were alone in this world and all at once you were told you were going to have to have an operation?"

She whirled back toward her mother. The two embraced and resumed their sobbing. Jeff and Isaac looked at each other. "What have we done?" asked Isaac.

"Nurse Waddle" appeared on the scene, in a posture that reflected much more friendliness than before. "He'll be in the operating room for about one hour. The surgeon doesn't think too much time has lapsed and that he will be able to save the testicle."

"Save the testicle? What's wrong with him?" asked Jeff.

"Oh, you haven't been told," she said, looking at Megan and Margarita. "He has torsion of the testicle—a twisted testicle. The emergency room doctor diagnosed it right away and notified the surgeon. It is not a serious procedure, but it has to be performed quickly or the testicle becomes ischemic—the blood supply cut off and it becomes nonviable."

"Will he be all right?" asked Jeff.

"He'll be fine, thanks to the fact that you brought him into the hospital quickly."

"How did it happen?" asked Isaac.

"It was bound to happen some day. In some children the testicles are not anchored sufficiently to surrounding tissue to prevent twisting. Then some unusual activity brings on the torsion. We think in Ignacio's case it probably was caused by his riding his bicycle."

Jeff grinned and looked at Isaac who returned an all-knowing smile. A silent message of camaraderie was exchanged between the two without a single word uttered.

* * * *

After Megan assured the hospital financial officer that ICE would be responsible for the hospital's and doctors' reasonable charges, Ignacio's discharge process was much smoother than that of his admission. It was even accompanied by apologies from administration.

On their return to Isaac and Margarita's home, there was a celebration fit for visiting royalty. Everyone had a present of some sort for Nacio. Celi knew just what special food to fix. He was asked at least every thirty minutes if he was hungry and if he wanted anything.

The room was quiet. Only Megan sat beside Nacio while he napped. When he awakened, Megan saw the tear stains on his pillow. He began sobbing again without raising his head. Megan took his hand in hers and gently patted his arm.

"What's wrong, Nacio? Do you need some more pain medicine?"

He shook his head in a negative gesture and turned away from Megan again.

"You can tell me what's wrong, Nacio. Maybe I can help you."

He was silent for a few moments before speaking. Finally he looked at Megan, his sad brown eyes glazed with tears. "Meggie, did Esme have pain when she died?"

"No," said Megan, realizing that Nacio hadn't had time to grieve over Esme's death. "We are told she jumped from the car and was killed instantly. She didn't suffer."

"Where do we go when we die?" he asked.

"I'm sure Esme went to heaven," said Megan as she continued patting Nacio's arm and pushed his hair back off his forehead.

"Will I ever see her again?"

Megan waited to answer. *How am I going to tell this child that our spirit goes back to God? That he will always remember how she looked, but that he will not ever see her again.*

"Her spirit goes to heaven, Nacio. But when people die and their spirits go to heaven, we bury their bodies."

"Did Mamá and Papá go to heaven?"

"Sure they did."

"Can I see where they are buried someday?"

"Of course. We will find their graves some day and take you there. But even though they're gone, you'll always remember them."

"If I die and my spirit goes to heaven, will I be with Esme again?"

"Your spirit will be with Esme's spirit."

"Did anyone you loved ever die, Meggie?"

Megan was startled at the question and bit her lower lip to try to maintain composure. Had she had the same questions in her mind when Andy died? She must have, but she didn't remember her mother and dad ever explaining death to her. So now she must answer Nacio's questions.

"I had a little brother who died when I was about your age. It was very difficult for me," she said and wiped her cheeks with the back of her hand. "When I get sad, thinking about my little brother dying, I just tell myself that he is now in heaven and that he is happy. You should think about Esme that way."

"Maybe Esme is with your little brother."

"I'll bet she is," Megan laughed. "They would have a lot of stories to tell each other, wouldn't they?"

"I don't want to die, Meggie," he said as he tightened his hold on her hand. "I don't want to leave you and Jeff."

"Don't you worry a minute about that."

As soon as she said those words, the stark reality hit her. She would have to give up Nacio some day. She dreaded the day when the message would come that a relative of Nacio's had been found and Nacio would have to be deported to Mexico. She was reasonably sure that Jeff felt the same way. But what could they do? Maybe they shouldn't have gotten so emotionally attached to Ignacio.

Nacio took a corner of the bedsheet and wiped his eyes. He then flashed the smile—complete with dimples—that always caused Megan to melt with affection. He closed his eyes, and soon fell asleep again.

Chapter 26

Isaac retreated to his private office and closed the door. Chacón answered on the first ring.

"Carlos," said Isaac. "I need to talk to you."

"I'm listening, Isaac."

"You've heard about Bernie, I'm sure. And where did this Tony come from?"

"Yeah, I know the story. I don't think there's much hope for Bernie. He's stupid and impetuous ... a bad combination. As for Tony—that was Bernie's idea. Another example of bad judgment. You must be getting soft-hearted, Isaac. A few years ago you would have wasted both of them."

"Yes, years that we'd like to forget, right?"

"Hard to erase. I still have flashbacks," said Carlos.

"Yes, I know what you mean. Those years did something to us, didn't they?" said Isaac.

"But we survived, didn't we? We survived then the same way we survive today."

"Carlos, get back to the present," said Isaac. "I have the package in the safe at my office. I want to get rid of it. Can you meet me there at your earliest convenience?"

"I'm at El Rancho Alegrón today. Is tonight all right with you?"

"Yes, I'll go across now and wait for you. You know how to get in the back door. The guards will be gone and it will be dark ... you should be safe."

"I'm always a target, Isaac," he replied. "I'll be careful ... I'll have two young Turks with me."

"Would you rather I bring it to El Rancho?"

"No … I want you to reevaluate the contents. It's passed through so many hands, we need to make sure before I send it on. You know how suspicious I am, Isaac."

"Yes, I know that. I can remember a few times when it kept both of us alive, Carlos."

"Do you still have that bottle of Scotch in your desk drawer?"

Isaac laughed. "You remembered. It's still there—also that box of cigars."

"Let's just sit together and enjoy a sample of each like we used to."

"I'll be waiting."

* * * *

Isaac arrived well ahead of Carlos. He punched in the code to open the safe room door and clicked all but the last of the keyboard numerals on the safe before settling in his desk chair. He checked the bottom drawer of his desk to confirm that the bottle of Scotch and the box of cigars were still there. No longer than ten minutes passed before the red alert light, signaling that the rear door of the store was opening, flashed in his office.

Without looking up he recognized the clop-clop of Carlos Chacón's gait, a carryover from his old injuries. When Isaac looked up and saw Chacón approaching—walking with the limp that had crippled him for so many years and wearing a black eye patch over his left eye—for a lightninglike second he recalled that fateful day. It was as clear as if it had happened yesterday:

"Dive, Isaac, dive!" Carlos yelled. "VCs at eleven!"

The rata-tat-tat from behind his right flank told Isaac that they had been ambushed. Bullets ripped through Carlos's leg, but he remained standing and wiped out their assailants just before the grenade exploded in front of them. Blood poured both from Carlos's face and his leg, as well as from Isaac's chest.

They both lay motionless, eyes closed, just as they had been trained to do. "Pretend to be dead," they had been told. By some miracle they stayed alive. A full hour lapsed before Isaac managed to stand, in spite of the excruciating pain in his chest. He fought the lightheadedness and mustered enough strength to hoist Chacón, now unconscious, over his shoulders. Somehow he managed to stagger into a medical field station before collapsing. Their actual war was over but the virtual flashback war would never totally end.

Isaac shook his head to break the trance. He stood to open the door. Looking beyond Chacón, he could barely make out the images of the two ever-present bodyguards standing in the shadows. He pulled up a chair to the small conference table for Carlos, and greeted him with an embrace.

"How are you, my friend?" asked Isaac.

"I'm doing fine, Isaac," he replied. "You know I had nothing to do with that stupid stunt Bernie pulled, don't you?"

"I know that," he said. "You said you thought *I* was getting soft. How do *you* put up with Bernie?"

"I guess because he has ties with the diamond cutters in Tel Aviv … and he's loyal. His protégé, Tony, has to go."

"Do you ever tire of this life, Carlos?"

Carlos laughed as he eased himself into the heavily upholstered chair. "What's this … soul-searching hour?"

"Call it that if you wish," said Isaac as he poured a generous measure of Scotch in each of two glasses and opened the box of cigars. "Somebody's gonna ice you, Carlos. You know that. You have too many competitors, too many enemies. It's not like it used to be."

"Yeah …" he paused for a moment. "I guess the risk is out there. I just don't care any more."

"Come on, Carlos," said Isaac. "Think about what we've been through to get here. Why not put aside all the bitterness over what happened to us? I know you're lashing back at society in America. That's why you keep pushing the smack—and whatever else they want—across the border. Get over it Carlos. Get out … get a life. You sure as hell don't need the money."

"If I show any sign of weakness, Isaac, they will devour me like a vulture on a road kill."

"What if you just disappeared? We can arrange that."

"What about Carmen? She depends on me."

"She'll get along fine. Her business is selling sex. She's well established. She'll do all right without you."

"Your pitch sounds inviting, Isaac," he said. He paused and looked into the distance with a vacant look. "I looked forward to getting the import business going again. It's clean, low risk. The wars in Sierra Leone are really heating up. We could have it like it used to be. The country owes us."

"I know how you feel. Every step you take now reminds you of what we went through. You were the real loser … losing an eye. When they told me you would lose your eye, I felt just like you do right now. I wanted to pay back the public for abandoning us over there. But it's over, Carlos. Let's get on to something else."

"What can we do?"

"Get out. Let it go … give it to your competitors."

"I wouldn't last the day if I announced that," said Carlos.

"So, you're staying in out of fear? Not like you, Carlos."

"I guess you're right, Isaac. I never thought fear would bother either of us, did you?"

"I want out, Carlos."

Chacón was silent for several moments. He gazed into vacant space before turning back to Isaac. They both sipped their Scotch and puffed away at their expensive cigars.

"What about you, Isaac?" Carlos asked. "Can you put it all behind you? Aren't you still fighting the same demons … since Andrew died? Have you forgotten how distressed you were?"

"I don't know … but I want to try to forget it all. I want out, Carlos."

"Tell me why. I know you're not into trafficking."

"I just don't want Megan and Margie to know everything about me."

"What would your contacts say about that?"

"I don't know. They sent the FBI here today to verify my status."

"What a joke," Carlos said with a laugh. "I'm sure you outmaneuvered them."

"No problem."

"It's ironic," said Carlos. "All these years you've been reporting to those guys and never once have they ever targeted me."

"You know that I would never incriminate you, Carlos."

"How do you do it?"

"Look … on the diamond deals, the only thing I've ever done has been to give you an appraisal. I don't have anything to tell customs."

"I made a lot of money, Isaac."

"And you've always been good to me, Carlos."

"I think you're saying you don't want to work with me any more," said Chacón.

"That's it to a limited extent. I just don't want either of us to take chances anymore. I would never do anything to hurt you, Carlos … you know that. If you stay in, I'll stay in to help you. But I want to get out and I want you to get out also."

The two old friends enjoyed their cigars and Scotch for a good half hour in silence. Finally, Carlos looked at his watch and looked at Isaac. He stood, stretched his injured leg, and took a few steps around the office. "Maybe you're right," he said. "Maybe it's time to get out. He looked away with an unblinking stare for a few moments before turning back to face Isaac again. "Look at the package … this might be our last."

Isaac pulled the package from the vault and laid it on the table. He brought out his most powerful loupe—the one that he always kept in readiness to examine and measure the quality of diamonds. He began opening the package, one layer of tape at a time.

"Carlos … look at this!" he said. "This wrapping has been tampered with. The tape that I applied after I finished examining the stones before has been cut and covered by new tape. Look at this cut edge."

Carlos moved closer to the table. "Open it, Isaac."

"I have a weird feeling about this," said Isaac.

"Open it."

The layers of tape removed, Isaac carefully opened the container. Inside were multiple, small, velvet sacks packed in the box. He opened one sack and sprinkled ordinary, worthless stones on the table. He quickly grabbed another … the same.

"Carlos, these are common pebbles. Someone has removed the diamonds. Damn! What has happened here?"

"Stay calm, Isaac. Who has handled the package?"

"Bernie, of course. That's the last I saw of the package, when I passed it on to him."

"Was it in the locked briefcase?"

"No, it wasn't. Bernie said he would take care of putting the package in the briefcase. I thought at the time it was a little irregular—not like we've always done in the past."

"Bernie then gave the briefcase to the *coyote*?"

"Yeah, the story we've been told is that after the accident, the boy found the briefcase, took the package out, and put it in his tote bag. Megan said that he wouldn't let anyone even touch it because he believed that getting it delivered to someone in Houston was the key to getting his sister back. If the case had been locked, as it was supposed to have been, Ignacio couldn't have opened it."

"So that narrows our suspects down to Bernie and the *coyote*," said Carlos. He hesitated a moment before continuing: "Unless …"

"No … no," said Isaac. "Impossible. They would have told me if they had opened the package."

"Come on, Isaac," said Carlos. "How could two young, curious lawyers keep a package in their possession that long without looking, trying to find out why someone would go to such extremes to recover it?"

Isaac stood and paced about the room. He picked up the phone once, started to dial, and then put it down. He began pacing again, a contemplative expression on his face. Carlos stayed quiet and kept his eyes on Isaac, as if he were waiting on some word of explanation.

"Jeff and Megan are innocent, Carlos. Jeff was right by my side when Bernie and the punk kid attacked. They both are clean."

"I trust your judgment; you're always right," said Carlos. "So we're back to Bernie or the *coyote*."

"Or maybe both," said Isaac, and then shook his head. "No, Bernie wouldn't have taken on all the risks in recovering the package if he had known that the contents were only a bunch of rocks. The *coyote* must have planned to pass the fake package to the contact and then race back to pick up the real stones, wherever he stashed them. He wouldn't have risked taking the diamonds with him."

"Maybe you're right," said Carlos. "However, if Bernie knew the package was fake, he would want to recover the package before I found out. But what happened to the real merchandise?"

"God only knows," said Isaac. He once again paused and stared into space. After half a minute, he turned back to Carlos. "We've got to have someone get the report on the accident scene ... might uncover some clue."

"Who could do that?" asked Carlos. "We can't hire a private detective agency to investigate the loss of contraband goods."

"No, it would be too risky," said Isaac. "Let me see if I can get Jeff to look into it. As an attorney, he can manage access to all of the accident report papers. Also the boy, Ignacio, is very bright. Megan can talk to him. If the *coyote* contacted someone while Nacio was in the truck, the boy would know."

"Good idea," said Carlos. "I trust your judgment. It kept us alive years ago."

"The feeling is mutual, my friend."

Carlos rose to leave. When he embraced Isaac again, he held him close for a few extra seconds. "Find the diamonds for me, Isaac. The syndicate people in Tampico are impatient ... I think you know what I mean."

"You don't need another enemy, Carlos," said Isaac as he grabbed his friend for another embrace. "Be extra careful and think about my advice. I'm ready to help you ... whatever you decide."

"Thanks, I know you are." Carlos took a step toward the door, stopped, and turned back. "We've had some exciting times, haven't we?"

"Right ... even some of the scary ones were exciting. We are survivors, Carlos."

"Yeah, we are. But I'm tired," he said.

"I can tell that ... think about what I want you to do."

"Isaac, if I'm hit, please check on Carmen occasionally. Horse is now one of my bodyguards. If I'm iced, he'll go down too."

Chapter 27

On the way back home, Isaac couldn't stop thinking about the damaged package and the missing diamonds. Who was responsible ... Bernie or the *coyote*? Whoever took the diamonds had to have figured that the Houston contact would be blamed. It must have been Bernie. He knew the package was worthless now, and he had to find it before Chacón found out what had happened.

The key to locating the diamonds could lie in a search of the accident site and in rummaging through the parts and pieces salvaged from the *coyote*'s truck. If Jeff and Megan would agree to do some sleuthing, maybe they could find a clue that would lead to an answer to finding the diamonds. But what reason do Jeff and Megan have now to play detective? They have to be told that the danger still hovers over all of us before they will even consider taking on that role.

His thoughts turned to his friend. *What ever will happen to Carlos? He must suspect that he is in greater danger now than ever, or he wouldn't even consider walking away,* thought Isaac. *He lives in danger from attack by rival competitors every hour of every day. Now, with the missing diamonds, he faces an added threat: The Tel Aviv and Tampico syndicates will be much harder for Carlos to deal with if the conflict diamonds are not recovered.*

Isaac drove into the driveway, parked, and left the car in front of his house. All seemed quiet; the off-duty police officers were still keeping the premises under close surveillance. Inside the house, he found everyone in the den except Megan. *She must be in the guesthouse with Nacio,* he thought.

"How is Ignacio?" he asked.

"He's doing exceptionally well," said Jeff. "I can't get Megan away from his bedside. Celi even has to take her meals to her." Jeff laughed. "The only time she comes in is when Nacio needs a dressing change. He is so embarrassed. He wants only me there when he has to take his pajamas off."

"Celi is worried about your going without your dinner," said Margarita. "She saved food for you if you haven't already eaten."

"I had some work to do at the office. Yes, I am getting hungry," said Isaac. He motioned for Jeff to follow him into the kitchen.

Without going into details, Isaac related to Jeff—out of earshot of Margarita and Celi—his visit with Chacón and how they found the worthless stones in the package. He touched on the need for an investigation of the accident site.

Jeff stood, his brow deeply furrowed, his unblinking eyes blazing. "Are you telling me, Mr. Andrade, that, after all we've been through, we now find that the package that we've risked our lives protecting contained nothing more than ordinary pebbles?"

"That's it, Jeff," said Isaac. "Neither Chacón nor I can explain how it happened. I received the package from our contact in Tampico; I examined the jewels and established a value for them; I then wrapped and sealed the package and gave it to Bernie."

"Once again, Mr. Andrade, you're involved no more than what you are telling me?"

"Right," said Isaac. "I never have been. That's always been my role in the past. Chacón sends in the shipment and I examine it for value—just as I would do for any customer. Then I package and seal the merchandise and release it to his runner."

"So the process has been revived?"

"Yes ... the wars in South Africa have been revived. The diamond smuggling has been revived. The rough diamonds from South Africa go to Tel Aviv for cutting and polishing and then are channeled to Chacón's contacts in Tampico and then here for the next stage of merchandising."

"How can you say you are not guilty of wrongdoing, Mr. Andrade?"

"I am a contractor, Jeff. I receive goods to evaluate. I don't know the history of the origin."

"My legal training tells me that you do know—that you are aiding and abetting an illegal act," said Jeff as he gazed at Isaac with a look of solemnity.

"That's *your* opinion, Jeff?"

"I think you know that there is something irregular about the request to appraise the merchandise when it's given to you—you know the diamonds are not imported according to legal standards. You went to great lengths to explain to all of us about the Kimberly Certificate, how it certifies that imported diamonds are mined and distributed legally. You know what you're doing is illegal."

Isaac showed no sign of anger or emotional response to Jeff's expression of suspicion. He delayed answering Jeff's accusations before speaking. He smiled, thinking, *This kid is bright. He needs to be told more if I am going to convince him that he needs to do any sort of investigation into the missing diamonds. I will need to choose my words carefully.*

"Jeff, you've been exposed to enough, since you've been around me, that you need to be made aware of the complete picture. Please listen and try to understand; also remember that neither Megan nor Margarita knows the full story. I won't go into details; I'll just touch on the high points."

"Yeah … I need some answers, Mr. Andrade. I have pretended to be your attorney. I have been your accomplice in what could be considered a criminal act. I have been an accessory in deceiving and insulting FBI agents … yeah, I need some answers."

"Carlos Chacón and I grew up together here in Laredo. We were like brothers. When we were just kids we defended each other in school. I helped him defend his sister when she was accused of promiscuous conduct. We enlisted together in the marines, trained together, and served in the same platoon. I survived because of Chacón, and he survived because of me.

"When we returned, we both had a drug problem to deal with. We both kicked the habit. I went into a legitimate business, but Chacón never got over his bitterness toward the government and the public. After a few years, he managed to become the don of the largest drug cartel in northern Mexico. His sole objective was to ship as much illegal drugs as possible into the United States. He saw that as a way of punishing the people of America for his personal loss … a crippled leg and the loss of an eye. I'm not sure he even realized what he was doing and why.

"You question my role, don't you?" said Isaac, his eyes locked in on Jeff's. "I made a vow that I would do everything in my power to help Chacón, just as he would do for me. I have spent hours trying to get him to turn his life around, but I understand his bitterness. I had trouble for years coping with the same feelings. I thought maybe the conflict diamond deal with the syndicate might get him away from drug trafficking. Although it was illegal—dealing with the syndicate's diamond smuggling operation—it didn't seem to carry the same risks."

"But you have connections with the government in some way, if I heard you right."

"Chacón and I were in a special unit in the marines. When we returned we were offered positions as agents in a special operations unit. Chacón declined. I joined and was assigned to the border to conduct surveillance of the diamond trafficking scheme."

"But your friend was involved in drug as well as diamond trafficking."

"But I never reported on what I knew about Chacón. He was aware of what I was doing, but he knew I would never rat on him."

"Did the government know you were protecting Chacón?"

"Right, I made full disclosure to the government and to Chacón. I reported activity without naming individuals."

"And when you helped Chacón during the height of the conflict diamond era, how did you manage to protect him and still perform for the government?"

"I notified the government of the appraised value every time there was a shipment, but I never let myself become knowledgeable of any other details of any transaction. I just evaluated the stones and gave my report, without incriminating Carlos."

"But you really knew Chacón was behind the scheme. It makes you guilty, Mr. Andrade."

"Then I was guilty, dammit," said Isaac. He shoved his plate of half-eaten food away ... almost off the table. His voice reverberated anger. "I would never do anything to betray my friend, Jeff ... my friend to whom I owe my very existence today. Chacón and I fought that fuckin' war, Jeff. We made it home because we protected each other. Can you understand that, Jeff ... could Megan?"

Jeff looked out the window and was silent for a few seconds as if contemplating what he had just heard. In the eyes of the law, Isaac was probably guilty as an accomplice to criminal activity. But the era of Isaac and Chacón's wartime service and the period that followed was an era of turbulence. He could understand Isaac's fierce loyalty to Chacón.

"What comes next, Mr. Andrade?"

"Jeff, I'm telling you all of this as a way to explain my actions with regard to our dealing with our present problem—the package. Here's the kick: our mission was to find Nacio's sister. Unfortunately, we discovered news that we didn't want to hear ... that Esmeralda is dead. I suspect that Carmen never intended to give up Esmeralda when the *coyote* returned anyway. The girl was a valuable commodity to Carmen.

"But now, Jeff, my friend desperately needs to determine what happened to the real contents of that package. We all need to know what happened. In doing so we have to consider who had possession of the package from the time it left my hands. Chacón knows that I personally would never do anything that would put him in danger. So we have to think: Who *did* have the opportunity?"

"You don't think that Megan and I took the diamonds, do you?"

"No, I know you wouldn't. But in the eyes of Chacón and the syndicate, you will be suspects until the stones are recovered."

"You mean Megan and I, and I guess Nacio, are in danger from some undefined syndicate?"

"I'm afraid so, Jeff … all of us are."

"What can we do, Mr. Andrade?" asked Jeff. "If I understand what you're saying, the diamonds are missing from the package. Anyone who has had access to the package is suspect and is exposed every minute to the wrath of individuals linked to some sort of diamond smuggling syndicate that wants the contents of the package recovered."

"That's it, Jeff," said Isaac. "We didn't anticipate this turn of events, but we have to take steps to protect all of us, including Ignacio."

"Do you have a plan?"

"I think the first step is to keep the guards on duty. As soon as Nacio is ready to travel, you, Megan, and Nacio should return to Houston. As attorneys, you and Megan have authority to see the police report of the accident and to examine the salvaged articles from the *coyote*'s pickup. There might be a clue that would explain what happened."

Jeff listened intently to Isaac with unblinking eyes and a furrowed brow. "I see where you're going with this. Are there any options?"

"Yes, we could engage a private detective firm in Houston to investigate and report their findings to us," he said. "That way you, Megan, and Nacio could stay here until it all blows over. But it would unwise to bring outsiders on the scene in a case like this. I think you know why."

"You're also thinking of finding a way to protect your friend, aren't you?" said Jeff. He watched Isaac closely. *Would Isaac put his daughter at risk to protect Chacón? What if we just return to our usual life? Are we really in as much danger as Isaac implies?* Jeff wondered. *But if Isaac's fears are valid, we could easily be found in Houston if we were targeted. We need to stick together and get this dilemma resolved and behind us.*

"Protect my friend … yes," he said. "But foremost, protect my family."

"My gut feeling is that we should follow your first suggestion … go to Houston and see if we can find something that will lead to a resolution of this threat to all of us."

"That's the way I look at it. Since Megan works for ICE, you should not encounter any major problems getting information."

"I think it's time we enlighten Megan and Mrs. Andrade on the dangers that we face if we don't recover the stolen diamonds," said Jeff. "What do you think?"

"I'm afraid you're right," said Isaac. "It's not going to be easy to explain to them, but it has to be done. We can't predict how deeply all of us will become involved before this is over."

"Looks like it's time for a family conference," said Jeff."

*   *   *   *

Nacio stayed busy in the corner of the room with his books while Isaac stood in front of the group—all with solemn expressions on their faces as they listened. Isaac narrated in scanty detail the dilemma that they all faced right then. He touched briefly on the threat of danger to anyone who had had contact with the package and the potential retribution by the Tampico Syndicate if the stolen diamonds were not recovered and returned.

After he finished, there was knife-cutting quiet for what seemed like a lifetime. Megan was the first to break the silence.

"So what I'm hearing is that we are all suspects until the diamonds are found," she said. "We can't just pack-up and leave—we are in danger wherever we are."

"Absolutely!" Isaac said. "Jeff, do you have anything to add?"

"Not a thing, Mr. Andrade," he answered. "You've covered it thoroughly. We have to find the diamonds before we are safe, and we need to stick together."

"What's the next step, Isaac?" asked Margarita.

"Jeff, Megan, and Nacio are going back to Houston to look for clues that might shed some light on what happened to the diamonds. We now know that the package that Nacio has been protecting did not contain anything of value."

Megan became contemplative, stared into space, her forehead creased by shallow furrows. After a few moments, she asked: "Dad, how did you get involved with these diamonds in the first place?"

"Megan, I am a certified appraiser ... have been for years," he said. "When diamonds are brought in for me to evaluate, I do just that. I have no way of knowing to whom they belong or to whom they are being sold. I did the original appraisal on these diamonds."

Jeff held his breath hoping Megan wouldn't get too inquisitive. *Apparently Mr. Andrade does not intend to make a full disclosure of his relationship with Chacón,* he thought. *A wise decision at this time.*

"There's more to this story than you're telling us," said Megan.

"It will unfold later, Megan," said Jeff, a stern tone to his voice, before Isaac could speak.

Megan looked at Jeff for a few seconds before speaking, her eyes fixed on his. Then she grinned and then laughed. "Jeff, I'm seeing you in a different light: you *are* a lot like my father."

Chapter 28

▼

Conversation was minimal on the return trip to Houston; each seemed engrossed in private thoughts. Ignacio slept most of the way. After entering the city limits, Jeff began looking for a motel—remote from their apartment building and their office addresses—where they could stay for a couple of days while they conducted their investigation. Nacio stirred about enough in the backseat that Megan could tell that he was awake.

"We're almost there, Nacio," she said. "Are you all right?"

"*S,* Meggie," he answered. He gazed out the window, avoiding eye contact with Megan.

"Are you having any pain?"

"*Nada,* Meggie."

"Jeff, he looks so sad. What could be wrong?"

"Maybe he thinks we're bringing him back to the detention center," said Jeff. "Does he know why we are coming back?"

"I just told him we had to go to Houston, but I haven't explained why," said Megan. "He has such a distraught look in his eyes. Maybe he's missing his parents and Esme."

Jeff looked in the rearview mirror at the downcast look on Nacio's face. "As soon as you get the chance you need to tell him why we're here."

* * * *

Because the day was almost over, they decided to wait until the next morning to begin their search. Jeff managed to give Nacio a sponge bath, change his dressings, and get him into clean pajamas for the night. As far as Jeff could tell, Nacio's operative wound was healing rapidly. Also, Nacio was able to be up and about, apparently with minimal discomfort. Celi had packed a cooler with more than enough rations to last their two-day stay in Houston, so they didn't have to go out for food.

Shortly after daylight the next morning, Jeff and Megan started their day by laying out their agenda. First, they both made phone calls to notify their offices that there would be a few days delay in their returning to work.

"I think we should go to the site of the accident next," said Jeff, as they munched on Celi's *taquitos*.

"Do you think it's wise for Nacio to go with us?" asked Megan. "It might be an emotionally traumatic experience for him."

"We can't leave him. Maybe you should have your talk with him before we go," said Jeff.

"I told him the whole story early this morning about the missing diamonds and what we're trying to do. He was very curious about the package, what happened to it. He wondered why we're looking for the diamonds, if they can't bring Esme back."

"Did you tell him about the danger we're all facing if we don't find the diamonds?" he asked.

"I explained that to him," she said. "He's very bright, Jeff. You were right. After I explained to him why we were back in Houston, he seemed relieved that we're not going to leave him. Actually, he seemed eager to help. I asked if he understood. He said, "¿Alguien sacó los diamantes del paquete, verdad?""

"What's the translation?" said Jeff.

"He said: 'The diamonds are missing, aren't they?' He's worried that the 'mean man' may try to injure us," said Megan. "He knows all about Bernie now."

"I hope he doesn't get upset when we go to the site where his parents were killed. Should we leave him in the car while we look?"

"He understands what we're doing. He wants to help."

* * * *

"From what we've been told, I think the overpass where the collision occurred is just ahead," said Jeff. "We'll circle under the next overpass and come back."

The steady stream of cars—all racing at top speed—roared by as Jeff parked on the wide shoulder of the freeway. They began their search of the ground alongside the highway and along the sloped bank. Nacio guided them down the slope and pointed out where he had picked up the package and the rosary.

They climbed back to the peak of the overpass where signs of the burning vehicle were still evident. Seeing the site must have triggered the memory of the nightmare Nacio had experienced. He turned his head away and started walking back toward the car. Megan followed him and knelt down so she could look straight into his tear-filled eyes.

"I'm so sorry, Nacio. You loved your mamá and papá very much, didn't you?"

Tears streamed down his face as he tried to answer. "It's all right to cry, Nacio," said Megan as she held him close. "Your mother and father loved you ... and they loved Esme also. They would be proud of you. Maybe they are looking down on you from heaven right now and they see how strong you are."

"Will you and Jeff die someday too, Meggie?" he said between sobs.

"We're going to be right with you, Nacio. We are not going to leave you."

Jeff climbed up the grassy incline and joined them. "I found a scattering of screws, small tools that were overlooked, and a couple of empty beer cans ... nothing else," said Jeff. "It looks like the ground has been cleaned thoroughly of everything else. Is Nacio all right?"

"He's handling it pretty well," she said as she wiped his wet cheeks. "Nacio, you picked up the package right there, didn't you?" asked Megan, pointing to the grassy incline.

"S, Meggie."

"Did anyone else ever hold the package?"

"No, no one," he promptly answered. "I wouldn't let anyone even touch it. They tried to take it ... I wouldn't let them."

"So, the only person you saw hold the package was Señor Jimbob?"

"S," he answered as he continued to hold on to Megan.

"I think we're finished here," said Jeff.

* * * *

Their next stop was the indoor storage pound where items salvaged from accident sites and the remains of the vehicles were kept. Megan tried to show her credentials to the guard, who was seated at a desk watching television. For an agonizing few seconds, he wouldn't take his eyes off the tube. Then he finally looked at Megan's identification and said, "You need something?"

After Jeff explained why they were there, the man slowly dragged his overweight torso to a standing position, unlocked the door to the warehouse, and allowed them to enter to make their inspection.

"Why is there so much interest in all this stuff?" the attendant asked. "We've had two other groups of people looking through these salvaged items."

"Did they identify themselves?" asked Megan.

"Yeah ... one bunch said they were with some government agency and another guy, the one who came here by himself, said he was an adjuster from the insurance company. But none of them seemed interested in the vehicle, other than the toolbox."

"They didn't take anything with them, did they?" asked Jeff.

"Oh, no," he said. "I watched them every minute ... have to stay with everybody while they are in here. The insurance adjuster kept looking at the briefcase that was found at the accident site. It was empty, but he kept looking in all the compartments."

"The adjuster ... what did he look like? I might know him," said Jeff.

"Big guy, never smiled ... short haircut. He had an unusual accent ... never heard it before."

"Not the man I know. Can you show us the briefcase?" asked Jeff.

"Yeah, I know right where it is. That guy from the insurance company tossed it on the floor over there and walked away scowling and uttering something under his breath. I couldn't understand him, but I could tell he wasn't very happy."

Jeff and Megan examined the briefcase carefully. The zippered top was open.

"Was there a lock on this zipper when it came to you?"

"Nah ... it came just as you see it," he said. "Here's the description of the case when it was logged in."

Megan and Jeff roamed around the scattering of tagged salvaged items without finding anything that seemed of value. Nacio stayed away from the wrecked vehicle but wandered through the other items laid out on the storeroom floor. He picked up a shovel and carried it around for a few minutes.

"What do you have, Nacio?" asked Megan.

"A shovel like Señor Jimbob's."

"You saw Señor Jimbob with a shovel?"

"*Si*, Meggie," he answered. "Señor Jimbob dug a hole with it at the river."

"You saw him dig a hole ... when, Nacio?" asked Megan.

"When we were in the boat going across the river. Papá was paddling. I was sitting in the back, watching. Señor Jimbob dug a hole and then threw his shovel into his truck ... I could see him. The moon was bright."

"Jeff, come here," yelled Megan. "Nacio has found something. He saw the *coyote* digging a hole at the river's edge with a shovel like this one."

Jeff took one look at the shovel and yelled, "You've found the answer, Nacio! Good going, buddy! I've got to call your father, Megan. Nacio found it. Your dad said we might find a clue."

"And we've found out that the briefcase was unlocked."

Nacio smiled broadly, and contorted every facial muscle to reflect a look of pride. Jeff grabbed him, lifted him off his feet, and swung him around a few times. Nacio laughed all the way. "Let me down, Jeff," he cried. Jeff dropped him to floor and gave him a hug.

"Nacio, you may have found the answer," Jeff yelled. "Tell him what I said, Megan. Let's go back to Laredo. Nacio can show us where the *coyote* buried the diamonds. Look at the shovel, Megan ... there are still traces of sand on the blade."

* * * *

"Mr. Andrade, listen to this: we found something and found out something that you need to know," said Jeff after he finally reached Isaac on his cell phone. Jeff was still so excited that he could hardly speak.

"I hope it's good news," said Isaac in a tone of despair.

"What's wrong, Mr. Andrade?"

"Jeff, please don't alarm Megan. The Tampico Syndicate guys are on their way here. Chacón and I are scheduled to meet with them this afternoon. They want some answers about the diamonds. I'm still at the store but will be leaving soon for the meeting."

"Look, we might have the answer. We might be able to recover the diamonds," said Jeff. He told Isaac about the shovel and about Ignacio seeing Jimbob dig a hole near the river. "Nacio says he can take us there ... to the place where they crossed. Oh ... one other thing, the briefcase was unzipped and no lock was on it."

"That's encouraging news. I'll pass it on to Chacón, but it may be too late," said Isaac. "These people are impetuous and impatient. I don't know if I can convince them to give us a chance to produce the merchandise."

"Sir ... do you have to go to the meeting?"

"I can't let Carlos down, Jeff," he said. "The one thing that worries me more than anything is the rumor that I hear from my friends in the AFI. The Fidencio Estrada gang, one of Carlos's fiercest competitors, has heard somehow about the diamond heist. These people are like animals. They know that, if Chacón is weakened by some slipup, the time is right for a takeover. I know how they operate. If I can't convince them that we are making progress, the Tampico Syndicate might contact Fidencio Estrada and put out a contract on Carlos."

"If you are along, aren't you a target also?" asked Jeff.

"I know what you're thinking. Chacón will have plenty of bodyguards wherever he goes."

"We're on our way back," said Jeff. "Can I help you in any way?"

"Jeff, you are unbelievable … after all I've put you through," said Isaac. "Just take care of my daughter. And Nacio."

"I don't like the sound of this, sir," replied Jeff. "Where will you be meeting these people?"

"We'll be at El Rancho Alegrón," he said. "Don't try any heroics, Jeff."

"We're going to recover the diamonds, Mr. Andrade. Just try to convince them that we know where to look."

"Thanks, Jeff. Let me say this: It's been a delight to get to know you these last few days."

"Thank you, sir," said Jeff. "You're going to get to know a lot more about me, sir."

"That's the best news yet," he said. "Oh … Jeff, a thought has come to mind. If the *coyote* buried the diamonds at the river, or hid them anywhere here, he would plan to return to recover them, wouldn't he? What do you think he'd do then?"

A brief silence followed. "Sure … he'd get out of there as quickly as possible—most likely out of the country, as far away as possible. And he would have to have an airline reservation to do that."

"And he wouldn't have had time to pick up his ticket when he left here for Houston," said Isaac. "He would plan to go after it when he returned."

"So it would still be at the ticket counter. How can we find out?" asked Jeff.

"I'm going to call my friend Chief López-Guerra and see if he will check the airlines for us. The *coyote* would likely have some sort of passport. The chief of police will be able to get cooperation from the airline."

"Good thinking, sir," said Jeff. "Be careful at the meeting, Mr. Andrade. I'm anxious to see what the chief finds out."

The phone clicked dead.

*   *   *   *

"You're driving so fast," said Megan. "What's the rush?"

"Uh … no reason really," he said. "Just think we need to get back and have Nacio show us where Jimbob dug that hole."

"Yeah … sure," she replied. "What did my dad say when you talked to him?"

"Just that he was pleased that we had found something to go on."

"Jeffrey … you are *not* telling me everything," she said. "What did he say?"

"He told me not to get you upset. We need to get back to Laredo as quickly as possible. Can you settle for that right now?"

"Are we fighting a deadline, Jeff?"

"Maybe so," said Jeff. He was quiet for a few seconds. He had to be honest with Megan. If they were to be effective in helping Isaac, he would need her help—and Nacio's help.

"Tell me," she said.

"He's going with Carlos Chacón to meet with the guys from the diamond syndicate from Tampico. They are pressuring for some answers. He's going to try to convince them that we have something that might mean recovery of the diamonds."

"So that's why you've been driving like a maniac ever since we left Houston?"

"Yeah, Megan, that's it," said Jeff in tone of irritability. "Now, please … no more questions."

"Okay, Mr. Grumpy."

"Look, I'll explain later. Right now, I need to get back to Laredo to help your dad."

Chapter 29

Margarita looked up from her desktop monitor. "Where are you going this time of day?" she asked, her brow furrowed. "The store has been packed with customers all morning. Our sales girls are running in circles."

"I have a meeting with some vendors," said Isaac. "It won't be a long meeting … new merchandise."

"I don't like being in a saleslady position, Isaac."

"You can handle it. I'll be back within the hour," he said. He pulled her out of the computer chair and held her close for a prolonged minute and then kissed her.

"What brought this on?" she said as she kissed him again. "Have you been taking those little blue pills again?"

"I don't need pills when I'm around you."

"Cut it out, Isaac."

"Sometimes I feel like we don't have enough intimate time together … always work, work, work."

"Have you heard from Megan and Jeff?" she asked.

"Not yet," he said, trying to avoid eye contact with his wife. "I'm sure they will call if they find anything important."

"Isaac, be careful," said Margarita. "I have an ominous feeling about your going out. Have you told me everything?"

Isaac laughed, kissed her again, and turned to leave. "Why are you always so suspicious?"

"Don't forget what you've always told me—being suspicious is the key to survival."

"All right, Miss Know-it-all, enough of that. See you after a while. I love you."

* * * *

Isaac waited as long as he could before leaving for El Rancho Alegrón. He glanced at his watch. He had hoped Jeff would return before he had to leave. But if he had returned in time, Jeff probably would have insisted on going with him. Definitely he wanted to avoid having to explain to Margarita and Megan where and why he was going right now.

His Glock was securely stored in his briefcase and was easily within reach if he needed it. What would he do if the meeting deteriorated to outright conflict? Carlos likely had enough armed support. The undefined element was the Fidencio Estrada gang. Hopefully, the warning from the AFI was not valid, but they had no reason to mislead him. Most likely the rumor was launched by the Tampico Syndicate to serve as a scare tactic so Chacón would cooperate.

As Isaac approached the gate to El Rancho Alegrón, his cell phone vibrated. It was Jeff.

"Isaac, we are just now arriving," said Jeff. "Do you have any last-minute news for us?"

"No, I don't. I'm at the entrance to El Rancho Alegrón now. I think I can handle it all right. Fortunately, I am armed with the information that you have found some proof that the *coyote* was the culprit."

"Do you want me to do anything?"

"Don't chance it, Jeff. Wait for me to get through this meeting. I have a friend who is a part of the Tampico Syndicate. I think I can depend on him to support my explanation for the loss since I have the information that you've uncovered."

"Just let me know," he said.

"Try to tell Megan no more than necessary."

"I will do that." Jeff nonchalantly clicked his phone shut and kept his eyes on the road, waiting for Megan's questions, which he knew would be coming.

"What's going on, Jeff?"

"Your dad is anxious for us to take Nacio to the site of the river crossing."

"Jeffrey, once again, you're holding something back."

Jeff chose not to respond to Megan's prodding, hoping she would let up while he negotiated the Bob Bullock Loop traffic on the way to the Andrade residence.

"Answer me, Jeff," said Megan.

"Megan, your dad is working hard to bring this dilemma to a satisfactory resolution. He does not want to disturb you or your mother. I agreed not to say anything more to you about it right now. I am not going to betray his confidence."

"You and my dad have developed a close relationship since we've been here. He's influencing your behavior—especially your behavior with me. I've seen him do this to my mom for years. I'm not going to tolerate that from you, Jeff."

"I'm sorry, Megan. All I can say is that right now you and your mother will just have to put up with our management of this current problem."

"You're willing to risk what this sort of secrecy will do to us … to you and me?"

"I won't talk about it, Megan. You will have to look upon my refusal as a test of your confidence of your dad's ability and mine to handle this adversity."

"I don't like it, Jeff."

The silence thickened in intensity as they pulled into the driveway and parked. Ignacio, now sitting upright in the backseat, looked at Megan with a wrinkled forehead as if he were aware of the discordance between Jeff and Megan.

"Meggie, Jeff will *help* you. He helps me. Don't get mad at him, please," said Ignacio.

"See, Jeff, you've upset Nacio," said Megan as she leaned over the seat and grasped Nacio's hand.

"It's all right, Nacio," she said. "We're not mad at each other. We're just worried about the diamonds … whether or not we can find them."

"We'll find them, Meggie," said Nacio.

"What did he say," asked Jeff.

"He said you are a despicable character and that he hopes you rot in hell." Megan tried to suppress a smile, but finally broke down with laughter. She pulled Jeff over for a kiss. Nacio's grin, as always, framed his dimples, causing them to look deeper than ever.

*   *   *   *

At the entrance to the mansionlike main building of El Rancho Alegrón, Isaac was met by the same two off-duty policemen he had previously used at the store, Victor and Sergio Gonzaba. *They must be brothers,* Isaac thought, *they look so much alike.* Isaac had never bothered to ask, but whenever he put out a notice that he needed someone, they always came together.

"*Buenos días,* Señor Andrade," said one brother.

"Nice seeing you again," said the other.

"*Buenos días,* Víctor and Sergio. Am I early?" asked Isaac.

"No, señor," they answered. "The others are already here. We'll take you to the library."

Chacón, seated at the head of the table, was flanked by Bernie and Carmen's husband, Horacio, aka Horse. *Is this all of the support Carlos has?* Isaac wondered. *Horacio is the only one he can depend on. I'm glad I came and I'm glad I'm armed. Why does Carlos trust Bernie? He'd betray Carlos any day for a dime, if he thought he could get away with it.*

Isaac glared at Bernie with a look that figuratively cut him into small pieces. Bernie shifted his chair to avoid eye contact with Isaac. *I should have wasted the son of a bitch when I had a chance,* thought Isaac.

At the other end of the library table, the unsmiling representatives from the Tampico Syndicate were clustered. There was no indication of any greeting when Isaac entered except from his friend, Moshe Rosen, who seemed to take a lead role in the meeting.

"How are you, Isaac," asked Moshe, as he stood for an embrace. "Nice to see you again."

"I'm fine, Moshe," said Isaac. He turned to Chacón. "Do we have a problem here, Carlos?"

Chacón turned to Moshe. "There seems to be only a misunderstanding, Isaac. Can you elaborate, Moshe?"

"We can make this quick, Carlos ... Isaac," he replied. "The Syndicate sent merchandise worth some twelve million dollars to Nuevo Laredo for distribution. We have learned from our contact in Houston that the package has not been received. Naturally we are concerned."

"Understandable. We think we have unraveled the mystery, Moshe," said Chacón. "We will need a few days to be sure. We are aware that someone took the diamonds. We think we know who."

"And who would that be, Carlos?"

Carlos described the sequence of events from the time that the *coyote* left for Houston to deliver the package until the present when they discovered that the package contained only worthless pebbles.

"What can you do to recover the diamonds?"

"I will let Isaac Andrade answer, Moshe. He has organized a recovery team, and he thinks they have made progress in solving the mystery."

All eyes shifted to Isaac. "We know the identity of everyone who had access to the package," said Isaac, his eyes fixed on Bernie. "And we are in the process of checking out every lead."

Isaac then recited the story of Ignacio recovering the package at the accident site, thinking it was the key to finding his sister. Without revealing specifically what they had found, Isaac stated that Megan and Jeff had discovered evidence that Jimbob had taken the diamonds and had substituted pebbles in the package.

Bernie slammed his fist on the table and stood. "That son of a bitch," he yelled. "He double-crossed us. Dying was too good for him."

"What if he had not died, Bernie?" asked Chacón, without turning his head or changing expressions on his face. "Your split with him would have been worth a fortune, wouldn't it?"

Bernie turned pale, and stammered his reply. "Wha … Wha … do you mean, Carlos?"

"I've known all along that you and Jimbob planned to make off with the diamonds. Carmen has good hearing, Bernie. You should have been more discrete. I was hoping you'd confess, return the diamonds, and save us all of this trouble."

"You're wrong, Carlos," Bernie said, his voice cracking and his hands trembling uncontrollably. "If I had known it was worthless, I wouldn't have worked so hard to recover the stolen package!"

"You tried to find it before I found out what happened," said Carlos. "Where did Jimbob stash the diamonds, Bernie?"

"I don't know, boss. Believe me … I don't know. If I did I would have brought them to you."

"I don't believe you, Bernie," said Carlos. He turned to Horacio. "Take him out, Horse."

"Wait, Chacón … wait," he pleaded. "I can help you find the diamonds."

"If you knew where the diamonds were, you would already be on a plane to Germany. Take him out."

Bernie struggled against the overpowering Horacio Carrillo, who had to practically drag him through the door.

"You need to get your organization cleaned up, Carlos," said Moshe. "I think we've seen enough. What are your plans?"

"Isaac, can you answer that?" said Carlos.

Isaac described in detail the recent information that pointed to a burial site for the diamonds near the river. "We will find the diamonds. If by some chance we are wrong, I am sure that Carlos will reimburse you fully for the value. I still have my evaluation notes on every stone."

"That seems more than fair," said Moshe. Each of the other three men from the Tampico Syndicate nodded his head in approval. "I think this meeting is over. Keep us informed on your progress, Isaac."

"We'll do that daily, Moshe."

* * * *

Chacón and Isaac were left alone in the one of the parlors of the mansion. A knock on the door signaled the arrival of Carmen Carrillo, whose face drooped in a downcast expression.

"I'll bring you each a Scotch and water," she said with a glaring absence of her usual joviality. "Carlos, I'm worried. I think you should stay here tonight."

"I can't," he answered. "I have an appointment in Monterrey early in the morning. My limousine is waiting for me to make the trip. Why are you so concerned?"

"Just a feeling I have and rumors I've heard."

"You mean about the Fidencio Estrada threat?"

"Carlos ... why ...? Carmen paused, turned her head and dabbed at her eyes. "What happened to Bernie, Carlos?"

"He's all right, Carmen." Carlos laughed. "I'm sorry ... I didn't tell you. That was an act for the benefit of the Tampico people."

"But what will they do when they find out?"

"Don't worry," he said. "Moshe Rosen knew what I was doing. The others ... we'll never see them again."

"Oh, thank God. When you told Horacio to take him out, I thought you meant ..."

"The other reason, Carmen, is that I wanted to see how Bernie reacted when I accused him. After I saw, I wanted Bernie taken out of the room. I didn't want him to hear Isaac's update on his recovery plan ... where we think the diamonds are buried. And I don't want you to mention to anybody about Isaac's efforts to find the lost merchandise—especially Bernie."

"How would I know anything about it, Carlos?" she said. "I wasn't in here when you were talking."

"Come on, Carmen," said Carlos with a chuckle, "you have at least four microphones hidden in this room alone."

Carmen straightened her back and held her head high. "There's safety in being kept informed," she said. Her look of concern returned. She put her arm around her brother's shoulder. "I'm worried about your safety when you leave here."

"Why are you worried? I think the Tampico crowd was satisfied with our plans. They aren't going to take any action."

"It's Fidencio Estrada that I'm worried about. He knows you're here."

"Have you heard something?"

"I hope it's just rumors. But you'll have Horacio and Bernie with you when you leave, won't you?"

"Stop worrying. We've been through this before."

"Just be careful. Wait … why don't you do this? Just to be safe, ride out with Isaac, then let Horacio and Bernie follow later and pick you up somewhere in town."

"I think that's a good idea," said Isaac. "I don't trust Bernie. He's an empty suit, Carlos. He'd betray you in a minute … even if you like him, Carmen. He has no loyalty."

"Oh, I like you too, Isaac," she said as she swept her hand through Isaac's hair. "Go out with Isaac, Carlos … please?"

"I don't think it's necessary, but if you're that worried, that's what I'll do."

"Thanks," she said, back to her playful mood. She stood behind Isaac and rubbed his neck and shoulder muscles. "Now I'll stop worrying. I don't want anything to happen to my dear Isaac … even my dear Bernie … and certainly not to my dear brother."

"Cut the shit, Carmen," said Carlos. "Bring us the Scotch."

✶   ✶   ✶   ✶

"Where is the best place to leave you … where Bernie and Horacio can pick you up?" asked Isaac as he drove into the center of Nuevo Laredo with Chacón at his side in the front seat.

"They won't be coming, Isaac. I'm calling another driver."

Isaac looked at Carlos with an unblinking, puzzled expression for a few silent moments. *Chacón didn't explain. Did Horse really take him out?* thought Isaac. *Carlos will not say and I'm not going to ask.*

"Stop at the Blue Eagle, Isaac," he said. "Do this for me: Go in and tell Beto I'm here. He'll let me in the back. I'll call my driver and tell him where I am. I'll stay here for a while until it's safe to go on down the road to Monterrey."

"What can you tell me, Carlos?" said Isaac.

"I can't tell you everything, Isaac, just this much: I'm getting out … just as you suggested. I'm going to disappear, Isaac," he said. After a long pause, Isaac remained silent until Carlos decided to continue. "I'm gonna miss you, old friend, and I'll never forget the times we've had together. Maybe you'll hear from me someday. I've arranged for a transfer of funds to your account … just in case you have to reimburse the syndicate. You're the only person in this world that I can truly say that I trust."

"Carlos, if there is anything—anything at all—that I ..."

"I know you would, Isaac," he said. They both climbed out and stood in front of the Blue Eagle for one last handshake and embrace. Isaac stood by the car for a few seconds and watched Carlos disappear into the shadows, limping to the back entrance of the Blue Eagle. *Whatever will happen to my friend—my "brother"?* he wondered. *Carlos is not running away from anything—he's running to something.*

Chapter 30

"Is Nacio still asleep?" asked Jeff, as they came to a stop at the guesthouse driveway.

"Hasn't stirred since we left Houston," she said. "I'm glad he didn't wake up to see how fast you were driving," she added with a smirk.

"I just wanted to get back to make some plans with your dad ... you know that."

"I guess we're both getting a little irritable," said Megan.

"And for good reason," he said. "Is Nacio all right?"

"He seems to be," she said as she exited and opened the door to the backseat to awaken Nacio. She felt his forehead. "He's cool."

She gently pulled the sleepy-headed boy out of the car and guided him into the bedroom. On the way, Nacio awakened enough to pull Megan close to his side.

"Can I ride the bicycle tomorrow, Meggie?" he said, his eyes still half-closed.

"We'll see how you are tomorrow, Nacio. It might be too soon after your operation."

"Will I ever get to ride the bicycle again?"

"Sure you will. Your doctor said you'd be able to do everything. And you know what? When you get well, we'll get you a boys' bicycle of your very own so you won't have to ride a girls' bicycle."

"My own bicycle?" he said, his eyes now sparkling.

"Your very own!"

"Do girls ever ride boys' bicycles?"

"Sure, sometimes."

"Then you can ride my bicycle sometimes."

"We can ride together," she said.

"Good ... does Jeff have a bicycle?"

"I'm sure he does. If he doesn't, we'll get one for him too. We'll all have bicycles," she said as she turned down his bed. "We can all ride together."

"That's what I want."

"Right now you need to get to bed and to sleep. Jeff will be here in a minute to check your bandages and help you to bed."

"Maybe I can do it, Meggie."

"Better let Jeff help. Good night, Nacio," she said. "You were a big help to us today." Megan bent over and kissed his forehead.

"Good night, Meggie."

* * * *

Isaac checked his watch. Margarita by now would have closed the store and would be either home already or on her way. He debated whether he should stay close to the Blue Eagle in case Chacón needed him. Carlos had made it clear that he was leaving—disappearing, he said. Something has happened to cause him to make the decision to go into hiding. Whatever the reason, he must have felt it imperative that he move in a hurry. *Maybe he's just doing what I suggested*, thought Isaac. *He's getting out. Maybe my old friend is thinking of me.*

As Isaac passed through customs, just for safety, he took his Glock out of the briefcase and pushed it under the front seat. If Chacón was pulling out, there probably would be no need for him to keep a gun around any longer. With Chacón out of the picture, he no longer wanted any part in the illegal importation.

Finally reaching home, he steered his car around the house and down the driveway to the garage. Seeing Jeff's car in the driveway reminded him that they probably were in for a busy day tomorrow, searching for the buried diamonds. If Bernie or Jimbob had had grandiose plans to heist the diamonds, they never would have believed that their scheme could have been spoiled by an eleven-year-old boy! Isaac laughed, thinking that now he depended on that same boy to lead him to the hiding place for diamonds worth twelve million dollars.

The house was quiet when he entered. Jeff, Megan, and Margarita were in the den sipping drinks and munching snacks that Celi had laid before them. Jeff jumped to his feet when Isaac entered.

"How did it go, Mr. Andrade?" asked Jeff.

"I think they are convinced that we are sincere," he said. "We have our work cut out for us. When can we start?"

"We want to start early in the morning—as soon as Nacio is up."

"Good," said Isaac. "The sooner the better." Isaac glanced at Margarita.

"It's all right, Isaac," she said. "Go ahead. I can handle the store. Maybe Carmen will come in and I can sell her some cheap quartz jewelry."

"Come off it, Margie," he said. "This is no time for remarks like that. Yes, I'm ready, Jeff, Megan."

* * * *

In spite of a tiring, action-filled day, Jeff spent a restless night thinking of the predicament they were in. When he woke, he was ready for resolution to the problem. What he dreaded the most was the time when Megan would receive a call from her office to return Nacio. It would be devastating to both of them to have to give up the boy. He found himself thinking of the joy he would have someday parenting a kid like Nacio … being the father that he himself had never had.

"Enough daydreaming," he said aloud as he hopped out of bed and made himself ready for the day ahead. When he entered the main house, he found everyone except Nacio and Celi. He turned to Isaac.

"Will we have any trouble taking Nacio back and forth across the border, Mr. Andrade?" asked Jeff.

"I don't think so. We'll go in my car," said Isaac. "We'll not likely have any problems crossing. The customs inspectors at the border nearly always pass me through when they see my car," said Isaac. "Are we ready?"

"As soon as Nacio is here. Celi is getting him ready to go," said Megan. She laughed. "He won't let anyone but Jeff change his bandage."

"Guess I'd better go help," said Jeff.

* * * *

After Jeff left the room, Megan's cell phone vibrated. She flipped it open. "Megan, this is Jaime Cordova. Rob Schneider has been looking for you. Is Ignacio all right?"

"He's fine, Jaime," she said. "Why is Rob asking?"

"We've found a relative. Rob needs you to bring Ignacio in as soon as you can so we can start the deportation process. Where are you?"

"I'm in Laredo, Jaime ... at my parent's home. I can't leave for Houston today."

"What do you want me to tell Rob?"

Megan couldn't speak for the lump in her throat. With cell phone in hand she walked out to the back terrace just in time to see Jeff coming in with Nacio holding his hand. She had to compose herself and say something to Jaime.

"Jaime, are you still there?" she said. "Try to find a reason to delay my return ... please."

"I know what's happened, Megan. You knew better than to get so attached. What about Jeff?"

"As bad or worse than I am," she said and paused again without speaking, trying to restrain sobbing.

"Megan, what can I do?"

"I can't do it, Jaime."

"Megan, don't be foolish."

"Help me, Jaime ... please help us."

"It's not going away, Megan. You'll have to face it sooner or later."

"Who is the relative?"

"We found one uncle, his father's brother, who lives near the village where Ignacio's family came from—a village named Cuauhtémoc. It's near Ciudad Mante."

"Has anyone talked to the uncle?"

"Yeah, he's a farmer, lives close to the village—looking forward to having his nephew come live with him."

"Jaime, tell Rob that we are *not* going to let Nacio go just any place, and certainly not until we have chance to check it out for safety."

"You're treading on dangerous ground, Megan," said Jaime. "We're dealing with international law."

"I'll talk to Jeff. Somehow or another, we are going to keep Nacio. He needs us. I'll call you back, Jaime."

"Megan, I knew this would be hard for you to take. It's been hard for me to even call. I'm going to tell the chief that I've been unable to find you."

"Thanks, Jaime. I won't betray you."

Jaime chuckled. "You have reacted exactly as I predicted. You owe me one, Megan."

"Thanks again."

* * * *

Jeff and Ignacio approached. Megan knelt to the floor, took Nacio in her arms and held him close for a few lingering moments. She tried unsuccessfully to hide her tear-filled eyes.

"How are you this morning, *mi hijo*?" she said.

"*Bueno,* Meggie," he said. He pulled away and looked at Megan. "*¿Qué Pasa,* Meggie?"

"I'm fine … I'm fine, Nacio."

Nacio looked at Jeff as if to say, *Do something.*

"We'll talk about it, Nacio … nothing for you to worry about," said Megan.

Celi, seeing Nacio's worry, took him to the kitchen bar to get him away from the scene and encourage him to eat his breakfast. He kept glancing back at Megan expectantly as though he sensed something was not exactly right. Celi continued to joke with him, trying to get his mind off of Megan's distress.

* * * *

"What is it, Megan?" asked Jeff as soon as they could get out of earshot range of the others.

"Jaime called. They've found a relative of Nacio's. We have to take him back for deportation." Megan started sobbing. "I can't do it, Jeff. I can't lose him … I just can't. I knew this was coming … but I can't do it." She sobbed as she threw herself in Jeff's arms. "Help me, Jeff … please help me."

Jeff held her for a few moments. "Let's look at the whole picture, Megan. Try to compose yourself. I don't want to lose him either. He has been a godsend for both of us. I feel the same way you do about this child."

She held Jeff away at arm's length for a second and looked into his eyes. "This is the first time you have ever said that."

"Look … I have risked my life, my license, my position in my firm—my very being—trying to unravel this web of complexity that has entangled all of us. Please don't make remarks that imply that I am not just as concerned about Nacio's welfare as you are."

"I'm sorry, Jeff," she said. "I guess we haven't had time to really talk about it."

"Let's think about what we can do to keep Nacio," said Jeff. "There has to be a way. Your dad will help us. First, we need to help your dad recover the missing diamonds … that's crucial right now."

"Sure, I'm sorry I got you so inflamed, but I'm glad to hear that you care."

"We're not going to let him go, Megan," he said. "We'll find a way to keep him."

Chapter 31

▼

As they crossed the international bridge and approached the inspection kiosk on the Mexican side, Isaac could feel a wave of anxiety sweep over him. He hoped the immigration officer wouldn't question any of the occupants in his car.

"All of you remain calm while we cross. If the officer is someone I know, he'll pass us on through. Try to keep Nacio engaged in something."

Isaac rolled down the window on the driver's side. The officer leaned over far enough to glance at the others and greeted Isaac with a smile.

"Good day, Mr. Andrade," he said. "A little unusual time of day to see you going across."

"This is my daughter and her friends from Houston, Alberto," said Isaac. "I'm taking them to visit the store. My wife is already there."

"Oh yes … I remember seeing her earlier," he said as he waived them through. "Have a good day, Mr. Andrade."

"Thank you, Alberto, and the same to you."

They wove their way through the crowded streets in central Nuevo Laredo, passed the city limits, and continued south on the main highway. A few kilometers down the road they turned onto Highway 2. Within minutes they were in Las Lomas.

"This is the closest the highway comes to the river," said Isaac. "We'll go through the village and find a trail to follow along the river's edge."

A short distance past Las Lomas the road narrowed. Heavy brush lined both sides of the road. Rarely did they see another vehicle of any kind—or even a pedestrian. They stopped momentarily so Nacio could crowd into the front with Isaac and Jeff.

"Nacio, was there a lot of brush where Señor Jimbob put you in the boat?" Isaac asked, speaking Spanish.

"S, señor ... mucho matorral y muchos arboles."

The road narrowed even more until there was only a path wide enough for one car leading toward the river. They followed the trail for a few minutes.

"I'm afraid to go much farther," said Isaac. "We don't want to get stuck in the sand. Jeff, let's you and I, with Nacio, walk along here for a while instead of driving. We have to be close to the site. There's no other place it could be."

"You're not leaving me in the car alone, you guys," said Megan. "I'm going with you."

"Good, you can carry the shovel," said Jeff, faking handing her the shovel.

Isaac, holding Nacio's hand, walked ahead of Jeff and Megan. Isaac and Nacio conversed in Spanish as they went along the path at a fast pace. Nacio laughed and giggled all the way in response to comments made by Isaac. The ground became softer as they approached a clearing alongside the river. Soon they came across deep ruts that could only have been made by a truck. Isaac looked back at Megan and Jeff and pointed to the ruts.

"Probably made by Jimbob's truck," he said.

All at once Nacio broke away from Isaac and started running ahead. He stopped in a clearing near the river's edge. In the center of the open area was a giant popular tree that rose above all of the others.

"Here it is; the tall tree. The painted pole was here," he yelled. He stood beside the gigantic poplar tree and pointed to the ground near the tree where the surface had been disturbed recently. "Here is where Señor Jimbob dug the hole and took out the painted pole. I saw him. I was in the boat out there," he said, pointing to the river. "But I could see him dig." He looked around. "There is the pole!" he shouted. He ran behind a nearby bush and reappeared waving the pole over his head, the pink end pointed to the sky.

"Good going, Nacio," said Megan. "We're proud of you." Jeff and Isaac gave him high fives.

Nacio's face sparkled with pride.

They all gathered around Jeff while he took the shovel and started digging in the soft sand at the spot that Nacio identified. After making a hole over a foot deep, he stopped digging.

"Nothing here, Isaac," said Jeff. "Could Bernie have gotten here ahead of us?"

"I don't think so. Megan, take Nacio to the river's edge," said Isaac. "Have him point back this way ... to where he thinks Señor Jimbob was digging."

Nacio stood by the river and motioned to Jeff to move farther away from the tall tree. Isaac grinned. "We forgot—Nacio was in the boat drifting downstream while Jimbob was digging … his sense of direction was distorted."

Jeff repeated the digging process. Soon he unearthed what appeared to be the edge of a plastic garbage bag.

"This must be it," said Isaac, kneeling down on the ground. "Be careful not to tear into the sack with the shovel, Jeff."

Jeff tossed the shovel away. He knelt alongside Isaac and the two finished excavating in the loose sand with their hands. They carefully pulled the sack out, brushed off the soil, and opened the bag. It contained multiple small zippered plastic bags. The sparkle from the contents of the bags left no doubt that they had found what they were looking for.

They all were so engrossed with the discovery that no one noticed the onlooker behind them until he stepped on a dry tree limb and made a cracking noise. Startled, they looked back down the path to see Bernie coming toward them at a fast pace, gun in hand.

"I'll take that, Isaac," said Bernie. "No one will get hurt if you just toss the bag to me. All of you, stand with your hands where I can see them."

"Bernie, you're making a mistake," said Isaac.

"Isaac, Chacón can't help you this time," he said, as he snatched the sack of diamonds from Isaac's hand. "He's left the country."

"How do you know, Bernie?" said Isaac. "And even if he did, you still have to deal with the Tampico Syndicate."

"That'll be your problem, Isaac," he said. "You should be more careful. You're slipping, old man—you never looked at your rearview mirror. Now look at you. I think I'll just shoot you all. Who would know … in this part of the country? Then no one could link me to the diamonds. But I'm just gonna let Moshe's bunch take care of that."

"You didn't look in *your* rearview mirror either, Bernie. Look behind you."

"How dumb do you think I am?" he said. "Now all of you get in the car. And Isaac, reach under your seat where you keep your gun and toss it on the ground by your car. No more tricks."

Behind Bernie, Horacio Carrillo—partially hidden behind the dense brush—called out in a booming voice.

"Drop the gun *and* the sack, Bernie! I have a message from Chacón."

Bernie whirled, aimed his gun, and fired wildly. Horacio fired one shot. Bernie fell to the ground, blood spurting from the hole between his eyes. Megan stepped in front of Nacio to block his vision. Horacio picked up the plastic bag and tossed it to Isaac.

"Isaac, get out of here in a hurry," Horacio yelled. "There's a trail up ahead on your right that leads back to the main road. Move fast. I'll take care of this mess."

"How did Chacón know?"

"Isaac, you've known him long enough to answer that question. He knew all about Bernie and Jimbob's deal. He knew Bernie would follow you, and he told me to follow Bernie."

"So it wasn't an act when he told you at the meeting to take Bernie out."

"He wanted to impress the Tampico bunch, but mostly he wanted to judge Bernie's reaction. Chacón sends his regards, Isaac—he said to tell you not to worry about him."

"There's no need to ask where he is, is there?"

"No," Horacio answered.

"Thanks, Horacio, and thank Carmen. I think she played a role here."

* * * *

The return trip was punctuated by absolute silence in the car. Each passenger portrayed solemn, sphinxlike expressions as they stared straight ahead, appearing to be waiting for someone to be the first to speak. Nacio sat in the backseat, leaning against Megan, his head turned to the side. Her arm around his shoulders, she held him close and rhythmically patted his arm. She asked herself, *How much more can this child take?*

Once in Nuevo Laredo, Isaac pulled into his parking place and left the others in the car while he took the bag of recovered diamonds into the store and put them in the safe. He tried to act casually in front of Margarita but found it was rather difficult to be nonchalant after finding the diamonds, being attacked and almost murdered by Bernie, and witnessing Horse put a bullet through Bernie's head.

"How did it go?" asked Margarita.

"We recovered the diamonds," he said, avoiding eye contact. "The others are in the car. I came in to put them in the safe and call Moshe Rosen. Has he called yet?"

"Only once," she said. "He's expecting your call. Any problems?"

"I'll take the others home and come back. I have to reappraise the diamonds and compare my findings with my first appraisal before I call Moshe."

"I'll take them home," said Margarita, "Get your work done and make the call. Isaac … answer my question. What kind of problem did you face?"

"All right … brace yourself," he said. Isaac described the ordeal that they had just gone through. "Yes, we had a problem … but everyone is fine. We haven't spoken to each other since we left the river site … everyone is so stunned thinking how bad it could have been."

"Thank God you're all right," she said after hearing the story and crossing herself. "Isaac, you all could have been killed by that crazy man. He was desperate and would have stopped at nothing; and that poor child … having to be exposed to another tragedy. How is he?"

"Megan has it under control. She's very protective of him."

"I see that and it worries me, Isaac," she said. "Celi overheard Megan talking to her office. She thinks the call meant Megan has to take Nacio back … that he has a relative who wants him. What can we do?"

"I don't know, Margie," he said. "I'll have to look into it."

"We can't let him go, Isaac. He's part of us now—we all love him. He's a very bright boy, Isaac."

"We have to follow the immigration laws, Margie," he said. "I don't know what the alternatives are right now. Jeff and Megan can help there. First we need to take everyone home. Everyone has been shaken over Bernie's attack and his threat, let alone his murder."

"Just do something to save Nacio,"

"I'll try."

* * * *

Isaac retreated into the safe room and closed the door. Using his most powerful loupe, he examined and recorded the cut, carat, color, and clarity of each stone. After he was satisfied that the appraisal of the diamonds matched his original assessment, he put in his call for Moshe Rosen.

"Isaac … good to hear from you. What do you have to report?"

"All is clear, Moshe," he said. "We found the merchandise. I just finished examining each diamond. The package is exactly the same as the original … nothing is missing."

"Good news, Isaac," he said. "We need to get those delivered. We have another shipment coming in soon. Can Chacón handle the delivery?"

"I don't think so, Moshe," said Isaac. "You will need to take Chacón and me out of the loop."

There was prolonged silence on the phone. Moshe finally spoke.

"What can I do to change your mind?"

Isaac delayed answering while he tried to think. Was Moshe leading up to a threat if he didn't continue cooperating with the Syndicate?

"I helped Chacón, Moshe, because he's my friend and I owe my life to him. Carlos has disappeared and I don't think he will return. We worked together. I am not comfortable working with anyone else on a project like this."

"And Carlos owes his life to you, Isaac. Now he has abandoned you. You have no reason *not* to inform the FBI and the AFI about our business venture."

"And I have no reason to do so. If I had wanted to incriminate the Syndicate, I could have done so years ago. I never betrayed Carlos and I will never betray you, Moshe."

"Then I have your word?"

"Yes, you do, my friend."

"And you have no hidden document or tape that you intend to rely on for your safety?"

"Moshe, as one old Jew to another: if you decide to waste me and my family, there is nothing that could stop you."

"Of course, you're right," said Moshe. "We'll find another port on the border. Shalom, my friend."

Chapter 32

Megan took Nacio into the guest bedroom, placed him in a chair, and sat in front of him. It was difficult enough to try to talk to him about the assault and the killing of Bernie, now she must talk to him about his uncle wanting him to come live in Cuauhtémoc. She decided to address first the chaotic event they had all just endured.

"Nacio, I know you have seen a horrible happening today … one man killing another. But you have to understand: the man, Bernie, was a mean man. He probably was going to kill all of us because we knew that he had stolen the diamonds. The other man shot him so we wouldn't get hurt."

"I understand, Meggie."

"But, Nacio, it is not right for one person to kill another. It's a mortal sin to kill. Do you know what that means?"

"It means that God doesn't want anyone killed."

"That's right. God wants everyone to love one another and to live in peace with each other. But sometimes mean people do things that cause other people to die. That's what happened today."

Nacio gazed out the window for a few moments without speaking. He turned back to Megan.

"Why did God want my mamá and papá and Esme to be killed? They weren't mean people."

"God didn't want them to die, Nacio. Sometimes God doesn't have control over what evil people do, and things happen that cause good people to die for no reason."

"My mamá always prayed to God. I've heard her at night. She would ask God to protect her family, her children. She kept her rosary in her hand when she prayed. So praying doesn't help, does it?"

"Yes, it does, Nacio! When you pray, it gives you strength to face bad things that sometimes happen. God kept you from dying, Nacio, and he brought you to us."

"How did that happen, Meggie? Did you ask God to bring me to you and Jeff?"

"Look at it this way, dear—God means for all of us to be right where we are and to do just what we're doing every single minute. We are always where we are supposed to be and we should always be doing the right thing. That's the way to live—the way God wants us to live."

"I'm going to pray for God to always let me be with you and Jeff," he said. "Right where I'm supposed to be."

Megan bit her lower lip and tried to muster strength to answer Ignacio. How was she going to tell him that his uncle wanted him to come live with him? That was where he belonged, according to the immigration laws.

"That's right, Nacio," she said. "God meant for us to take care of you until some member of your family could be found. My office called. Do you remember Jaime Cordova who works with me? They have found an uncle—your father's brother—who lives on a farm near Cuauhtémoc. He wants you to come live with him."

Nacio withdrew, his eyes widened, his mouth dropped. "No ... no, no," he said. "No, Meggie, I can't live with him. Those boys are mean. He beats them. Makes them fight with each other. No, Meggie ... don't make me go. I won't go there."

"But he's your only relative, Nacio. The law says he has custody of you since your parents are gone. He'll take good care of you."

"Meggie, I'm scared," he said as he started sobbing. Megan tried to comfort him. He pulled away, crying. "You said you wanted me to be with you and Jeff, Meggie. You lied to me. You don't like me. God didn't send you to me. Why are you doing this? I wish I was dead. I wish I had died with Papá and Mamá. I want to die, Meggie, like Esme and Mamá and Papá. I want to die."

Megan started sobbing, covering her face with the palms of her hands. What had she done? She had wanted to comfort this child and now she had blasted him with this news. She was no better than the worst child abuser. Wait ... what had he meant when he'd said "he beats them?" *What boys?* She needed Jeff to hear this.

"Nacio, I do like you. I *love* you," she said. "I'll never be very far away from you, Nacio. Let me talk to Jeff. Maybe we can do something."

"I'm so scared, Meggie. I am all alone. I have nobody now."

"Yes, you do," she said, trying to hold his hand, but he quickly pulled away. "You have me and you have Jeff, my dad and mother, and Celi. You have us all and we won't let anything happen to you … ever, wherever you are."

"You don't care what happens to me." He jumped to his feet and edged toward the door. Megan remained seated on the bed and called after him.

"Come back, Nacio. Jeff and I will do everything possible so you can stay with us."

"No, you won't, you want to get rid of me. I can tell. You found the diamonds … now you don't want me around. You don't need me."

"No, Nacio, no … that's not true."

"You said that God meant for me to be with you and Jeff. You lied to me about God."

"No, Nacio," she said. "Come sit back down and talk to me."

Nacio turned and went to the door. "I'm not going with that man, Meggie. I'll run away … I'll hide. I'm not going. You can't make me." He threw the door open and, in a flash, he was outside running down the driveway.

Megan ran after him. "Nacio, wait … wait. We'll do something so you don't have to go … wait Nacio," she yelled as she started running faster, trying to catch up with him. Nacio raced into the street without looking.

"Nacio! Watch out!"

An oncoming car braked trying to avoid hitting Nacio. It swerved, skidded, and barely grazed the leg of his pants. Nacio, in his fright, jumped aside. In doing so he stumbled over the curb and landed on the grassy parkway. He immediately tried to stand but slipped and went down again into a sitting position, just as Megan got to his side. Megan knelt in front of him, her arms outstretched. She smiled, her softened eyes glued to his. Nacio hesitated for a few moments and then fell into her arms, crying hysterically.

"I don't want to go, Meggie," he said as he buried his head on her chest.

"It's all right, Nacio. Let's see one of those dimpled grins. You're not going anywhere. We love you, Nacio. You're staying right here with us."

"I love you, Meggie. I'm sorry I made you cry."

"It's all right, Nacio," she said. "I've hurt you and I wish I hadn't. It's too much for you in one day. Let's go back inside and find Jeff so he can check your bandages."

How could we ever stand to let him go? I will never be able to erase the memory of Dad walking along that path today—holding Nacio's hand—the two of them laughing and talking all the way. Dad has become just as attached to Nacio as we have, she thought. *We just can't give him up; Jeff and Dad have to find a way for us to keep Nacio.*

*   *   *   *

Megan found Jeff in deep conversation with Isaac. "I need you to talk to Nacio," she said to Jeff. "I told him about my call from Jaime. Now I wish I hadn't. He's so upset."

"I was just talking about that with your dad. We were discussing some possible options when you came in."

"You come too, Dad," she said. "Listen to what Nacio says about his uncle."

Nacio was curled up on the floor in the corner of the room when they entered. He didn't look up when Jeff went to him. "Hey, big man, it's time to check your bandages."

He didn't move. Finally he looked up at Jeff and said, "I can do it myself."

"Nacio, I'm so sorry you're upset and scared," said Jeff. "We need to talk. We all love you and we want you to live with us. We want to help you. You helped us today. We're so proud of you ... all of us."

Megan turned to her father. "Dad, I'm going in to tell Mom and Celi what happened," she said as she left the room. "Translate for Nacio, please."

"I made Meggie cry," said Nacio, as he stood and climbed on the bed for Jeff to examine him.

"She's just sad about the call she received from Jaime today," said Jeff. "Tell me about your uncle."

"He's not my uncle, Jeff. He married my aunt. My papá hated him."

"What about your aunt?"

"She died. My papá says that man killed her."

"Did they have children?" asked Isaac.

"Just those boys ... they don't belong to my aunt or to that man."

"Where did they come from?"

"I heard my papá say that man bought them. They came in one at a time. He keeps them in the barn."

"And they do work on the farm?"

"Every day ... all day. If they try to run away, Papá said he catches them and beats them."

"Nacio, don't worry, we're not going to let you go there," said Jeff as he taped down the dressing. "Mr. Andrade and I will talk about it. We'll do something." Jeff held up his hand. "Now … give me five!"

Nacio's grin once again deepened his dimples until they almost disappeared, as he hopped off the bed and slapped Jeff's hand. "Run in the house and give Meggie a hug," said Jeff.

Chapter 33

"What do you think, Mr. Andrade?"

"We have work to do," said Isaac. "First, we need to find out more about the so-called uncle. I smell child exploitation here."

"I'm going to call Jaime and see if he'll give me the uncle's name and where we can find him," said Jeff.

"If the 'uncle' is the type of person I'm thinking he is from what Nacio told us, I think we should pay him a visit and lay a few pesos on him," said Isaac. "He'll sell out his rights in a minute … if he has any rights."

"Let's call Jaime right now while we're alone."

"Good idea," said Isaac.

Jeff sat at the desk in Isaac's private office, drumming his fingers restlessly on the arm of the leather-upholstered chair, waiting while the ICE office telephone routing system connected him to Jaime. Isaac alternately paced the floor and thumbed through folders in his file cabinet. He stopped pacing when Jeff was able finally to reach Jaime Cordova, and strained to understand sketches of the conversation.

"Jaime," said Jeff. "This is Jeff Harrison, Megan's friend."

"Sure … sure, Jeff," said Jaime. "I know who you are. And I know you're gonna tell me how upset Megan is about Ignacio having to be deported."

"Okay, Jaime, so you know Megan's upset. I'm upset. Megan's father and mother are upset. We're all upset. There has to be some way we can keep the boy in this country. He has so much potential."

"I understand, Jeff," said Jaime. "I didn't make the laws. Right now, with the immigration thing being front page, we have to adhere to the letter of the law."

"Jaime, Megan said a relative has been found."

"Yeah, he has an uncle. His father's brother. The guy is eager to take Ignacio to live with him."

"Did anyone check him out? What kind of home can he provide for Nacio?"

"Jeff … we're not dealing here with social service standards that you are familiar with in this country. We can't do an in-depth analysis of this person. If this guy says he's Ignacio's uncle, we return the boy to Mexico, to his nearest relative … the uncle."

"I just think the government has some responsibility for placing the boy in a safe, desirable environment. You know what I mean … assurance that he has a comfortable existence, that he is not being exploited."

"You're living in a dream world, Jeff," said Jaime. "Look, wherever he goes will be the equivalent of what he came from originally."

"I'd like to check it out, Jaime," said Jeff. "Can you give me the name and location of the uncle?"

"Jeff, that's confidential information. I can't give you his identity. You know that."

"Are we dealing with a national security issue here, Jaime?"

"Come on, man," he said. "Where are you going with this?"

"Simple answer, Jaime," he said. "Are you familiar with the Freedom of Information Act?"

"Oh … shit, Jeff," said Jaime. "Don't pull that shit on me, man. I don't have time to fight a battle with the Justice Department. I don't even have time to take a crap in the morning anymore. What do you want, Jeff?"

"Give me the name, Jaime, and where I can find this so-called uncle."

"You're dragging me down, Jeff … you know that." Jaime was quiet for a prolonged moment. "Jeff, wait right where you are for a few minutes. Damn … what am I doing? Jeff, if you tell a living soul what I'm doing, I'll kill you … a slow painful death, Jeff."

"Cool it, Jaime," said Jeff, straining to restrain outright laughter. "You are simply upholding the constitutional right of a U.S. citizen."

"Will you visit me in prison?" he said. "I'll fax all the information we have on the uncle. Before you ask—we don't have DNA evidence of kinship."

"Jaime, thank you. Megan thanks you, and Nacio thanks you. You'll be glad you did this."

"Keep reminding me. Oh … God, what am I getting into?"

"You're a good person, Jaime. I'll be here," said Jeff, and he read Jaime the Andrade fax number.

* * * *

"Well done, Jeff," said Isaac as they both looked at the fax that had arrived in a surprisingly short time.

"What can we do, Mr. Andrade?" said Jeff.

"We can get a charter flight to Ciudad Mante," he said. "I know a pilot who operates a charter plane service out of the Nuevo Laredo airport. We'll find a car and driver and see what we can do to find this man."

"Jaime gives the name as Enrique Narváez, but Nacio says that this man is not his father's brother."

"The guy probably assumed the name Narváez as soon as he learned that Nacio might be available to capture," said Isaac. "This sort of thing goes on all over the interior of Mexico. Once we get into the village of Cuauhtémoc we will find some leads. Someone will remember Nacio's aunt ... especially if she died under unusual circumstances."

"What should we tell Megan and her mother?"

"Try to avoid saying anything right now. I'll say you're going to Nuevo Laredo with me to consult an attorney who practices in Mexico who might be able to help us with an immigration problem."

* * * *

Within the hour they were airborne. Jeff saw that Isaac had brought his heavy leather briefcase along. He knew that it contained papers—documents that that they hoped to get the purported uncle to sign. Jeff didn't know what else Isaac had stashed away in the briefcase, but he had his suspicions.

After a three-hour, smooth flight they landed at the airport in Ciudad Mante. Isaac negotiated with the driver of a vehicle—one of reasonably recent vintage—and they were on their way to nearby Cuauhtémoc. The driver dropped them off at the plaza in the center of the village and agreed to wait until he was needed again. A short walk took Isaac and Jeff to the local church where they found the priest, Father Armando Alvarez, in his study. Isaac had said that this was the place to get information.

"Thank you for seeing us, Father," said Isaac after introducing himself and Jeff. The priest looked askance at the two with skepticism.

"We seldom have the pleasure of visitors," said Father Armando. "How can I help you?"

Isaac briefly described their purpose for being there, including the question of the relationship of Enrique Narváez to Nacio. Father Armando sat with his hands resting on his generous abdomen, fingertips touching. His eyes narrowed to slits as he listened and stared at Isaac. Isaac stopped talking, and they waited for the father's response, which was slow in coming.

"As you might imagine," Father Armando said finally, "it's hard to keep up with the migration of young men from the village. Many seem obsessed with the desire to travel to *El Norte*, thinking everything will be better. I try to discourage them, but usually I am not successful. They go on anyway and often meet with some tragic occurrence. I'm not sure what your interest is in this case—enough interest that you have made this trip."

"Let me be honest with you, Father. My daughter and her friend here—as well as my wife and I—have become attached to Ignacio, and he to us. He is a unique child. He is very bright and we think that, given the educational opportunity, the boy has significant potential."

Once again the priest became somber. He gazed out the window for a few silent moments before he spoke. "The boy you are talking about is the son of Rafael and Rosa Narváez. The parents and their two children, Ignacio and Esmeralda, left here about a week ago for *El Norte*. I heard that it turned out to be an ill-fated trip, and that the boy was the only survivor. Rafael, the husband, had a *sister* ... no brother. She married a farmer who has a small place near the village ... on the river. His name is Enrique Gomez."

"Could that be the person who claims to be Enrique Narváez ... Ignacio's uncle?"

"Very likely. As far as I know, Rafael and Rosa have no living relatives. Rafael's sister, Señor Gomez's wife, died a couple of years ago. There was considerable speculation on how she died. Rafael was convinced that the husband killed her. Enrique said she fell on a knife one day when he was not at the house. Rafael was enraged and threatened to kill Enrique."

"Did Rafael turn to you for counseling?" asked Isaac."

"I'm sorry, sir. I cannot discuss my relationship with the man."

"We understand that, Father. Perhaps you can answer this question: Why did Enrique tell the United States immigration people that he is Rafael's brother and that his name is Narváez?"

"I will answer that if you give me your word that you will not reveal that I gave you any information about Señor Gomez."

"You have my word, Father. Mr. Harrison is an attorney and is very sensitive to issues of confidentiality. I can provide you with personal references if you would like."

The priest smiled and looked Isaac in the eye. "Mr. Andrade, Mexico is a large country. But those of us in the clergy enjoy an enigmatic network of knowledge that transcends myriad socioeconomic strata. I know more about you than you would believe."

"How could that be? I live in Laredo …"

"And you own Andrade Jewelry in Nuevo Laredo. And we have a mutual friend—a man who is indebted to you for his very existence—a man who has helped the poor people of this community immeasurably."

"You need to say no more, Padre."

"I trust you to keep your word. Enrique Gomez is one of the most wicked individuals on the face of this earth. He has done this before. If a boy of Ignacio's age is orphaned—for whatever reason—this man claims kinship and represents to the authorities that he can provide a golden environment for the child. He then places the boy in his workforce of children that he keeps locked up in a barn. He works the boys like he would animals … actually uses a rawhide whip to discipline them. It's criminal. But he has been getting away with it for years. The boys are prisoners. If you can prevent it, don't let this boy get placed in that prison."

"Thank you, Padre," said Isaac. "We plan on visiting this individual. We want his full release that he will not claim kinship to Ignacio."

"That might prove to be difficult. Having the boy in his custody means dollars to him. He is ruthless, gentlemen."

"We will try to reason with him."

"Be careful, please. I wish you luck; I don't want to see any more of these boys exploited."

* * * *

For an extra few pesos, the driver of the car agreed to take them to the countryside and to Señor Gomez's farm. They stopped in front of what appeared to be a residence, surrounded by multiple sheds and lean-to shelters. They stayed in the car waiting for someone to appear.

"Mr. Andrade," said Jeff. "I think I know how you have planned to handle this, but this is really my problem. Do you think I can do it … with your help of course?"

"Jeff … I am delighted and honored that you want to try."

"Can I see what's in the briefcase? I think I know already."

"Sure, you need to know what your props are," Isaac grinned. "Let me tell you right off—the Glock is not loaded."

Soon a rotund, heavily bearded man, with a moustache stained with cigarette smoke, came toward them in a lordly swagger, still chewing something, and picking his teeth as he approached. Jeff and Isaac exited the vehicle to meet him. The man kept eyeing the interior of the car as if expecting another occupant.

"Señor Narváez, I believe," said Jeff in a silky voice that didn't sound like him. "Nice place you have here. We are from UNICEF, Mr. Narváez. I'm sure you are familiar with UNICEF, the international child protective agency. We have been given your name as a potential custodian of … let me see. Oh … here it is: Ignacio Narváez. I believe he is your nephew."

"Yeah, where *is* the kid … my nephew? I thought he'd be here by now," he said, his eyes again searching the backseat of the car. "You didn't bring him?"

"We just need to verify that his living conditions will meet our standards."

"What the shit are you talking about? He's my brother's son. He's supposed to come live with me. Where in the hell is he?"

"Mr. Narváez, UNICEF must be assured that placement of international orphans is in keeping with the highest standards for young people to thrive and excel to their maximum potential."

"I still don't know what the shit you're talking about."

"We just have to inspect your home and your facility. And, of course, you can expect us to return every three months to resurvey the environment. We have to be accurate in our assessment. I'm sure you understand the need for thoroughness where our children are concerned."

"Look, I'm sorry that my brother and his wife were killed. I'm willing to take the boy, even though it will be a financial hardship on me … another mouth to feed. Now, bring him here and stop all of this nonsense talk that I don't understand. Where is the kid?"

"I'm sorry, Mr. Narváez. We have to look around first."

"I'll tell you what you can look around for—a way out," he said. He opened the door to a nearby shed and grabbed a long rawhide whip. "Now get the hell off my property. And don't either of you come back until you can bring the boy."

Jeff ignored the threat and calmly opened the briefcase and rummaged around inside as if looking for something. Señor Gomez appeared stunned at Jeff and Isaac's cool, stubborn response and kept his eyes glued to the briefcase. Finally, Jeff pulled out the Glock as well as a neatly stacked bundle of pesos of large denomination. He handed both to Isaac.

"Hold these for me, please, Mr. Andrade, while I look for the papers I need to give to Señor Narváez," said Jeff while he continued a mock survey of the contents of the briefcase. He turned back to their assailant. "They are in here somewhere … the papers you will need to sign, so we can place the young man in a safe home."

"Hurry it up," said Enrique, eyeing the money and the gun. "I don't have all day."

"Sir, perhaps you don't fully understand the importance of our visit," said Jeff, his eyes blazing, and a furtive, twisted smile on his face. "Now, put the whip aside, Señor Gomez," Jeff added, with emphasis on the name, Gomez. "And come talk sense to us." Enrique paled and quickly tossed the whip aside.

"What do you want from me?" he said as he cowered away from Jeff and Isaac. "I just wanted to take my nephew in so I could care for him."

"Cut the shit, Enrique," said Jeff. "He's not your nephew and you know it. Now we have some papers for you to sign saying you are not a blood kin to Ignacio Narváez. Sign these in a hurry before we continue an investigation of your treatment of other young boys on your farm. And what we find will be reported to the Mexican government agency that protects children from exploitation. Then you'll face some real investigations and charges that will place you right where you belong—in the rottenest jail in Mexico. Your fuckin' whip won't be of any use to you there."

"You can't force me to do this."

"You're right. But we can report that one Enrique Gomez was found dead from a gunshot wound and is not capable of assuming custodial care of this boy."

"Hell, I don't need any more of those little fuckers anyway. Where do I sign?"

"Right here, shit-ass."

"Does this mean that if I sign, you won't be back?"

"Can't promise," said Jeff as he pocketed the signed statement. "Thank you, Mr. Gomez. You've been very cooperative. Have a nice day, sir."

"Go to hell, you bastards."

Chapter 34

On the way back to the airport Isaac threw the palm of his hand in the air toward Jeff, to be met by the loud slap of Jeff's hand.

"You did it, Jeff!" said Isaac. "Señor Gomez crapped in his pants when he saw the gun, and he couldn't take his eyes off the money. You were perfect, Jeff. We could make a good team."

"Thank you, sir. I don't think I could carry that banner alone for very long. I learned it all from you, Mr. Andrade."

"Let's pray that you never have to face another occasion where you have to do the same."

"I don't know, Mr. Andrade, I'll have to admit … I enjoyed it," said Jeff. "I certainly have gained a lot of respect for what you've been through."

"Thank you, Jeff," he said. "Those are delightful words to hear."

"And I know you don't hear that very often."

"We'll be back before dark. There will be a happy gathering tonight," said Isaac. "I'm going to miss having you around here, Jeff. Have you ever had any interest in the jewelry business?"

Jeff chuckled. "The only interest I have in jewelry is to find a ring for Megan and try to talk her into marrying me."

"If she refuses, I'll disinherit her."

* * * *

"Where have you two been?" said Megan, her forehead creased in a frown. Margarita and Celi echoed the question. "We have been worried sick ... and we are waiting to have dinner."

Nacio, playing with the Legos on the floor, scowled at the women, jumped to his feet, and ran to stand between Jeff and Isaac, as if ready to protect them. Jeff tossed the signed release on the table. As soon as the women realized the significance of what they read, their demeanor abruptly changed.

"How did you do it?" asked Megan.

"Don't embarrass Jeff by asking," said Isaac.

"It's time for a celebration," said Celi. "I'm off to the kitchen to prepare."

"Good. We have a lot of planning to do, now that we know Nacio has no living relatives," said Jeff, as he looked at Megan. "We have to decide what we should do next."

"In the meantime, I'm opening a bottle of champagne," said Isaac.

"Before you do," said Megan. "Chief López-Guerra called to talk to you. He wouldn't say what he wanted."

"There's no telling what he's been up to now," said Margarita.

"Margie, I asked him to look up some information for me ... that's all."

* * * *

Isaac went into his office to make his call and motioned for Jeff to follow.

"What did you find?" asked Isaac, on the speaker phone to the chief.

"You were right, Isaac. A James Robert Clifton made a one-way reservation on a flight to Rio de Janeiro, to leave three days ago. He never picked up his ticket. He was supposed to pay for the ticket at the airport. He hasn't been heard from."

"Thanks chief," said Isaac.

"Anything else you need from me, Isaac?"

"Nothing, chief ... thanks again."

"Oh ... Mr. Andrade, one thing more, there was another reservation on the same flight that wasn't picked up, made at the same time—adjacent seats—for a Bernie Hefferman."

"Probably just a coincidence," said Isaac.

* * * *

After dinner, Jeff and Isaac sat on the patio sipping their after-dinner drinks. Megan, Margarita, and Celi gathered in the kitchen while the clean-up ordeal took place. Outbursts of laughter from Nacio told the group that he was busy playing video games.

"What comes next, Jeff?" said Isaac.

"Do you have any suggestions, Mr. Andrade?" asked Jeff.

Isaac's eyelids narrowed. He looked into Jeff's eyes with a flat, masklike face. "A lot depends on your long-range plans, Jeff."

"You want to know what Megan and I intend to do, don't you?"

"I think your next step depends on that very thing."

Jeff gazed across the terrace at the swimming pool and delayed saying more for a few moments. He envisioned Megan in that pool, fighting to save her drowning brother. He thought of the emptiness that loss had created in Megan's life … and how being with Nacio had helped soothe some of the pain from that emotional wound.

He had already told Isaac that marriage to Megan was his ultimate goal. Now he had to make a commitment. He was sure that there was no way they could adopt a child from Mexico unless they were married. *Stop debating in your mind, stupid,* he told himself. *You could never give up Megan and now you couldn't ever give up Nacio. They are now a part of your life."*

"Right now, Mr. Andrade, I am going to ask Megan to marry me … as soon as possible. And then I am going to start an adoption process for Nacio. I hope I have your blessings, sir."

Isaac tried at first to conceal a grin, but to no avail. "Of course you do. How could I say no to my partner in crime? I know everything about you that I need to know."

"Thank you, sir," he said. "And I have to say the same about you."

Isaac extended his hand. "Now, go see Megan. Afterward I'll talk to you about some suggestions."

* * * *

Jeff rushed inside and pulled Megan aside. "I need to talk to you for a minute."

"It had better be important. Are you sure you can drag yourself away from my father for a while?"

"It's important," he said as he escorted her into the next room, gently eased her into a chair, and knelt in front of her. "Will you marry me? I don't have a ring to give you right now ..." He grinned. "We've had our fill of diamonds lately anyway, haven't we? I asked your father, and he gave his blessings."

Megan tried to keep a straight face. "Come off it, Jeff, and stand up! You asked my father? This is not the nineteenth century! No one does that anymore."

"Megan ... this is a serious time in our lives and you are making jokes."

She laughed while tears flowed across her face. She jumped up from the chair and threw herself into his arms. "I love you, Jeff. You are one big, unpredictable fool. I'll be a good wife."

"And a good mother," he said with a chuckle. "We're starting an adoption process for Nacio. Don't say anything yet, I need to talk to your father again."

"My father ... again?" said Megan with mock consternation

* * * *

After Jeff and Isaac had closeted themselves in the office once again for about half an hour, Jeff gathered everyone together—after dragging Nacio away from his video games. When they were finally all gathered in the kitchen, he announced that he had proposed to Megan and that she had accepted. The room erupted in applause. After Megan translated for Nacio, his smile was so wide that his dimples had never been deeper. He threw his arms around both Megan and Jeff and pulled them into a "group hug" that nearly sent them all sprawling to the floor. The room was full of laughter. Isaac busied himself with opening bottles of champagne and filling glasses. As soon as the toasts quieted the questions started.

"When ... Jeff, Megan?" said Margarita, "I need to go to Joe Brand for a new dress. And we've talked about redecorating the house, Isaac. We need to start on that right away. I need to call Diane Whitworth. Everyone says she does a beautiful job with flowers. Oh ... there's so much to do. I need to know when, Megan."

"We need to start thinking about a menu, Mrs. Andrade," said Celi, bouncing around like a monkey freed from a cage. "I can put together a lot of hors d'oeuvres and pack the freezer. Of course, you might want a reception at the country club, but I'm sure we'll have guests here at the house too."

"Wait … wait, all of you," said Megan. "Jeff and I want a family-only wedding right here in the house. No one except family. We don't have time for a big wedding."

"We're sorry to disappoint you," said Jeff. "But there's more to the story. Mr. Andrade's friend, Judge Jorge Maldonado, one of the U.S. District Judges for this district, has agreed to come here to the house to perform the rites. And more news—he has been kind enough to help us with the DIF in Mexico to allow us to adopt Nacio as soon as we are married."

"How did he do that?" asked Margarita. "I've always heard that it was almost impossible to adopt a child from Mexico."

"You're right, if an orphaned child has relatives. But since we now have verification that Nacio has no relatives, one barrier is out of the way," said Jeff. "There are other obstacles that a judge in Mexico can waive. Judge Maldonado was able to convince the DIF and the Mexican judge to follow his recommendations."

"What is the DIF?" asked Margarita.

"It's *Desarrollo Integral de la Familia,*" said Megan. "It is the equivalent of our Child Protective Services. One of its functions is to protect the rights of orphaned children in Mexico. It enforces some very strict rules, but a judge has the power to waive certain regulations on waiting times. Nacio is in our custody now with full benefits of a dependent.

"And as soon as Judge Maldonado completes the marriage rites and provides the Mexican judge with his findings and rulings, we can adopt Nacio. The day the adoption is finalized, he will automatically become a U.S. citizen," said Jeff. "Thanks to Mr. Andrade, it's going to happen. Oh … a collateral benefit from visiting with the judge: he's going to follow up on what we discovered about Señor Gomez and the child labor on his farm."

Margarita listened. While she sipped her champagne, she began sniffling and assumed a downcast countenance. Isaac put his arms around her.

"I know what you're thinking, Margie," he said. "You've looked forward for years to a grand wedding and reception for our girl. Look, after the dust settles, let's do this: we'll have a gargantuan announcement party at the Country Club and invite everyone we've ever known. Jeff's family will have a list of friends that will want to come from Houston. We'll make it formal. Will that be all right, Jeff?"

"Sure … a good idea, Mr. Andrade. And we can repeat our vows if Megan agrees."

"I want to see Nacio all dressed up in a tux," said Isaac. "He'll be handsome, Margie. And we'll tell Diane to buy as many flowers as she wants and to go all out to make the occasion something memorable for the two Laredos."

Margarita, now all smiles and glowing from the thought of the event, came alive. "We'll need to clean out the den to make a place to display the wedding presents ... there will be showers for the bride. You know we'll have people coming here to visit. Celi, we need to start planning the menu. Can you get together with the chef at the country club?"

"Sure ... and you need to call Diane early enough for her to start planning," said Celi.

"It's going to be the party of the year in Laredo," said Isaac. "Make sure José knows, so he can plan an upgrade to the landscaping.

*   *   *   *

The following morning every one wandered in one at time for breakfast. The women, still full of exuberance, resumed their planning and comments. Isaac came in from his early-morning jog and joined the others. Jeff and Nacio tackled breakfast.

Jeff dropped out of the group and quietly went to the terrace outside and punched numbers into his cell phone.

"Jaime," said Jeff. "I have news for you. One of your deportation problems will be resolved before the day is over."

"What do you mean, Jeff? Are you bringing Ignacio back for deportation?"

"Try again, Jaime," he said. "Megan and I are getting married at two o'clock today. Right afterward, the judge will grant us full, permanent custody and parental rights of Ignacio Narváez."

"Jeff, are you serious?"

"Absolutely, Jaime," he said. "We wanted you to be the first to know. Megan asks that you tell the chief."

"What about the uncle?"

"He doesn't exist, Jaime. We are sending you copies of the papers. It is all self-explanatory."

"I can't believe it, Jeff," he said. "Congratulations! I wish happiness for all of you. You'll be a good father, Jeff."

"Thanks, Jaime," he said. "We'll see you in a couple of weeks."

* * * *

Megan and Jeff sat as close to each other as possible—with Nacio, dressed in newly purchased clothes, insisting that he sit between them—while they awaited the arrival of Judge Jorge Maldonado. They all jumped when Celi announced that he had arrived. Jeff leaned across Nacio and gave Megan a kiss.

"Can you believe it? This is our wedding day!"

"Are you ready for this?" asked Megan.

"Never been more certain of anything in my life," he said. He chuckled and tousled Nacio's hair. "And all because of this kid."

"Not altogether," said Megan, pulling Nacio close. "But he helped."

After brief introductions and greetings, the group stood before Judge Maldonado. The room became quiet and the air thickened with solemnity.

Jeff had asked Isaac and Nacio, to be his "best men." Megan had asked Celi and her mother to stand as her maid and matron of honor. Celi and Margarita competed with each other in wiping tears from their eyes. The ceremony was short but to the point.

Next, the judge, speaking fluent Spanish, asked Nacio to step forward and answer a series of questions. As a formality, the judge asked Nacio about his expectations of a future relationship with Jeff and Megan. In short order Nacio declared his opinion. The judge then counseled Jeff and Megan on the responsibility of taking on a child to raise.

"I am pleased to declare that the two of you are now man and wife and are, as of this day, the legal representatives and guardians of this minor, Ignacio Narváez. And you will be so until he is eighteen years of age. You will be accountable for his every deed and for providing for him the benefit of a family unit in a domiciliary environment until he reaches the age of eighteen years. This is a solemn pledge that you must make and I expect both of you to live up to your responsibilities. If you agree to do so, please answer for the record: We do."

Jeff and Megan responded simultaneously. The newly created family unit hugged and kissed each other, held their embraces for a memorable minute, and then turned to the others for repeat embraces.

CHAPTER 35

▼

Eight Years Later

Houston, Texas

Ignacio awakened before dawn. Lying in bed, he rehearsed his speech over and over again in his mind. He still wasn't comfortable with it. It just didn't seem to carry the punch that he wanted to deliver. He was proud to be valedictorian of his high school class, and he wanted to make Meggie, Jeff, and Andy proud of him. Graduation was only a week away, and he wasn't ready. Maybe if he just put it aside for a couple of days—put it out of his mind—he could come back to it with fresh thoughts.

He had a few days completely free of classes; his grade-point average was high enough that he was exempt from exams during finals week. If he did take two or three days off from rehearsing his speech, what could he do? Where could he go? He laughed thinking: *Wherever I go or whatever I do, Andy will want to tag along. How can I slip away without Andy?*

Graduation! It signaled the beginning of major changes in his life: he would start college in the fall where he would work to earn a bachelor's degree so he could enter law school. And again this summer he would work in Jeff's law office, just as he had done every summer for the last three years. It didn't seem like work … it was really fun being around Jeff and his partners.

Neither Jeff nor Meggie had mentioned any plans for a family vacation this summer. He knew it would be coming soon—just as it had every year, except seven years ago when Andy was born. At seven years of age, Andy should now be more fun to be with on a trip. Last year, when they went to Washington DC, Andy was a pest—no interest at all in anything they visited, except the National

Air and Space Museum. *I think that trip was mainly for my benefit,* he thought, *Both Jeff and Meggie made it an educational experience for me.*

It *had* been an education. He had developed a keener appreciation for the country's history and for his citizenship. Every immigrant should spend time visiting the Capitol, the White House, the museums, the war memorials, and the government centers in Washington DC. But maybe this year they would decide to go to Disney World. He would have as much fun as Andy with all of the rides and the attractions to visit.

Being on the threshold of transition into a life of advanced education had triggered memories of all that had transpired over the last eight years, ever since he had become a part of his new family. There was one big question still, however, that had lurked in the depth of his mind for years—and continued to surface periodically to haunt him—what really had happened to Esme?

I can remember when that weird guy took me into a huge mansionlike house and turned me over to some woman—I can still smell her perfume. I thought he said he was taking me to Esme, but then he disappeared and Dad Andrade and Jeff picked me up and took me back to Meggie. Then Meggie told me later that the same person had told Dad Andrade that Esme had been killed. What happened? It just keeps nagging at me—I've got to find out.

He had wanted to talk to Jeff about it, but the time had never seemed right. Maybe he just didn't want to bother Jeff and Meggie about his thoughts. *Who can I talk to?* He wondered, then he thought: *Wait ... I know just the person who can help me learn the true story. Dad Andrade! If anyone can help me, he can. Esme might even still be alive somewhere. But ... no, if she were alive, she would be looking for me.*

As soon as he was up and dressed, he grabbed a sweet roll and juice, staying as quiet as possible, trying not to awaken Andrew. If Andy found out what he was doing, he'd come bouncing in, ready to go. And it was always difficult to tell Andy no. Nacio left Jeff and Meggie a note, and slipped out of the house and into the garage. He opened the garage door manually to avoid the noise made by the mechanical opener. As he backed his car out, he flipped his cell phone open and clicked on Dad Andrade's cell phone number.

"Hey, Nacio, is that you?" asked Isaac. "What's going on?"

"I need some help, Dad," said Nacio.

"I'm right here, Nacio," he said. "Anything serious?"

"I guess not, sir," he said. "I just need some help working through a quandary. I'll be there in about five hours."

"Is everything all right there?" Isaac asked. "The sound of your voice worries me. We're looking forward to seeing you next week ... at the graduation."

"Everyone's fine, sir," said Nacio. "It's just my own personal problem."

"I'll be in the store," he said. "Call me when you get to the house. Celi will be ecstatic about seeing you. She asks every day about you."

"You *will* bring her to the graduation, I hope."

"Absolutely," said Isaac. "We couldn't get away without her."

*   *   *   *

Nacio maneuvered his GT Mustang—his graduation gift from the family—through the sparse early-morning traffic and found the entrance ramp to Highway 59. Soon he was on his way to Laredo. While he cruised along the highway, he reminisced about the time when Jeff had taught him to drive. He could laugh now at the memory of some of his mistakes early on during the process. He wanted to give up, but Jeff wouldn't let him.

He thought about all that they had been through over the last eight years. It didn't seem as if it had been that long since he had come to the United States. He marveled at how quickly he had mastered the English language with Jeff's and Megan's help, and he chuckled thinking of how Jeff had been determined to learn Spanish. They had taught each other.

On rare occasions, Jeff had taken the family to visit Jeff's mother and father in their River Oaks home in Houston. What a drag. He hated every minute of it. It never seemed to bother Megan, but their frequent questions about his birthplace and about his parents cut through him like a knife. When Jeff's mother made statements that bordered on racism, both Megan and Jeff came forward and put a stop to it. Fortunately their visits were infrequent and short lived.

How was he going to approach Dad Andrade about his problem? He had coped with it for so long and now he just had to seek some answers. He just didn't want to bring it up to Jeff and Meggie, but he somehow felt obsessed with wanting to know the truth. Dad Andrade would either help him or—with words of wisdom—ship him packing back to Houston. Either way, Dad Andrade would make him feel better. Nacio was confident of that.

*   *   *   *

The miles raced by—his car performed beautifully on its first out-of-town trip—and, well within the time predicted, he drove in the driveway of the

Andrade home. He saw José, busy as always with his gardening. His flowers were always vibrant in color no matter what time of year. José stood to greet him with a hug.

"Celi's waiting for you. Señor Andrade called her earlier."

"You know what she's gonna ask, José: 'Are you hungry, Nacio? You've lost weight.'"

"I'm sure you're right, Nacio," said José. "How are Megan, Jeff, and Andrew?"

"They're fine, José. Andy is a live wire ... keeps all of us jumping."

"Here she comes," he said, pointing to the front door.

Celi came bursting through the door, ran to Nacio, and smothered him with a close embrace and a kiss on his cheek.

"Come in, come in, *hijo mo,*" she said, dragging him toward the door. "Are you hungry, Nacio? You look like you've lost weight."

Nacio glanced at José, and they exchanged grins.

"Thanks, Celi. Anything you fix will be good," he said. "I need to let Dad Andrade know I'm here."

"I've already called him. He's called here every fifteen minutes checking on you ... worried about your making the trip by yourself."

"Celi ... I'm almost nineteen years old. I start college this fall."

"Of course, dear. But we still think of you as a child. Your grandpa was worried about your call."

Celi had already put together some of his favorites snacks, and she went to work spreading them all before him. Within a few minutes Isaac came through the front door. Nacio jumped to his feet and met Isaac with open arms. Isaac joined him at the table as Celi quietly retreated into the kitchen.

"Hey ... Nacio, what a nice surprise. I see Celi has already welcomed you," he said, glancing at the dishes of food.

"Dad ... I didn't mean to worry you," said Nacio.

"No problem, man," he replied. "I know something is worrying you and that's what's important."

"You're gonna think I'm foolish."

"Never ... what are grandpas good for if they can't stop and listen every once and a while. First, tell me about Megan, Jeff, and Andrew."

"They're fine, Dad," he said. "Andy is a remarkable kid, but he's a little imp. He hangs onto me like a pet puppy. But I like having a little brother. He's always getting into my things, but I don't mind ... really."

"You're good for him, Nacio," said Isaac. "He sees the world through your eyes. Most kids aren't that fortunate."

"I like teaching him. He catches on quickly. It reminds me of the way Esme taught … He paused, his voice breaking. "And the way … the way she watched over me," said Nacio. He dropped his head for a few moments, tried to blink the tears away, and stared at the floor. Finally, as he looked up at Isaac, a wave of tears flooded his eyes. "I'm sorry, Dad."

"Nacio, being an old guy gives me an insight into a situation without anyone describing it to me," said Isaac, as he put his arm around the boy and pulled him close. "You want to know something about your sister, don't you?"

"I don't know what's happening to me, Dad," said Nacio, rubbing his shirt sleeve across his eyes. "I can't get it out of my mind. What really happened to her?"

"I'll tell you what," said Isaac. "You stay here and visit with Celi for a while." He chuckled. "Make sure you eat some of the food she's prepared for you so she doesn't get her feelings hurt. I'm going to make a few calls and then you and I are going on an exploratory, fact-finding mission."

Nacio dried his eyes and grinned at Isaac. "Thanks, Dad," he said. "I'm ready. I'll tell Celi that we are just going for a ride."

"Good … that's the spirit," said Isaac. "We'll go in my car."

Chapter 36

"Do you think this is a waste of time, Dad?" asked Nacio as they drove toward the bridge.

"No … not at all, Nacio," said Isaac. "I think I know what you're feeling … it's hard to explain, but it's something you have to do."

"It won't change anything, though."

"I think it will," he said. "Sometimes we have miniature, boiling caldrons in the depths of our brains that keep erupting over and over again. If we don't cap them some way—close the lid, so to speak—they just keep on eroding our thinking."

"And that's what's happening to me?"

"I think so. What you need, I think, is called closure," he said. "We need closure any time we suffer a loss … we need to bring it to a close and get on with our lives."

"How do you know all that, Dad?"

"I've been there, Nacio … more times than I like to remember," he said. "The worst was when our boy, Andrew, drowned. Every day I would go outside and sit by the pool for a whole hour and just stare at the water. Once I realized what I was doing, I learned to accept his death. It has taken Megan years to do the same. You never get over it, but you learn to compensate for the loss by thinking about those areas in your life where you've gained."

"I have a lot to be thankful for right now. I guess that's what I should be remembering."

"Sure. You can't just pull the curtain and put your memories of Esme out of your mind. But you need to remember the fun times you had together and you need to focus on the great things happening to you today."

"Do you think there's any chance that she could still be alive?"

"Always a chance," said Isaac. "That's another demon that's eats away at your brain if you let it. Until you find proof that she's not alive, your mind will always ask the same question: What if she's still alive?"

Nacio was silent for a few minutes while they cruised along the highway. Soon they came to the road that led to El Rancho Alegrón. "We'll start here," said Isaac, as they pulled into the entrance driveway.

Carmen met them at the door. She hugged Isaac for a few seconds and then pushed him away, but still held onto his shoulders, and scrutinized him from head to toe with a frown on her forehead.

"You've been bad, bad, bad, Isaac. You never come to see me any more."

"I've been busy Carmen."

"You always say that."

Nacio stood back, trying to suppress a grin, while the scenario played out. Isaac's face was beet red. Carmen turned her attention to Nacio.

"You've brought this dear, sweet boy back. How he has grown. You're out of school for the summer, aren't you, dear?" she said.

"Yes, ma'am," he said.

"Why don't you come spend the summer with me ... here at El Rancho?"

"I'll be working in Jeff's office," he said, trying to move away from the cloud of strong perfume.

"Well, maybe later," she said as she stroked the back of his neck and plucked at his chin. "You would have fun if you stayed at El Rancho Alegrón for a while."

"Carmen, we have some serious issues to discuss," said Isaac.

Carmen looked at Nacio. "See how serious he is. And here is the place to come to forget all your worries."

"Ignacio needs to hear the true story about his sister's death. Is the driver that she was with still around?"

"Oh ... you mean Ziggy. Isaac, the poor boy has just disappeared. The same time that Carlos left."

"Then Ziggy was Carlos's driver?"

"Yes, and no word from either of them since they left. And my poor, dear Bernie. I guess you heard that someone shot and killed him. It must have been one or those Fidencio Estrada thugs. So much killing, Isaac. Thank God, Horacio has been spared."

"You're fortunate that you still have Horacio here with you," said Isaac. "Carmen, where do you think Esmeralda jumped out of the car?"

"Not far from here. It's the first bridge you come to going up the highway toward Piedras Negras—the one with the wide concrete barriers on each side. I made Ziggy take me there the next day to look. Someone had already removed the body." She looked at Ignacio. "I'm so sorry, sweetie. She was such a lovely child."

"Thank you, Carmen," said Isaac. "Have you ever heard anyone say where they took the body?"

"No … nothing," she said. "I imagine they went to the hospital. I never heard anything more."

"We're going to look around, Carmen."

"Sure, I knew you would sooner or later," she said. "Be careful, Isaac."

* * * *

Isaac parked along side the road. He and Nacio inspected the concrete wall.

"According to the story, Nacio, her head crashed into this wall, and she was thrown over the barrier into the creek below. Ziggy reported that she was covered with blood and showed no sign of life."

"I'm gonna climb down there, Dad," he said.

"I'll go with you."

At the bottom of the ravine, which was overgrown in weeds and grass, Nacio stood still for a minute without speaking. Isaac stayed by his side with his arm around Nacio's shoulders.

"Do you think she felt anything?" he said finally.

"Not likely. It all happened so fast."

They climbed out of the creek bed and sat in the car for a couple of minutes.

"I guess that's it, Dad," said Nacio. "Let's go home."

"Let's check the records at the hospital first," said Isaac. "You need to be sure about this."

* * * *

With only scant information on date and time of day of the accident, the manager of medical records at the Nuevo Laredo hospital kindly searched the archives for some clue to the identity of the patient that Isaac and Nacio had described. The manager perused all of the old emergency room records of admissions during that time period, looking for one that could possibly be Esmeralda's record.

"The only case that even comes close to matching the girl you have described is this one," said the manager as he thumbed through the pages of an old record. "This girl—identified only as Jane Doe—had a severe head injury, was unconscious and near death when brought in. There are no notes on how she was injured. She had a deep cut through her scalp that extended all the way across her forehead and eyebrow. She must have almost bled out. The ER nurse signed out at daylight the next day. Her notes indicate that she didn't expect the patient to survive the day."

"Do you have any record of what happened after that?" asked Isaac.

"No, the pages are blank after that entry."

"Does that mean that she died?" asked Nacio.

"Either that or that she was transferred somewhere else, which is unlikely in this case; but she could have been sent to a hospital in Laredo if there was any hope for her survival."

"Was there any identification of the girl, other than the Jane Doe name?"

"None ... I'm sure they made little effort to identify her, from the description of the way she was dressed."

"What do you mean?"

"From the notes here she was dressed like every other prostitute you see on the street. They never carry any identification. They're brought in here dead or half-dead after they're thrown from a car."

When he saw the tears forming in Nacio's eyes, Isaac gently rubbed his shoulders and patted his back. "This is not what we were hoping for, Nacio."

"I know, Dad, and I know that girl was not Esme."

Isaac turned to the manager. "Thank you, sir, for your help. One more question—if she did die, where would she have been buried?" asked Isaac.

"In the pauper cemetery ... there likely would have been no grave site marker for this girl."

* * * *

Celi met them at the door. "Megan's looking for you. I didn't know what to tell her. And Margarita is hopping mad that you and Nacio are up to something and haven't let her know. She didn't even know Nacio was here."

"Oh ... I failed to tell her," said Isaac. "In my haste to get here to see Nacio, I forgot."

"And I didn't call Mom Andrade," said Nacio. "We are both in trouble,"

"Let me call Margie and you take on Megan."

Nacio laughed. "Boy, you were quick to pick up on that. I've got the hardest job."

"I don't know ... you don't have to live with Mom like I do," said Isaac, joining Nacio in chuckles. "Maybe if you don't say anything about going to El Rancho, it won't be so tough."

"It's a deal ... if you promise you won't tell Meggie and Jeff why I came. Can you just say I was trying out my new car on the highway?"

"Then it's our secret," he said as he held up his palm for a high five.

✳   ✳   ✳   ✳

"Hey, Meggie. It's me," said Nacio.

"Nacio, we've been worried sick," said Megan. "Where've you been? I saw your note but, when I called to check on you, your cell phone was off. Celi said you and Dad had gone somewhere. What's going on?"

"Uh ... uh ... Dad Andrade was just showing me around," he said. "I'm sorry if I upset you. I didn't think you'd mind. I just wanted to visit Mom and Dad Andrade before summer work started. And I wanted to drive my car on the highway ... it drives great on the road."

"Did Dad take you across the bridge, Nacio?"

"Uh ... well ... yeah," he said. "We just drove around."

"Stay right where you are, Nacio. I'm going to get Jeff to talk to you."

"Nacio ... hey, man," said Jeff. "How was the trip?"

"Fine, Jeff," he said. "My car performed like a well-tuned watch. What's Meggie upset about?"

"Did Mr. Andrade take you to Carmen Carrillo's El Rancho Alegrón?" he asked, unable to suppress a stifled chuckle. "You can tell me, partner."

There was a long silence on the phone.

"What's that phrase I hear you guys use in the mock trials at the office ... 'I refuse to answer on the grounds that ...'"

Jeff laughed. "Way to go, buddy! I can handle it on this end, Nacio. Be careful on your trip home. You will spend the night there, won't you?"

"I plan to. Jeff, I came because I just had to talk to Dad Andrade. I would never do anything that would hurt you and Meggie."

"I know that. I'm here if you need me."

"You always have been. How's Andy?"

"Fussing about where you are and why you didn't take him with you."
"Tell him I'll explain tomorrow. Thanks, Jeff."
"We love you, Nacio," Jeff said as he passed the phone to Megan.
"Nacio, please be careful," said Megan. "We worry about you so much."
"I will, Meggie … please don't worry."
"I love you, Nacio," she said. "Drive carefully."
"I'll do that … and I love you all. I'll be home tomorrow."

Chapter 37

▼

Nacio slept fitfully during the night. Mom Andrade and Celi had grilled him incessantly, any time Isaac was not around, about their activities of the day. He did the best he could to avoid full disclosure of their visits to El Rancho Alegrón and then to the hospital in Nuevo Laredo, but he could tell they were skeptical of his answers. He wanted to start back to Houston early the next morning. He needed some more time to work on his speech before graduation.

After an early breakfast and farewells to everyone, he struck out for the return trip. To break the monotony of the long stretches of highway, he kept his radio tuned to a rock music station for a while, keeping time with the beat with gyrating head and neck movements. Tiring of the music—already past Freer and now on Highway 59 toward Houston—he turned off the radio.

With the "loud" beat-free quietness, the steady hum of his car on the road lulled him into a state of reminiscence about his and Dad Andrade's time together. After hearing the report from the Nuevo Laredo hospital's record keeper, he felt sure Esme had been killed and was buried some place, probably impossible to find. His heart had skipped beats when they had been told that a girl had been picked up and taken to the hospital. For a brief time he had thought that maybe she was alive.

But then, when they were told that the girl was dressed like a hooker, he realized, no way! Esme would never dress like that or even let anyone force her to dress that way. Unless ... someone did force her under some pretense. Or someone drugged her first and then dressed her to look like a hooker. She had been taken to Señora Carrillo's bordello. Anything could have happened while she had been with that woman. But, no, if there was a chance for error, Dad Andrade would have picked up on it.

Still, that lingering feeling had *not* completely vanished. The man who read the record at the hospital described a deep wound on the girl's head that extended into her forehead and eyebrow. If he ever saw someone with a scar like that, he would be suspicious that it was Esme. But right now he had to put those thoughts aside.

* * * *

Nacio had no sooner driven off than Margarita started in on Isaac at the breakfast table about the day before.

"I've already talked to Megan," she said, standing, arms folded across her chest, facing Isaac, now seated in his desk chair like a prisoner being interrogated, "She told me how Jeff had laughed when he talked to Nacio. Ugh ... men! You're all alike. Trying to make a man out of that poor child."

"Margie ... please," he said. "Come sit down. We need to talk about Nacio's visit. Forget about El Rancho Alegrón. When you hear the story, you'll understand why Nacio needed to talk to me."

Isaac told Margarita every detail of their conversation and their travels and their findings. True, he had promised Nacio he wouldn't reveal the reason he had come to Laredo, but with the uncertainty that had crept into his mind, he needed Margie's support on what to do next.

"Then Nacio left here thinking there was no hope that Esmeralda might be alive somewhere?"

"What I'm saying is that we have not proved in my mind that the girl described to us was *not* Esmeralda. It could have been and she could be alive. Nacio thinks that, if it were Esme, she would try to find him. But if she had a severe enough head injury, she could be amnesic for anything that happened in her life prior to the accident. I saw that in 'Nam more times than I like to remember."

"So you decided not to pursue it any further because of the upcoming graduation, didn't you?"

"Right," he said. "I'll follow through on it ... by myself later. I didn't want Nacio having that same doubt hanging over him during the graduation celebration."

"Are you going to tell Megan?"

"No, and I hope you won't. I promised Nacio I wouldn't. I think he was afraid that Megan and Jeff would get their feelings hurt if he came to me with a personal problem instead of talking to them."

"Yes, and it made you feel ten feet tall that he did, didn't it?"

Isaac chuckled. "What do *you* think?"

"That you are pretty wonderful."

"You know what, Margie? If that girl is alive, she will have a terrible scar on her forehead—from the description by the hospital people. If I ever see someone with a scar like that I'll be suspicious that it is Esmeralda."

* * * *

Nacio parked in the garage and eased into the back door of the house. But no one would be home at this hour, so he didn't feel a need to be quiet. Andy would be in school and Meggie and Jeff would both be at work. He needed every minute to work on his speech. With no one at home, he would be able to practice aloud in front of a mirror. He had been told to make a video of his talk and look at it closely to pick up any changes in speech or body language that needed attention. He laughed thinking that maybe Andy could help him.

He glanced at his watch, a few minutes before 2:00. Andy would be bouncing in at about 3:30 or 4:00. That would give him time to practice a few times and make some revisions. No more than two hours later he heard a car door slam and looked out the window to see Andy getting out of the carpool vehicle and running toward the front door. *Meggie must have told Andy I'd be here,* thought Nacio, *he isn't searching in his pocket for his key.*

Nacio met him at the door. Andy looked as if he'd been run over by a bus—shirttail out, grass stains on his shirt, hair tousled, and a red streak across the side of his face.

"Hey, cowboy, what happened to you?"

"I hate school," he said as he marched straight to the kitchen. "And I hate everybody that goes to school."

"Did you get into a fight, Andrew?"

"They called me names … said I was just another Mexican from Mexico," he said, while he started building a peanut butter and jelly sandwich. "Now Mom has to go to the school and talk to the teacher."

"Why is that …? Oh, I know. You clobbered one of the other kids, didn't you?"

"Yeah. Remember that neck hold you showed me? While we were rolling in the grass, I wrapped my arm around his neck. He started crying ... said I was killing him. That's when the teacher came."

"What brought all of this on, Andy?"

"You want a sandwich, Nacio? I'll make you one."

"No thanks, Andy," he said. "Answer my question: what brought this on?"

"Oh, that stupid teacher told the class that I knew how to speak Spanish ... that students should think about learning Spanish so they could be bi ... something. So they all blame me that they are going to have to study Spanish. That's when they started yelling at me—on the playground. They said, 'you're nothing but a dumb Mexican, your mother is a Mexican and your brother is a Mexican.'"

Andy brushed the long black locks of hair out of his eyes long enough to chomp on his peanut butter sandwich. Grape jelly dripped from his chin.

"I'll bet they wouldn't say those things to you, Nacio," said Andy. "I told them you were going to whip their asses if they didn't stop."

"Watch your language, Andrew."

Nacio tried to restrain laughter at Andy's remark; he knew he had to assume a serious demeanor when he turned back to his brother. *This little kid just had his first taste of it. But now is the time to learn how to cope with racist remarks. I'll try to find the right words.* He hesitated for a few moments before speaking.

"Andy, there's nothing wrong with being Mexican. Everyone in our family, except Jeff, is Mexican, and we're proud of it. Jeff is proud of the way he's learned Spanish and how much he's learned about Mexican culture."

"Now Mom is going to be mad at me for hurting that kid. I don't even know his name. She's gonna have to go talk to the teacher."

"Meggie will understand, Andy," said Nacio as he wiped the jelly off Andy's chin and off the floor.

"What's the difference in being Mexican and not being Mexican, Nacio?" asked Andy. "Is everyone else smarter than we are? Is that why they call me a dumb Mexican?"

"Andy! Look at your grades—all As. Look who's going to give the valedictorian address at the high school graduation. You can't be dumb and do those things. Look at Mom and Dad Andrade, Look at Megan and Jeff. You're a smart kid, Andy. Don't pay any attention to those kids. Maybe being Mexican is a challenge for us. Know what I mean?"

"Tell me, Nacio."

"A challenge to show everyone we can do as well or better than most if given a chance."

"Yeah … like that racehorse you told me about … what was his name?"

"Seabiscuit."

"Yeah … nobody thought he could win a race, and he fooled everybody, didn't he?"

"Now you've got it. Sure, as minority citizens, we have to show the world that we can achieve more than we are expected to achieve. Do you understand what I'm saying, Andy?"

"Yeah, I think so. You went to see Dad and Mom Andrade, didn't you?"

"Yeah, they asked about you."

"Will they be here for your graduation?"

"Everybody, including Celi."

Chapter 38

Nacio sat in his chair alongside the smiling school board members and the other graduating seniors who would be receiving awards. He found himself struggling to keep his eyes open during the long address by the school board president. Fatigue from staying up so late the night before was catching up with him. He had read his speech over and over again, making changes and corrections with each reading. Now he was ready to stand before an audience of over two thousand parents and friends and give his valedictorian address.

He scanned the myriad faces in the large convention hall hoping to find his family; he knew they were out there somewhere. He wished now that they had planned on some special sign to show where they were seated in the auditorium, like so many other students' families had done—colorful banners, signs written in large letters, or just bright swatches of cloth.

While waiting his turn to speak, he once again rehearsed his speech in his mind. He had been adamant against using notes; instead, he wanted to speak extemporaneously so he could place emphasis wherever it was needed. Jeff had offered to help him, but Nacio had declined. He wanted the words he was going to utter today to be heard by Jeff, Meggie, and the others for the first time.

Finally the superintendent motioned for Nacio to come forward. After an introduction complimenting him on his achievements, the superintendent handed him the microphone. Nacio felt his knees weaken. His chin and lower lip quivered, his throat tightened, and the lump in his chest grew into a "fist." *No one ever told me I would feel like this,* he thought. *This sure is a little different from practicing in front of a mirror.*

He hesitated a few moments before speaking while he gazed across the ocean of attendees, each with posture poised as though waiting to hear him begin. Just before he spoke his first word, he spotted his family: Meggie, Jeff, Andrew, Mom and Dad Andrade, and Celi. They were seated fairly close to the front, all with smiles of pride on their faces.

Andrew—restless as usual and already bored—was pestering everyone, scooting on and off his seat, and trying to converse with anyone around him who would listen. Jeff had his arm wrapped around Meggie's shoulders. Nacio relaxed and waited even longer before beginning, thinking of the blessing he had enjoyed for the last eight years—his family. Any time he needed them, they were there … all of them. *And now they are here.*

Andy came alive when he realized that Nacio was standing before the lectern and when he saw the screens flash Nacio's image. "Hey, Nacio!" he called out, waving his arms. He then turned to face the attendees seated behind him. "That's my big brother. That's Nacio. Hey, Nacio!" Megan grabbed him and pulled him down into his seat amid the roar of laughter all around them. Nacio waved to Andy, then stood still for a few moments more until the auditorium was quiet again.

After thanking the superintendent for the introduction, Nacio stepped away from the podium, cordless microphone in hand, and walked to the edge of the stage. All eyes followed him as he turned and pointed back to the two giant video screens placed high on each side of the stage—each carrying his projected image. He turned around to face the audience again and paced back and forth at the edge of the stage a couple of times. Finally he began.

"Do you see that kid on the screens up there?" he said. "Can you see him? He's a Mexican immigrant. Can you believe that? That's me, the kid of two poor, undocumented Mexican peasants from Cuauhtémoc, Mexico, who lost their lives during their illegal immigration to America. But that kid you are looking at is now a citizen of the United States. Do you detect any accent when I talk? Of course you do. Do I look like a Mexican? Of course I do.

"But let me tell you this: I am proud of my heritage. I am proud to say that my existence in poverty as a child, before coming to this country, is responsible, to a great extent, for my appreciation for my citizenship today—for the opportunities I see ahead for me everywhere I look.

"I am honored to be here to talk to you and to the student body. I am truly overwhelmed. There are many of my fellow students who are just as deserving of this honor, but none could be more appreciative. My being here is a reflection of the excellence of the education system in this school. I am grateful for all of my teachers and mentors to whom I give credit for where I am this very minute.

"When I look at all of you out there, I wonder how many of you are thinking: 'How did that dumb Mexican kid ever get to be Valedictorian? There must have been some political pressure from somewhere.' Let me tell you how I got here: there were no politics involved. I was fortunate to have had loving, caring, compassionate adoptive parents who saw to it that I learned English, who saw to it that I was given the opportunity for an education, and who saw something in me that no one else, including myself, had recognized.

"I was fortunate to have two adoptive grandparents who were always there, showing concern and ready to give wise counseling when needed. And I was fortunate to have our long-time family friend, Araceli Talamantes, who to this day worries that I don't eat enough and that I am too thin." A roar of laughter followed.

"I want to give credit to these people who mean more to me than anyone or anything else in the world: Megan, Jeff, and my bratty brother Andrew Harrison, Mom and Dad Andrade, Celi, please stand. I love you all."

They all stood. Megan, Margarita, and Celi blotted their eyes, Jeff kept his arm around Megan, Megan held on to Andy with a firm hand, and they all waved to Nacio. He waited a few moments until the applause died down to resume his speech. He wiped a tear from each of his cheeks, and then resumed speaking, but he never stood still; he paced back and forth on the stage.

"I have only a few words more to say. I'm not going to address my fellow students now with any words of wisdom about what they are facing in this world or how prepared they are to deal with the future; they hear that at every turn. Instead, I am talking to their families and to their friends—all of you in this hall: This country has an immigration problem ... has had for years. There's no question about it. And there is not one good answer to the problem. But there *are* answers. The problem can be resolved only slowly over the years to come.

"I will list what I see as a beginning solution:

"First, let's recognize the benefit of assimilating into our communities those legal immigrants who meet reasonable standards of behavior. They will set an example for all immigrants and many will make good citizens that communities can be proud of.

"Next, let's show respect for every immigrant, legal *and* undocumented, as fellow human beings. Recognize their potential for enhancing the culture of our country—contributing to our art, our music, our architecture, out technology, our sciences, and our civic responsibilities for human rights. Give them the opportunity to work toward citizenship.

"And next, let's provide opportunities for our new citizens in the workforce ... in keeping with their skills. Let's provide educational opportunities for all immigrants—regardless of where they might have originated—without prejudice based on ethnicity or religious beliefs.

"And finally—which actually should be first—let's follow the example of Jeff and Megan Harrison and every other member of my adopted family ... just provide plain, everyday, nonjudgmental love and compassion at any time the opportunity presents itself.

"I am thankful that I have been given a chance for an education, and I am appreciative of my many mentors in this school. I have enjoyed the comradeship of my many friends among the student body. But most of all ... Meggie, Jeff, Mom and Dad Andrade, Celi ... and you too, Andy, I thank you from the bottom of my heart. I owe my life to you.

"Thank all of you for listening today to this Mexican kid."

* * * *

There was dead silence when Nacio finished his speech and turned back toward his seat. He looked up to see everyone on the stage standing, and then turned around to see everyone in the audience standing and applauding. He started to sit in his chair when the superintendent motioned him to come to the rostrum by his side. He put his arm around Nacio's shoulders.

When the applause died down, he spoke. "Ladies and gentlemen, I have been superintendent of this school system for several years and have heard valedictorian addresses from more classes than I can remember. Never have I experienced the emotional impact that has equaled what I've felt here tonight.

"All of us need to remember what made this country great—freedom of speech and the assimilation of ethnic cultures from all over the world into our country nationwide. We have never, *ever*, been xenophobic in this country and this young man has reminded us that this is not the time to start. Thank you, Ignacio, for a stirring speech that has prompted our memory."

* * * *

The summer passed with the speed of light. They vacationed at Disney World just as Nacio had hoped, and they all had fun. Andy dragged him from one attraction to the other. On the wild rides, Andy—squealing all the way—clung to him with viper tenacity. *He needs me,* Nacio thought. *It's a warm feeling and I like it—I like being needed. Meggie would say that God brought me to him. I love this little kid.*

* * * *

Ignacio had worked in Jeff's firm during the summer. But fall wasn't far away, and the day finally arrived for his orientation at the University of Houston where he was to begin his pre-law curriculum. He checked in with admissions to get his assignments. He was scheduled for a meeting with a counselor—along with a few other new students. He found the room and discovered that he was a few minutes early, but he entered the classroom anyway and took a seat.

Soon afterward, the door behind him slammed shut, loud enough to vibrate the windows. *It must be the orientation person,* he thought as he shuddered. *The instruction sheet said it would be a woman.* He listened to the clog of sandals as the person came closer.

"I'm sorry for the noise of the door. I didn't know anyone was here already." The voice was distinct, flavored with Hispanic accent ... silky and feminine. He thought he had heard that voice before somewhere ... why would he think that?

"I just wanted to capture a good seat," he said as he stood and slowly turned to look at the instructor. The girl walking toward him was lovely, but she had the most atrocious disfigurement imaginable on the right side of her forehead. The deep scar started in her scalp, passed through her hairline, and coursed across her forehead all the way across her eyebrow. Any movement of her facial muscles distorted her eyebrow and eyelid, giving her an almost gargoylelike appearance. But her smile ... it was captivating and diverted attention away from her deformity.

"Hi, my name is Olivia ... Olivia Guzmán, she said. I am a third-year, pre-law student at U of H. I've been assigned to be your counselor for your first year in pre-law. Is anyone else in this panel?"

Nacio was so awestricken that he couldn't answer for a few seconds.

"Are you staring at my scar?" she said.

"Oh ... no ... I just had the feeling that I've met you before."

"With my face, you wouldn't forget," she said with a laugh. "No one ever forgets me."

"You just look familiar some way," said Nacio.

"I was just thinking the same about you," she said. "Where are you from?"

"Originally from Cuauhtémoc, Mexico," said Nacio. "But now I live right here in Houston." When Nacio mentioned Cuauhtémoc the girl jerked her head around abruptly to look closer at her pupil. She became quiet and stared out the window for an almost full minute without speaking.

"Are you from Houston originally?" asked Nacio.

"I'm not sure. I can't remember anything about my life before my injury. It's weird. Sometimes a word that I hear will sound familiar—like Cuauhtémoc—and I don't know why."

"Maybe you'll find out someday," said Nacio.

*　　*　　*　　*

Nacio walked away from the meeting hall after his orientation session, a tight feeling in his throat. Could that have been Esmeralda? She didn't look at all the way he remembered her. But there had been something about her voice ... and her eyes. And Cuauhtémoc *had* sounded familiar to her.

978-0-595-47471-4
0-595-47471-3

Printed in the United States
108253LV00005B/264/P